# THE UNKNOWN WOMAN

## THOMAS FINCHAM

**The Unknown Woman**
Thomas Fincham

**AUTHOR'S NOTE**
This book is a work of fiction. Names, characters, places and incidents are products of the author's imagination or are used fictitiously. Any resemblance to actual events or locales or persons, living or dead, is entirely coincidental.

The scanning, uploading and distribution of this book via the internet or any other means without the permission of the publisher is illegal and punishable by law. Please purchase only authorized electronic editions, and do not participate in or encourage electronic piracy of copyrighted materials. Your support of the author's rights is appreciated.

Visit the author's website:
**www.finchambooks.com**

Contact:
**finchambooks@gmail.com**

Join my Facebook page:
**https://www.facebook.com/finchambooks/**

## LEE CALLAWAY SERIES

1) The Dead Daughter
2) The Gone Sister
3) The Falling Girl
4) The Invisible Wife
5) The Missing Mistress
6) The Broken Mother
7) The Guilty Spouse
8) The Unknown Woman
9) The Lost Twins

# ONE

The gun rested on his lap as he sat behind the wheel of the black sedan. He was wearing a dark trench coat that reached his knees, with black military-style boots that were scuffed and dirty. His left hand clutched the steering wheel, his right hand gripping the butt of the gun. A silencer was attached to its muzzle.

Kristoff was well over six feet in height. He weighed close to two hundred pounds, and he knew how to use his size to his advantage. He'd been in many fist fights—some in prison, some outside. After each one, his opponent required immediate medical attention, while Kristoff required nothing more than ointment for his bloody knuckles.

He moved his left hand over his buzzed hair, something he had kept after his brief stint in the Russian Army. He was kicked out for insubordination after only one year. They tried to instill discipline, obedience, and loyalty in him. They failed. Kristoff was not good at following orders. He was too restless. He felt his superiors knew far less than he did.

But Kristoff had to quickly change his way of thinking. He realized that societies survived on hierarchy. No matter what you did in life, there was always someone you reported to. Complete freedom was an illusion. Someone was always dictating some aspect of your life.

After arriving in the United States, Kristoff knew he had to get in line if he wanted to survive. He had to find people who required his special set of skills. Those skills meant doing whatever was necessary to get the job done, no matter how dangerous or risky.

He felt movement in the passenger seat.

Andrei was half his size, but he still weighed as much as Kristoff. Like him, Andrei wore a dark trench coat and black military-style boots. He, too, sported a buzz haircut. Unlike him, Andrei was never in the Army. His nearsightedness prevented him from passing the medical examinations. Without the use of his thick glasses, he couldn't shoot a person ten feet away.

Kristoff met Andrei when he moved to Moscow. The man lived in the same building as him. What Andrei lacked physically, he made up in tenacity. The man could be a Pit Bull when he wanted to be. He was also deeply loyal. And his loyalty was only to Kristoff.

There weren't many employment opportunities for someone like Andrei, and he was smart enough to know that his survival depended on people like Kristoff. People who made things happen for themselves, no matter how impossible they seemed.

When Kristoff decided to move to America, Andrei followed him. When Kristoff told Andrei what they had to do, Andrei followed him without question.

They were parked across from a bungalow. The house needed some exterior work—a new paint job, some roof shingles replaced—but overall, it was in good shape.

They had been waiting here for over an hour, and they weren't sure how much longer they'd have to wait.

*As long as necessary*, Kristoff thought.

His palm began to sweat as he gripped his weapon. He debated wiping his hand on his trench coat but decided against it.

*You always keep your eyes on the target*, his training sergeant had told him. *And you always keep your weapon in a ready position at all times.*

But he was in a suburban neighborhood, not some battlefield. The worst thing that happened here was package theft.

But training was training. He would stay alert.

Andrei had a similar weapon—one with a silencer on the muzzle as well. His was tucked in his trench coat pocket. Kristoff knew that when it came time to act, however, Andrei wouldn't hesitate to draw his weapon and fire.

He glanced at his wristwatch.

He then saw a white sedan pull up to the bungalow and park in the driveway.

A woman got out. She had short, dark hair. Her eyes were brown, and they were squinting in the sunlight. She wore a light coat over green scrubs. They knew she worked at the hospital as a nurse and that she was just returning from a twelve-hour shift.

They saw no one else in the sedan. This greatly disappointed Kristoff. He was hoping the woman's daughter would be with her.

*No worries, though*, he thought. *She will have to do.*

He got out.

She was pulling her purse out from the sedan when he approached her.

"Patricia Callaway?" he asked.
"Yes?" she replied, turning to him.
He aimed the gun at her head.

## TWO

Six Days Earlier

Motel 86 was on the outskirts of Milton. It was a U-shaped structure with an open space in the middle that was used as a parking lot. The motel had two levels with eight units on each, and it was built in 1986. By the looks of it, the place had seen better days.

The exterior paint was fading, cracks were visible on the walls, and the roof had missing tiles.

Detective Dana Fisher pulled into the parking lot and parked next to a police cruiser. She was five-five, weighed one hundred and ten pounds, and she had dark, shoulder-length hair. Her green eyes were large and expressive, and her thin nose pointed upward, moving whenever she opened her mouth. Her eyes were a source of benefit and weakness. They could comfort those who were grieving, and they could make others see what she was feeling just by looking at them. As a ten-year veteran of the Milton Police Department, Fisher had worked hard to control her emotions. She looked around the motel. Tenants were already outside their rooms. They were staring in the direction of room ten, which had yellow police tape across the front door. Something bad must have happened in that room for the police to show up, and the tenants were curious to know what it was.

Fisher only hoped that none of them had tried to access the room. There was nothing worse than a contaminated crime scene.

Room ten was on the upper level. Two sets of stairs—one on each side of the U-shaped building—went up to that level. Fisher took the stairs closest to the room in question.

The officer at the door was older, with gray hair and a protruding belly. He was a walking cliché of the type of officers seen in movies or TV series.

He had gray stubble on his chin, a sure sign that he had forgotten to shave in the morning.

*This is not promising*, she thought.

The first officer at the scene had the most crucial role. He or she had to evaluate the scene and make sure there was nothing that posed a threat. Once the scene was secured, he or she had to make sure it was preserved for the investigators. The worst thing an officer could do was trample through the scene and destroy crucial evidence.

Fisher prayed this officer didn't do the latter.

She flashed her badge and asked, "What have you got?"

"Call came in twenty minutes ago," he replied in a hoarse voice. "I was about a mile from here, so it was a quick drive over. When I arrived, I went to speak to the owner. He had no idea someone had called 9-1-1."

Fisher's brow furrowed. She would have to find out who made the call. But that would be later.

"Okay, let's take a look," she said.

They ducked underneath the police tape and entered the room. There was a bed in the middle, and a large table was next to the front window, the blinds closed. An old CRT television was wedged in the corner, and next to it was a VCR.

*People still have those?* she thought.

She looked around at the space. There were things everywhere—on the bed, on the table, even on racks mounted on the wall. Books, cardboard boxes, VHS tapes, and even cassette tapes.

The side table was covered with small bottles of prescription medications and tubes of creams.

Just when she thought she'd seen everything, she spotted a small stove next to the bed.

*It looks like someone's been living here for a long time*, she thought.

Motels were for a short stay—a day or two perhaps—but she'd heard of instances where people lived there for months or even years. With rent so high in Milton, Fisher wouldn't be surprised if that was the case here.

She turned to the officer. "Was the door locked when you came in?" she asked.

He shook his head. "No, it wasn't, ma'am."

Fisher thought of something. "How did you know which room it was?"

"The dispatcher told me," he replied.

She squinted.

*This is getting interesting.*

"Where is it?" she asked, referring to the crime itself.

He took her to the back of the room and opened the bathroom door.

In the middle of the space, between the toilet and bathtub, was a chair. A man sat on the chair. His hands were tied behind his back, and his head was bowed low with his chin touching his chest.

Fisher got closer. The man's hair was receding, but strands of silver hair had fallen across his wrinkled face. His eyes were closed, and there was a black hole in the middle of his forehead. Dark liquid oozed from the hole and ran down the bridge of his nose.

*Gunshot wound to the head*, Fisher thought.

# THREE

The dead man's hands were restrained by zip ties. This told Fisher she was dealing with someone who knew what he was doing. Regular folks didn't walk around carrying zip ties. They used rope, duct tape, or whatever else they could find lying around to bind someone.

Also, the man was killed in the bathroom. Why? Because bathrooms can buffer a lot of noise. Especially if the air vent was turned on. She flipped the switch on the wall, and the vent inside the bathroom whirred to life. It was old and loud. It would be hard for someone outside to hear a man's screams.

Then there were the bruises across the man's arms and neck. The bruises weren't visible at first glance. The light in the bathroom was yellowish and not at all bright. But upon closer inspection, she spotted red and purplish marks.

She removed a pen from her pocket, and using the tip, she lifted his shirt above his belly. She saw nothing troublesome, but when she moved the shirt up to the chest, she saw more bruises around the rib cage. Someone had punched or kicked the man.

Fisher felt movement behind her. She turned and saw a large man standing in the doorway.

Detective Gregory Holt was six-four and weighed over two hundred and fifty pounds. He had thick arms, thick hands, and a thick neck. His shirt collar was tight around his neck, but he made no effort to loosen it. He liked his clothes fitted. His shaved head was smooth to the touch and glistened even in the poor bathroom light.

Holt was Fisher's partner. He was also her friend.

Over the years, she had come to trust him more than she trusted anyone else in her life. After all, he had saved her life on numerous occasions. But if you asked him, he was just doing his job.

His eyes darted from one spot to another, taking everything in.

"It looks like he was tortured," he said.

"That would be my guess, too," she said.

"And that wound on the forehead had to have come at close range," he added.

"I'm guessing it's someone with experience in these kinds of things."

Holt looked back at all the stuff in the room. "Robbery can't be a motive."

"Don't be so sure," Fisher said with a grin. "As they say, one man's garbage is another man's treasure."

He looked at the room again. "I'm not sure you'll find any treasure in there."

Holt was not known for his sense of humor, but she understood where he was going with this. He was trying to eliminate all possibilities, starting with robbery.

"The door was open when the officer came in," Fisher said.

"So, the victim let his killer in?"

"Maybe he knew him."

Holt stared at the man slumped in the chair. "I'm not too certain about that."

They were silent for a moment.

Holt asked, "Do we even know his name?"

"Good question." Fisher checked the man's pockets for a wallet. "Nothing here." She then went out into the room. She looked around and then came back into the bathroom.

"What are you looking for?" Holt asked.

"He must have a jacket." Fisher scanned the bathroom and found a blue jacket hanging on a hook behind the bathroom door. She rummaged through the pockets and pulled out a wallet. "Trevor McGinty," she said. "Age fifty-three. And based on the driver's license, his address is at this motel."

"How long has he been here?" Holt asked.

"We'll have to ask the owner."

"The victim was shot in the bathroom, right?" Holt asked.

"By the looks of it, yes. Why do you ask?" Fisher replied.

"While you were outside looking for the ID, I checked the bathroom, and you know what I didn't find?"

"What?"

"Empty shell casings."

"So, the killer took time to clean the scene?" Fisher said.

"Looks like it."

Fisher frowned. "Which means we might be dealing with a professional," she said.

# FOUR

Wayne Lemont was rail thin. His face was pocked with marks from adolescent acne, and his teeth were yellowish from years of heavy smoking.

Wayne was the owner of Motel 86, and he was already on his second cigarette as he stood outside his office, speaking to Holt and Fisher.

They found out that Wayne's father had built the motel from the ground up. He used money borrowed from Wayne's grandfather to make his dream come true. It used to be derelict land. There was nothing for miles except for a highway. Wayne's father saw the potential and made a down payment. He believed that truckers and travelers needing a break would stop over at the motel, and to make that happen, Wayne's father placed large billboards along the highway pointing to the motel. And the timing was just perfect for Wayne's father.

During the seventies, gas prices shot up because of the formation of OPEC. They cut oil production drastically to inflate prices. But by the early eighties, prices had started to go down. Demand fell following the energy crisis of the seventies, and when combined with a surplus of crude oil, prices fell by half by the mid-eighties.

More and more people began to get behind the wheel, and by the end of the eighties, the motel was hardly ever vacant.

Wayne and his siblings worked alongside their father and mother to keep the motel running. They cleaned the rooms, did the laundry, and at one point, his mother and his sisters prepared breakfast for the tenants at an additional fee. That service ended when Wayne's mother couldn't work for health reasons. Wayne could never get a cook to stay long enough, so he decided to close the kitchen for good.

Plus, business wasn't what it used to be after his father died suddenly of a heart attack. He was only sixty-one. It was a shock to Wayne and his family, but Wayne was grateful his father never saw what ended up becoming of the motel.

Other motels opened nearby, and they were backed by corporations with big money. They priced aggressively, cutting into the already meager profits of the business. It didn't take long for them to steal his customers. The other motels offered more for less money, something Wayne couldn't do.

Eventually, he stopped spending money on the motel's upkeep. He knew his new clientele wanted a cheap place to stay and didn't care whether it had all the amenities or not. As long as there was hot water and no bed bugs, they were fine.

"How long has Trevor McGinty been staying at the motel?" Fisher asked.

Wayne took another drag of his cigarette. "About four years."

"Why that long?"

Wayne shrugged. "He moved in and never left."

Holt said, "Doesn't the law say the maximum you can rent out your room is for less than a month?"

Wayne shrugged again. "Yeah, sure. But the law doesn't pay my bills. If someone is willing to stay longer than that, who am I to turn them away?"

Fisher could see Holt wasn't pleased with Wayne's response. He was a stickler for rules and regulations. He followed them, and he expected others to follow them, too. But they weren't here to bust Wayne for infractions related to the motel industry.

"What can you tell us about Trevor McGinty?" she asked.

"Not much, I'm afraid," Wayne answered, dropping his cigarette to the concrete and stubbing it out with the heel of his boot. "He paid on time at the beginning of each month. But he kept to himself. I asked him what he did. He said he was retired."

"He's only fifty-three," Fisher said.

"I know," Wayne agreed. "Once, though, he let it slip that he worked for D&G Wholesale."

"Where's that?"

"I don't know. I never bothered to check."

Fisher made a mental note to look into it when she got back to the station.

"Did he own a car?" Fisher asked.

"It's the gray Ford over in the corner of the parking lot."

"I see that you have security cameras on the property," Holt said, pointing to a camera just above the door of Wayne's office. "We need to see all the footage."

Wayne looked down at his boots. "That's the thing, though. When I heard about what happened in room ten, I quickly went to check the recordings. And you know what? They're gone."

Holt's face turned hard. "What do you mean they're gone?"

"My security is old. I still rely on tapes to record the footage. And this morning, someone took the tapes."

"How did they *take* them?" Holt growled.

Wayne took a step back. "I… I don't know. I usually sleep in one of the empty units. I don't have a place of my own. And if the motel is full, which it hasn't been in a long time, I'll sleep on the mattress in the office. Last night, though, I slept in room sixteen. The one in the far corner." He pointed to it. "And when I came to the office, I found the office door was not locked."

"And you weren't bothered by this?" Holt asked.

Wayne shrugged. "I thought I might have forgotten to lock it. I mean, sometimes I'll have a beer or two before going to bed, so I can be clumsy."

Fisher asked, "You went to your office before or after you found out about Trevor McGinty?"

"Before," he replied. "I was on my laptop when the officer showed up to tell me something had happened."

"Was anything stolen?" she asked.

"No, nothing. Everything was where I had left it the night before."

"Except for the security tapes."

"Yes, only the security tapes were missing."

*We are definitely dealing with a professional*, she thought.

# FIVE

Lee Callaway stood in the front of a classroom and felt cold sweat roll down his back. Callaway was tall and tanned with silver around his temples. His eyes were emerald green, and they were staring at the students gathered before him.

Nina, his daughter, was among the twenty-two students looking at him intently, each waiting for him to enthrall and impress them.

Callaway was at Nina's school to participate in career day. Each parent was invited to talk about their profession, and Nina had begged Callaway to come and speak about what he did.

Callaway was a private investigator—a job he loved doing—but he was not particularly impressive when compared to the other parents who had spoken before him. One parent was a surgeon, another was head of a private equity firm, a third worked in television, and a fourth was an information specialist.

Callaway wasn't sure what the last position entailed, but when you had the word *specialist* in your title, it must be important.

He saw Nina smiling at him. She was glad he was there. He wished he could share her enthusiasm, but he didn't.

He took a deep breath and then spent twenty minutes going over all the cases he had worked on. And there were many, each more complex than the last. Murder. Missing persons. Unjust incarceration. He had seen it all.

He tried to avoid parts that were gruesome. After all, they were only nine years old. He also didn't mention the times he was broke, with not even two cents to rub together. Times where he was literally kicked out of his home for not paying his rent. Times when he went to loan sharks and had to work for them because he couldn't repay the money he had borrowed. Times where he skipped meals because he had blown all his money at the casino.

In short, Callaway was a man no parent would want their children to grow up to be. He was impulsive, irresponsible, and selfish. And it took him a long time to realize the errors of his ways.

He was working hard to change himself. He had sobered up and had not set foot inside a casino in months, and he was taking responsibility for himself.

He was here speaking to these kids not because he wanted to, but because it meant a great deal to his daughter.

He had not known unconditional love until now.

Callaway had walked out of his marriage when Nina was just a baby. His ex-wife had to raise their daughter as a single parent. During those times, he saw his daughter occasionally, but each time he did, she always embraced him like he was the most important person in her life.

Even when he decided to be more involved in her life, she never held his actions against him. She was more forgiving than he could ever be. Maybe she was still young and not yet jaded. Maybe when she became a teenager, she would resent him for what he had done.

Until that time came, he had to do everything in his power to make it up to her.

When he was done with his spiel, the teacher asked if anyone had any questions.

Several hands shot up. One student—a girl with braces—said, "My mom says private investigators spend all day drinking."

Callaway stared at him, unsure of how to answer. "We drink occasionally, but not all day," he replied.

*Precocious kid*, he thought.

In reality, Callaway would frequent bars so often that he would sometimes wake up somewhere and not know how he got there.

A second student—a boy—asked, "I heard private investigators sleep with a lot of women."

The teacher jumped up from her chair and scolded him.

Callaway said, "That only happens in the movies."

*That's a* really *precocious kid. How much TV does he watch?*

The truth was, Callaway had been with a lot of women. Married women, to be exact. And those married women were his clients.

It was another part of his life he was not proud of.

Another girl asked, "Is it true that you are a private investigator because you are not qualified to be a real police officer?"

"As a matter of fact, I used to be a deputy sheriff," he replied with a touch of pride.

He smiled and winked in his daughter's direction.

She beamed back.

While he was married, Callaway worked for the sheriff's department for several years. It was a sleepy town where nothing really happened. The only excitement he ever saw was picking up drunks for urinating on people's property. Bored out of his mind, he quit the department and walked out on his marriage at the same time.

Another boy asked, "Do you own a gun?"

"I do."

The boy's eyes glinted with excitement. "Can we see it?"

"No, you can't," the teacher interjected.

Callaway grinned. "I don't carry it with me all the time. Only when I go into a dangerous situation."

"Have you shot anyone?" the boy asked, looking at Callaway like he was an action hero.

Callaway opened his mouth but then shook his head.

*How many action movies have you watched, kid?* he thought.

Callaway was a pacifist. He didn't believe in using violence to solve problems. If he could talk his way out of a situation, he did. But that didn't mean he didn't have his share of altercations. He'd been left with a split lip, broken nose, and swollen cheeks— usually by an irate husband of one of his clients.

The bell rang, saving him from more questions he was not comfortable answering.

As he walked back to his car with Nina, she said, "I'm proud of you, Daddy."

"Thanks, honey," he said, managing a smile.

Deep down, though, he felt like he had let her down.

*I must have looked like a complete fool*, he thought.

## SIX

Holt and Fisher returned to room ten, where they found members of the Crime Scene Unit combing through the room.

One CSU member came over to them. She was holding a shoebox. "You have to see this," she said. She opened the lid, and inside the box, wrapped in Ziploc plastic bags, were bundles of cash.

With a gloved hand, Fisher lifted a bundle. Hundred-dollar bills were held together in elastic bands. And from the size of the bundles, Fisher estimated there was probably ten thousand dollars in each bundle.

She quickly counted the bundles.

"There's over seventy thousand dollars in that box," Fisher said.

"But that's not all," the CSU member said. She took them over to the other side of the bed. "I was looking underneath the mattress and I noticed this." She held up the mattress, and they could see the bottom hung low. "So, I searched and saw one side of the mattress fabric had been stitched up. I cut it open." She shoved her hand into the opening and pulled out more Ziploc bags. Each had a bundle of cash. She handed one bag to Fisher.

Fisher's eyes narrowed. "This looks like Canadian currency."

"How much is inside?" Holt asked.

The CSU member stuck her hand back inside the mattress and began to remove all the Ziploc bags. When she was done, they counted over two dozen of them.

Fisher did a quick calculation. "By my estimate, that's another hundred thousand."

"But why in Canadian dollars?" Holt asked.

"That's a good question," Fisher replied. "But the more important question is, why is someone carrying over two hundred thousand dollars in cash living in a motel like this?"

They thought for a moment.

"Drug money?" Holt asked.

"That'd be my guess," Fisher replied.

A second CSU member approached them. "Can I show you guys something?" he said.

He took them over to the front window. He pulled the drapes aside and pointed to the upper corner of the window.

"Is that a camera?" Fisher said, squinting.

It was small and black, and the lens was pointing outside the motel room.

"That's great," Holt said with excitement. "We can see who entered the room at the time of the murder."

"That won't be possible," the CSU member said.

"Why not?"

"The camera is not wireless. It was connected to something, I'm guessing a laptop, but the laptop's not here."

Holt let out a dismissive grunt.

Fisher said, "I wouldn't be surprised if the killer took it."

"But why didn't the killer take the money?" Holt asked.

"Maybe the killer wasn't here for the money."

"Then why torture the victim?" Holt said.

Fisher was silent. She and Holt liked bouncing theories and questions off of each other. They did this at the beginning of every investigation. They wanted to discard anything that might steer them in the wrong direction. There was nothing worse than wasting valuable time and resources on a lead that went nowhere.

"We can be certain of one thing, though," Fisher said.

"What?" Holt asked.

"The camera was set up because of the money. The victim was probably worried someone would break in and steal the cash." Fisher then walked over to the door and pointed at a second bolt lock on the door. "This was likely installed by the victim."

"But it was unlocked when the officer came in earlier," Holt added.

"It was," Fisher agreed.

There was a moment of silence.

Fisher pulled out her cell phone and dialed a number. She spoke a few words, listened, and then hung up.

"Who did you call?" Holt asked.

"The 9-1-1 dispatcher. She played the call that came in. The voice was low and muffled as if someone was cupping the telephone receiver."

"What did they say?"

"That someone's shot in room ten of Motel 86. Then they hung up."

"Where did the call come from? Do they know?"

"Not far from the motel."

They left the room, went through the parking lot, and walked along the side road until they stopped at a traffic light.

In the northeast corner of the intersection was a phone booth.

The city had started to get rid of pay phones. Almost everyone had cell phones now. But in some neighborhoods, particularly those less affluent, pay phones were still in existence.

*The 9-1-1 call had come from there*, Fisher thought.

She knew the caller would not be dumb enough to leave fingerprints behind, but she could not take any chances.

She turned to Holt. "Let's get someone to dust it for prints, just in case."

# SEVEN

They decided to speak to the motel's residents. There weren't that many, to begin with—the motel was never fully booked—so they figured the task would be simpler. But even so, Holt and Fisher decided to split up.

Madison Dier was staying on the upper level, two rooms over from Trevor McGinty. She was in her late thirties, with dirty blonde hair and pale skin. Her eyes were glassy, and lines had begun to emerge underneath them. She had dreams of making a career as an actress in movies and television. She moved to Los Angeles in her early twenties and spent years trying to break into the business. Like many young and beautiful women, she was used and tossed aside by the system.

"I got some bit parts in TV shows," she said, looking down at her feet. "But my career never took off. I made the mistake of getting involved with a married director. He promised he would make me a star, but then his movies started to flop, and he couldn't get another movie off the ground. It wasn't long before we broke up. Last I heard, he was still living with his wife and kids, and I'm... *here*." Her eyes suddenly became misty. "They should name this place the Motel of Shattered Dreams."

"Why would you say that?" Fisher asked.

"I've seen a bunch of people come and leave. Actors like me. Single mothers running away from their abusive husbands or boyfriends. A bigshot from Silicon Valley who lost everything in the dot com crash. Veterans suffering from PTSD who desperately needed help but didn't get any from the government. We even had a former athlete stay here for a bit. His career was over, and he was broke and on drugs."

"Why do all these people come here?"

Madison looked at her. "Why do you think? The rent is cheap, and Wayne doesn't ask too many questions. He'll rent out the place to anyone, just as long as they pay in cash and on time."

"How long have you lived here?" Fisher asked.

"About a year," Madison replied. "My family lives not far from Milton, but I don't have any contact with them. My parents were never happy when I packed up and went to LA. Especially my dad. He told me I would come back penniless and heartbroken. And he was right. I have no real education. My acting is far behind me, and I barely make ends meet by working at a food processing plant three miles from here."

"I'm sorry to hear that," Fisher said. "I can't believe your family has abandoned you."

Madison fell silent. "I don't blame them, though," she said. "After my breakup with the director, I starred in some risqué films. My parents found out about them, and they said it brought shame to the family. And since then, they have not spoken to me."

Fisher could sense Madison had nobody, and she was desperate for human connection. From experience, Fisher had learned to let people talk even if it had nothing to do with the case. The worst a detective could do was cut someone off and ask them direct questions. People were not obligated to provide information. There was no law to compel them to do so—unless they were under arrest, of course. Also, most people were hesitant to speak to the police. They feared saying something that might incriminate them.

Madison clearly had a lot to say, and Fisher didn't want to interrupt her.

"If I could afford it," Madison said, "I would leave this place in a snap."

"How come?"

"Wayne gives me the creeps," Madison said, hugging herself.

"In what ways?" Fisher asked.

"It's the way he looks at me. It's like he knows something about me, but he won't say. I've thought about confronting him, but I don't want to get kicked out. I need a place to stay." She shrugged. "He's probably seen my risqué movies, and so he thinks he knows me."

Fisher saw her opening. "How much do you know about your neighbor, Trevor McGinty?"

"Not much, really," Madison replied. "He would say hi or bye whenever I saw him. I tried conversing with him a few times, but he mostly kept to himself."

"Did he tell you what he did for a living?" Fisher asked.

"No, he didn't."

"Did he have a lot of people visit him in his motel room?"

Madison shook her head. "He didn't get many visitors. I usually saw him alone. Once in a while, though, I would see him with another man."

Fisher's eyebrows shot up. "What did this man look like?"

Madison thought for a moment. "Um... I can't say, really. He was probably about the same age as Trevor. He always wore sunglasses, and he always had on a newsboy cap."

"Newsboy cap?" Fisher asked, confused.

"Yeah, you know, the one where the front of the hat looks like a duck's bill."

"Oh, right," Fisher said. "Last night, did you hear anything from Trevor McGinty's room?"

Madison thought for a moment. "No."

"No gunshots?"

"No."

"Are you sure?"

Madison looked away. "To be honest, since I've come back to Milton, I haven't been sleeping well. So, I take medication before bed. And I also..." She paused.

"Also what?" Fisher prodded.

"I've been drinking a little too much as well, so I'm usually passed out all night."

*That would explain the glassy eyes*, Fisher thought.

"Thank you for your cooperation, Miss Dier," Fisher said.

# EIGHT

Freddie Iseman had long hair that reached down to his shoulders. He looked like he had not shaved in months, but instead of growing a thick beard, he had whiskers on his chin and cheeks. He wore a hoodie that bore the name of a college. And even though it was a bit cool this time of year, he had on shorts and sandals.

He stood outside his motel room, which was on the lower level, right below Trevor McGinty's room.

Freddie had dropped out of college a couple of years ago, and he was currently unemployed, which wasn't a big surprise to Holt. Freddie didn't come across as someone who took responsibility seriously.

Freddie stood outside his motel room with the door closed behind him. There was a good reason for that. Freddie reeked of marijuana. It was on his breath, his clothes, even his hair. And when Freddie had answered the door, the smell was even stronger inside.

Holt had no choice but to go inside and search the room. If there was anything illegal happening inside the room, as a law enforcement officer, Holt had to find out. Holt didn't have a warrant to search the premises, but he did get permission from Freddie before he entered the room. He found small bags of pot, a bong, edibles, and joints ready to be smoked.

The smell was so pungent that Holt decided to conduct the interview outside, in the fresh air.

"I hope the marijuana is for medical purposes," Holt said.

"It is," Freddie said.

"Do you have a doctor's note?"

"I'm sure I do, but I don't know where it is."

"You're not dealing, right?" Holt asked.

"No, man. I don't deal. I don't have enough stash to sell. You saw that when you went inside."

Freddie was telling the truth, Holt agreed. Freddie had just enough marijuana for consumption. But then again, Holt hadn't turned the place upside down. He wasn't sure what he'd find if he checked the oven, toilet bowl, and air vents—the places drug dealers tended to hide their goods.

Against his better judgment, Holt was willing to cut Freddie some slack. Holt wasn't here to arrest someone for possession. He had bigger and more important matters to deal with.

Holt sensed Freddie was harmless. A surfer or skateboarder who was always looking for a good time. The future mattered not, only the present. In some ways, Holt envied people like Freddie. He was enjoying his life even if he was accomplishing very little.

But there was another reason Holt was not going to throw the book at Freddie. If Trevor McGinty was involved in the drug trade, leading to his murder, Freddie might know something that could help.

"Did Trevor McGinty ever sell you any drugs?" Holt asked.

"The guy who lives upstairs?"

"Yes."

"Isn't he dead?"

"He is. But how did you know that?"

"I heard people say that."

"What people?"

Freddie shrugged. "The people who live at the motel."

"How long have you lived here?"

Freddie looked up, thinking. "I can't remember. What's today's date?"

Holt told him.

"Then a couple of years, I guess."

"How do you pay for the room if you don't have a job?" Holt asked.

"My mom sends me money. She works on Wall Street."

Holt's eyes narrowed. "And you prefer to live here than with your mother in New York?"

"I visit my mom once a month. But I want to be independent. Make my own way in life, you know?"

"But she pays for your lodging, and I assume she pays for your food as well."

"It's only temporary. I got big plans in life."

"And they are?"

"I don't have plans now, but I know I'll have them in the future."

Holt felt like his head was going to explode. *This is like talking to a five-year-old*, he thought.

"Okay, let's go back to Trevor McGinty. Did he ever sell you marijuana?"

"No, man, I never bought anything from him," Freddie replied, shaking his head. "I asked *him* if he wanted a joint from me."

Holt stared at him. "I thought you said you didn't deal."

Freddie put his hands up defensively. "I don't. I swear. I was trying to be friendly, you know. I even give joints to Wayne. That's why he lets me stay here long-term. And he also doesn't care how much I smoke inside."

"Right. You never sold Trevor McGinty any marijuana, and he never sold you any, either."

"That's what I said."

"Did you at least talk to him? Get to know him?"

Freddie thought for a moment. "Not really. He didn't really come out and talk to other guests. In the summer, we'll hold a barbecue in the parking lot, grill some ribs, drink a few beers, play some music, have a blast. The guy would stay in his room. I think he was paranoid."

"What makes you say that?"

"He had a camera in his front window."

"How did you know?"

"Easy. Whenever you walked by his room, you could see a red light blinking. That told you he was recording you."

# NINE

The gray concrete building was cold and unwelcoming. It was built during the cold war, when tensions were high between the United States and Russia. At the time, the government decided to erect buildings that could withstand enemy fire in case of invasion, and some of those buildings still stood.

One of those buildings was now used for commercial purposes. Start-ups, IT companies, cyber security firms, and various other corporations occupied floors of the building.

In the basement, one floor below the underground parking, was a level exclusively used by companies who valued anonymity. One of those companies was Dark Box. And in order to get to Dark Box, you had to go through several security checks.

The elevators on the main lobby could only be accessed using a scan card. Even after gaining access to the basement level, you had to go down a narrow hall and find the right door for Dark Box. There were no signs, which made this task all the more difficult, unless you knew where you were going. The door was made of steel, and next to it was a keypad that required a PIN—which changed on a daily basis—and also a thumbprint. Only then were you able to get inside.

The space was small and confining. Several people worked behind computer terminals that were connected, not to the local internet, but to secure networks. These individuals came from all over the world. They were hired not only for their technical skills, but also for their ability to do things normal people would hesitate in doing: accessing personal information and using it against people. And their boss was a man who prided himself on being able to do just that.

Howard Crenshaw sat in his tiny office with a glass of bourbon in his hand. He was not prone to drinking during the day, but today was an exception. Crenshaw was in his early sixties. His dyed black hair was thinning. He sported a thick mustache that covered his upper lip, and he wore round spectacles. Crenshaw always donned a three-piece suit. He also wore an expensive watch and expensive shoes. He drove a Rolls Royce and lived in a five-bedroom house just outside the city.

Crenshaw was able to afford all these luxuries because he was ruthless. He was willing to destroy people's lives, as long as he got paid.

Dark Box operated in the shadows; it didn't advertise itself to the general public. They were an exclusive service provider. People came to them via word of mouth. And even then, Dark Box thoroughly investigated them before taking them on as clients. On top of that, Dark Box was not cheap. Only the rich could afford their services.

Dark Box used surveillance, counter-intelligence, and black-hat tactics. They didn't work for any government, though they had clients who held high positions in the US government.

Their sole mission was to make money. And the only way to do that was to ensure they made their clients' problems go away.

To accomplish this, a lot of money needed to change hands. Bribery was a common practice. They had people all over the city on their payroll. They also had an encrypted telephone line specifically for their informants. If the information turned out to be useful, a payment in cash would be made to them.

Crenshaw had installed a safe in the concrete wall behind his desk. There was close to a million dollars in various currencies stored inside. It was risky holding that much cash on hand, but it was out of necessity. Nothing was ever paid in credit or debit. Even the hackers he employed were paid in cash.

His employees were aware of the safe in his office, but they would never dare try to break into it. Crenshaw had people who were loyal to him. They did whatever was asked of them—even murder.

He took another sip from his glass. He didn't like getting his hands dirty. Once the police were involved, things became complicated. He had people on the force who provided information for a fee, but dealing with them required extra precautions. He could never be sure if someone was doing it for the money or if they were doing it to set him up.

For that reason, Crenshaw relied on his employees to do most of the heavy lifting. He just wrote the checks, so to speak.

Right now, though, one of his employees had taken a step he hadn't approved. He knew it could come back to bite them.

But there was a bigger problem to deal with.

Someone from their past had returned, and what they knew could unravel everything he had worked so hard to build.

Crenshaw tightened his grip on the glass. He would not let that happen. He would not let this person threaten his existence.

He would do everything in his power to destroy that person.

# TEN

Callaway entered the restaurant and beelined for a table in the corner. It was his favorite spot in the restaurant, and he was relieved whenever it was unoccupied. On the occasion when someone was sitting in it, he'd grab a stool and have his meal at the counter by the cashier.

The main counter wasn't a bad spot, either. It gave him the opportunity to chat up the waitress.

Joely Paterson had blonde hair that she kept pulled back in a ponytail. She wore a tight-fitting T-shirt with an apron over it. She was behind the cash register, ringing up a customer's order. She caught his eye and smiled.

He smiled back and then sat down at the table.

Someone had left the morning newspaper behind. Callaway grabbed it and quickly flipped through it. There was always some tragedy gripping the city. If it wasn't drive-by shootings at a children's park, then it was a hit-and-run involving the elderly, or a case of a hate crime where someone had posted vitriol on a mosque, synagogue, or temple.

Callaway had long ago given up on the idea of world peace. It was something to aspire to, but it was not something that was attainable. And this was coming from someone who was not a pessimist.

Callaway had always tried to look for the good in people. He didn't believe people were inherently bad; it was their circumstances that made them do bad things. But there were those who were born to do evil. Serial killers were a prime example of that. No amount of nurturing could change who they were. They had no feelings for humankind. And as such, they took it upon themselves to play God by hurting and murdering others for their pleasure.

Joely came over to his table. "Why so glum?" she said.

He pushed the newspaper aside. "I should stop reading the news. It's depressing."

"I steer clear of the news," she said. "I know bad things are happening around me. I just don't want to constantly be reminded of it."

"How's it going with you and Mike?" he asked.

Joely was divorced. Her ex-husband, Dean, used to work as an equipment manager for a rock band. One day, while on the road, he called Joely and told her he wasn't coming back. Joely had her own dreams of becoming a singer, but with a child to care for, she had to abandon those dreams. Josh was now six years old and the apple of her eye. She knew he would one day make something of himself.

Joely had no luck when it came to dating. She met enough scoundrels to turn her away from the whole thing. Most were looking for a one-night stand or someone to support them. Plus, when they found out she had a child, they quickly looked for the exit.

Callaway, however, encouraged her not to give up. He was once a scoundrel, but now he was doing everything to win his family back. If he could change, there was still hope for a better ending for her and Josh.

Reluctantly, she had gone out on a date with a regular from the restaurant. The customer ran his own construction company, and he was also divorced and had a son. His wife had run away with her dance instructor, leaving him to care for their son on his own. Last he heard, his ex-wife and her boyfriend owned a salsa studio in Brazil. Mike understood exactly what Joely had gone through with her ex, and he agreed to take it slow in their relationship.

"It's going great with Mike," she said. "I'm hoping to introduce him to Josh soon. We are planning to take the boys to a baseball game. Hopefully, the boys can hit it off and become friends."

Callaway smiled. He was happy for her. But at the same time, his feelings were tinged with sadness. If Joely and Mike got serious, Joely might decide to leave the restaurant. There were too many instances where he was broke and looking for a free meal, and Joely had never turned him away. He enjoyed her company as well. But above all, she had become a trusted friend.

"How did it go at Nina's school?" she asked.

Callaway's shoulders slumped, and he sighed.

"That bad, huh?" she said.

"The other kids' parents were far more accomplished than I was. I felt like an idiot standing in front of them talking about a career that people have only read about in detective novels or seen in movies or on TV. I feel like I let Nina down."

Joely sat across from him at the table. "Let me tell you something, and I want you to listen to me good."

He started at her. "Okay."

"Kids don't care what you do. They don't care how much money you make, how famous you are, or what your position is in society. They only care that you love them and give them your time."

Callaway looked away, feeling ashamed. "I never gave Nina much of my time when she was growing up."

Joely smiled. "I know that. And you know what? There is nothing you can do about the past. But what you can do now is be there for her, which is what you are doing. You are giving her the attention she needs and wants. You went to career day, and you spoke to all the students in her class. Believe me, she will remember that more than what you did for a living."

"Really?"

"Look at me," she said. "I'm a waitress. I barely make minimum wage. But I know this for a fact: When I'm at home reading a book to Josh before bed, he's the happiest kid in the world. And you know why? He's got his mom all to himself."

Callaway thought for a moment, then he smiled. "Thanks, Joely."

# ELEVEN

Fisher knocked on the door of the room down the hall from Trevor McGinty. Wayne had given them the names of all the guests staying at the motel. She and Holt had interviewed them all. Except for this one.

She knocked again and waited.

The tenant's name was Karla Johnson. Wayne told them she'd checked in the night before. She said she was passing by and needed a place to stay for a couple of days.

Fisher squinted. *A couple of days.*

If she'd said she was staying for only a night, it would make sense that she would be gone by morning. So far, Fisher nor Holt or any of the CSU members had seen anyone come out of the room.

Fisher found this strange. Whenever the police arrived at a scene, it was not uncommon for people to be curious about what was going on.

She reached down and touched the door handle. It was unlocked.

She slowly pushed the door in. "Police," she said, in case Karla Johnson was sleeping. "Can I have a word with you?"

She waited and then took a step inside. Instead of finding a second dead body, she found the room empty. The bed was not made up. The bedsheets were unruly as if someone had woken up and just left. Most people didn't make their beds at motels. It was the management's job.

She looked around and saw a bag next to the bed. She reached down and looked inside. There were some articles of clothing, but no personal items.

She went into the bathroom. It was empty. She was about to leave when she noticed that the window above the bathtub was open. She walked over and examined it. It was big enough for someone to fit through. She stuck her head out. There was a water pipe that went along the wall next to the window.

She debated whether to close the window or not. She decided against it.

She went outside and stood looking out into the parking lot. She saw that the media had already gathered around the motel. The only thing keeping them away was the yellow police tape.

Fisher knew all too well that, if given permission, the media wouldn't hesitate to trample through the crime scene. They only cared about their ratings. The more sensational the story, the more people would tune in.

She then saw a man standing across the street, just behind the cameras and reporters. He had his hands in his pockets, and he was staring at… *her*.

When he caught her staring back, he lowered his head and quickly left the scene.

Fisher wasn't sure what to make of it. He could be a curious bystander, eager to get a glimpse of what all the commotion was about.

Or he could be someone of interest.

But she knew running after him would be of no use. By the time she reached the sidewalk, he'd be long gone.

# TWELVE

The Callaway Private Investigation Office was above a soup and noodle restaurant. In order to get to it, you had to go behind the restaurant, up a flight of steep metal stairs, and then knock on the metal door.

Even if you got to the door, you still didn't know if you were at the right location. There was no sign anywhere to indicate such an office existed. There was, however, a telephone number taped to the door.

If someone was eager to speak to him, they could call that number. And if Callaway was interested in speaking to them, he'd answer the phone.

Over the years, Callaway had seen his share of bad luck. He'd owed money to the wrong people, and these people didn't take kindly to not being paid on time. These people were also inclined to use brute force to get their way.

And then there was the matter of his clients' ex-spouses. They, too, didn't take kindly to being photographed with their mistresses. Not to mention the impending divorce that ruined them financially.

Callaway couldn't care less about his clients' ex-spouses. They deserved what came to them. They wanted to have a good time without repercussions. *You do the crime, you do the time*, Callaway always thought. *If you are going to cheat on your husband or wife, then you better be prepared to pay for it. Even if that means losing half of your assets.*

Fortunately, though, Callaway had been getting fewer of those cases. The money was good in them, and the amount of work was substantially less when compared to some other types of cases. But following a cheating spouse in order to catch him in a compromising position left Callaway feeling dirty and in need of a cold shower. Plus, what he unearthed destroyed marriages and homes. He wasn't concerned about the spouses; they'd find someone else. He was concerned about the children. It couldn't be easy on them being in the middle of warring parents, having to constantly shuttle from one house to another. The emotional damage that did to them was enormous.

He always reminded himself that he wasn't to blame for this. The people who betrayed the trust and the sanctity of their marriage vows were to blame.

He looked up at the camera just above the door. Ever since he installed it, he could breathe a little easier. If someone showed up unannounced, he could refuse to open the door and hide in his office until they left.

This was easier said than done, though.

He unlocked the office door and entered. The space was small. With no windows, it looked even smaller. His office had no air conditioning, and the heating barely warmed it in the colder months. He could manage without the air conditioning, though. He would open the door and place a running fan in front of it. But when it was blistering hot outside, the fan would only circulate hot air.

There was no bathroom, either. In an emergency, he could either run to the noodle shop below or a coffee shop down the block. He preferred the latter. He would get behind on the rent, and as such, he avoided the noodle shop at all costs. It didn't help that his landlady owned the entire building, which included the noodle shop.

Callaway could try to find another place to rent, somewhere with a view of the city, a fully functioning bathroom, and proper heating and cooling. But those places cost money, and in his line of work, there was no such thing as stability.

Some days he was inundated with work. Other days, he had nothing to do but stare at his phone all day.

Lately, he was spending more time solving puzzles on his phone than solving actual mysteries.

*It comes with the territory*, he thought.

# THIRTEEN

Callaway shut the door behind him. Next to the door was a small desk with a laptop on it. The desk had a drawer, and in it he kept one item: a handgun which he had legally purchased from a gun shop. He also had a license to carry concealed firearms. He had considered keeping the weapon in his apartment, but now that Nina was sleeping over once a week, that was out of the question. His ex-wife, Patti, had conditions before she allowed Nina to stay over. No drugs, which was not a biggie for Callaway; he'd never dabbled in narcotics. No drinking alcohol in front of Nina. Again, something he could do without. And finally, nothing that could potentially harm her. So, no weapons of any kind.

Callaway was a responsible gun owner. He would store the weapon in a safe. But Patti was a nurse, and in her line of work, she had seen her share of accidents. Kids shooting other kids because the parents failed to properly secure their weapons.

Callaway wasn't going to try to change her mind. The only thing that mattered was that he got to see Nina regularly.

Next to the small desk was a sofa, which at times of desperation, he had come to use as a bed. Across from the sofa was a flat-screen TV hanging on the wall. The TV was a gift from a client, and it was the only valuable item in the office.

Callaway reached over and grabbed the remote on top of the desk. He clicked the TV on. It was tuned to the 24-hour news channel. Callaway never knew where he'd land his next case, and the news was a great place to get a heads-up.

He turned the laptop on. It was ten years old and took a good twenty minutes to boot up. Callaway always debated about getting a newer model. In fact, he recently saw a laptop on sale. He went to the store to take a look. But in the end, he didn't have the heart to replace the older laptop. It still worked fine, and it never crashed once it was fully up and running.

While the computer loaded, he decided to take a walk to the convenience store around the corner. As a creature of habit, he poured himself a cup of coffee from the vending machine, grabbed a granola bar, and made his way to the cashier. At times, when he had little money, the coffee and granola bar were just enough to satisfy his hunger.

The owner was behind the counter. Callaway hadn't seen him in weeks. His son had minded the store in his place.

"Your son told me you were sick," Callaway said. "How are you doing?"

The owner looked at him. "Much better. Thank you for asking."

"What was wrong?" Callaway asked.

"I had pneumonia. I was bedridden for two weeks."

"I'm sorry to hear that. I'm glad to see you back." Callaway meant it. He had come to the shop dozens of times, but he never made an effort to speak to the owner. Not even once. He always paid and left.

"That's very kind of you," the owner said with a smile. He then pointed to the items in Callaway's hands. "No need to pay for those. It's on me."

"Thanks," Callaway said, surprised. "By the way, I'm Lee."

"Nadeem," the owner replied.

"Nice to meet you, Nadeem."

"See you next time."

Callaway smiled and left the store. As he walked back to the office, he thought, *It doesn't take much effort to be nice to people.* Life was hard. Life was complicated. And everyone was doing their best to get through it. A smile. A tiny gesture. Some kind words. They went a long way in making someone feel better.

He got back to the office, put the granola bar and coffee to the side, and began checking his emails. Apart from relying on word of mouth, the only advertising Callaway did was through his website, which had been created by another client of his. That client was tech-savvy, so it took him only a few hours to set something up for Callaway.

If anyone was looking to hire a private investigator, everything they needed to know about him was on the site: his bio and a photo of his smiling face.

After ten minutes of checking his emails, he sat back in his chair with a frown on his face.

*If I don't find another case soon*, he thought, *I'll have to start looking for a job.*

## FOURTEEN

Trevor McGinty was seventy-one years old. He died in his sleep after a long bout with Alzheimer's. His obituary read that he was a loving husband and father, and that he had left behind his wife, two children, and four grandchildren.

What was even more shocking was that Trevor McGinty had died twenty-three years earlier.

Fisher looked at Holt. He was staring at her laptop screen.

"This must be a mistake," he said.

Fisher picked a plastic baggie up from her desk and held it up for Holt. "The driver's license has the victim's photo with the name Trevor McGinty next to it. You saw me find it in the victim's jacket pocket, so it can't be a mistake."

"Check the database again," Holt said, his voice taut with disbelief.

Fisher punched in the name, and several Trevor McGintys popped up. One lived in Alaska. His driver's license indicated that he was twenty-nine years old. The second Trevor McGinty was in Las Vegas. His driver's license showed an age close to the victim's, but this Trevor was black, while the victim was not. The third was in Florida, and his age was ninety-two. The only Trevor McGinty in Milton was seventy-one years old, and the victim was fifty-three.

Holt was silent for a beat. He was going through the information on the screen again. He then fell in his chair and rubbed his eyes.

"Satisfied?" Fisher said.

"If the victim isn't Trevor McGinty, then who is he?" Holt said.

"If he's not in the system," Fisher said, "then that means the driver's license is a fake."

"What about a social security number?" Holt said.

Fisher checked the system and shook her head. "I can't find any Trevor McGinty on file for our state."

"But didn't Wayne Lemont say he worked for a company called D&G Wholesale?" Holt asked.

Fisher got to work and then replied, "There is a D&G Wholesale in Torrens County. It's about thirty miles from Milton."

"Should we go take a look?" Holt said.

"We will eventually…"

Fisher fell silent, lost in her thoughts.

"What's bothering you, partner?" Holt asked.

"I'm still thinking about the money we found in the victim's room."

"It was a lot of cash," Holt agreed, "but what about it?"

"There is no way this Trevor McGinty could have saved that much money working for a wholesaler."

"Unless that wholesaler is doing something illegal, you mean?"

"We can't be sure of that. According to D&G Wholesale, they sell organic fruits and vegetables directly from farmers to customers. They even donate a portion of their profits to farmers in third world countries. They believe in sustainable living, and they've also won several environmental awards."

"So, what you're saying," Holt said, "is you don't believe they are using their business as a front for distributing narcotics?"

"I'd be surprised if they were. They are already getting too much attention with their environmental initiatives. I doubt some cartel would want to work with them. The exposure would be too risky."

"We should still talk to them."

"First, I think we should talk to Trevor McGinty's family," Fisher said.

Holt frowned. "But he doesn't exist."

"Not this one. The one who died twenty-three years ago."

# FIFTEEN

Callaway was staring at his laptop when he heard footsteps on the stairs leading up to his office. The door was closed. He pulled out his cell phone, opened an app, and stared at the image on the screen. The camera outside his office was feeding live footage via the app to his cell phone.

Callaway wasn't expecting company, and if it was someone he didn't recognize, he would not open the door.

To his surprise, his landlady appeared on his tiny screen.

*That's odd*, he thought. *I'm not behind on rent.*

His landlady only ever came up to hound him for the rent if it was past due.

He got up from his chair and opened the door before she knocked.

His landlady was short, slim, and Asian. Her hair was always tied in a ponytail. She had on a colorful patterned dress and flat walking shoes.

"Ms. Chen," he said. "To what do I owe the pleasure of your visit?"

"Can I talk to you?" she said hesitantly.

"Um… sure. Do you want to come inside or talk outside?"

She took a peek into his cramped office space. "Maybe we can talk in the shop."

He shrugged and then followed her down the metal stairs, through the side alley, and into the noodle shop.

The shop was closed at this time of day, but he could hear the chef in the back preparing for the opening, which would be soon.

They took a table by the front windows. Ms. Chen said, "Can I get you anything? Rice? Noodles? Soup?"

He stared at her and then blinked. He had been at the shop multiple times and never once did she ask if he wanted anything. Maybe because she knew he didn't have the money to pay for it. She was already charging him rock bottom rent prices. She wasn't about to give him a free meal on top of it.

"Um… I'm fine. Thank you," he said.

She sat across from him and stared at the table.

"What's wrong?" he asked, sensing something was amiss. She wasn't acting like she normally did. She hadn't insulted him once. And those insults were usually warranted.

"It's… it's about my son…"

"Bruce?"

She nodded.

Callaway had met Bruce on many occasions. He would see him at the shop helping out. Bruce had a degree in chemistry. He was currently working at a pharmaceutical company.

Ms. Chen was proud of her only child. She had doted on him and encouraged him to excel in his education. The day Bruce graduated was the happiest Callaway had ever seen Ms. Chen. She was smiling from ear to ear. Callaway remembered that day well. It was the first of the month, and he was short on rent. Ms. Chen gave Callaway an extension without him even asking for one.

"What happened to Bruce?" Callaway asked, suddenly worried.

"He got himself in trouble," Ms. Chen replied.

"With who?"

"Scammers."

"How?"

"I don't know the details, but he told me last night that all our savings are gone."

"Gone? How?"

"I think he invested it in something, and it's not there."

"Okay," he said slowly. "But why are you telling me this?"

"I want to hire you."

"Hire me for what?"

"To get our money back."

"How can I do that?"

"I don't know," she replied. "But don't you help people who are in trouble?"

"Yes, but—"

"We are in trouble," she said, putting her hands over her face. "The shop is not making money, and your rent is not enough to cover the expenses. But our savings were helping us get through, and with that gone, I don't know what to do." She stifled a sniff. "Bruce won't talk to me. I know he is hurt by what happened. I will pay you. How much do you charge?" She looked up at him. Her eyes were suddenly raw.

Callaway paused for a moment. "We'll discuss money later," he replied. "Where is Bruce now?"

## SIXTEEN

Gordon McGinty was turning seventy soon, a fact he was most proud of. He had a full head of silver hair, wrinkled skin, and bright blue eyes.

When Holt and Fisher called, Gordon was more than happy to see them. They were now seated in his living room, surrounded by framed photos of his family.

"My wife, Ethel, passed away a few years ago," he said. "She was a great host. She always had things to serve when guests dropped by. Can I get you anything? Tea or coffee?"

Holt and Fisher declined.

"I don't get many visitors, so I like to stare at all the wonderful memories of my past." He waved at the photos on the walls. "Unfortunately, like my dad, I'm also in the early stages of Alzheimer's. I'm just glad Ethel didn't know about it. She had her share of health problems: breast cancer, brain tumor—which was thankfully not malignant—and then the arthritis. When she fell and broke her collar bone, she was in the hospital for weeks. After she came home, we thought everything would be back to normal. But then she was hit with pneumonia. She never recovered from that." Gordon's face creased with sadness. "On the phone, you said you had questions about my dad. He died over twenty years ago, so I'm not sure how I can help."

Fisher asked, "Did you notice anything odd after your father's death?"

"Odd? What do you mean?"

"Anything that surprised you."

Gordon thought for a moment. "I did get a lot of calls and letters after his death."

"What kind of calls?" Fisher asked.

"Calls from credit card companies, for example."

"And what was surprising about that?"

"They were confirming if my dad had received the new credit card he had requested. I mean, this was kind of expected. After my dad died, I had to call his bank, his doctors, and his telephone provider to let everyone know he was gone. So, I assumed the credit card company was not informed or maybe misinformed when they called about a new card."

"And the calls came to *your* house?" Fisher asked.

"Yes. At the end of his life, with the Alzheimer's in full effect, my dad lived with me. So, all his mail and calls came to this address."

"And after you informed the credit card company of this, did the letters and telephone calls cease?" Fisher asked.

"As a matter of fact, no. Every few years, I'd get another letter informing me about some change to my dad's account."

"What kind of change?"

"Address change, change of PIN... stuff like that. And these were from companies I had never heard of."

"Can you remember their names?"

Gordon thought again. "I can't. I'm sorry. But one call came a few years ago."

"What was it about?"

"It was from some company—I can't recall the name of it right now. My Alzheimer's has started to impact my memory. But I do remember that the guy was very nice and polite. He said he was calling about some job and that he wanted to confirm if this was his address. I told the guy the address was right, but I wasn't aware of any jobs. I regret not telling him that my dad had died years ago. I just hung up."

"Do you have any mail you got for your dad?" Fisher asked.

"I threw them all out. A lot of them were from subscription services, so they were useless." He fell silent as his mind drifted elsewhere.

"Mr. McGinty?" Fisher said, fearing it was the Alzheimer's.

"One time…" he began, but he paused, trying to get all the facts properly aligned in his head. "There was a time I would gather all my dad's mail and put them in the corner. I don't know why. Maybe I liked having his stuff around the house, to remind me that he once existed. That he had a life. One day I decided to get rid of them. It was around the time of Ethel's brain tumor prognosis. I didn't want to be reminded of death, and seeing those envelopes in the house reminded me that he was no longer here. And I feared that Ethel would be gone too, just like him. I remember I grabbed the stack and dumped them in the garbage bin outside the house. A few days later, I was returning from my walk, and I saw a man rummaging through the bin. When he saw me, he quickly left. I checked the bin and I found that most of my dad's mail was missing."

"You believe this man had taken it?" Fisher asked.

Gordon shrugged. "He may have, but I'm not sure. And after that day, I didn't get any more of my dad's mail."

Holt pulled out a plastic baggie and held it out for Gordon. "Can you tell me if that's the man you saw rummaging through your garbage?"

Gordon took the baggie. His brow furrowed. "That's my dad's name," he said. "But that's not my dad on the driver's license."

"Do you recognize the man?" Holt asked.

"I don't think so." Gordon stared at the card. "How come the license is still valid? My dad passed away years ago."

Fisher didn't want to tell him that someone may have taken over his father's identity and that this person was now brutally murdered. Gordon was suffering through a debilitating illness. No point in aggravating him at this point in his life.

She said, "It's someone that has the same name as your father's. We just wanted to make sure he didn't contact you."

"No. I would remember him if he did."

## SEVENTEEN

Bruce Chen lived in a one-bedroom condo, not far from his mother's house. He had bought it pre-construction. After three years and several delays, he was able to move into it at the beginning of the year.

Ms. Chen told Callaway that Bruce had not left his building ever since he found out he'd been taken by scammers. He had even refused to see her. Callaway decided he would drive over there himself. He doubted Bruce would answer his calls. But if he showed up in person, he just might speak to him.

After announcing himself at the front lobby, and a bit of back and forth, he was buzzed in. Callaway took the elevator up to the nineteenth floor, where he found Bruce waiting for him by his door.

Bruce had jet black hair, smooth skin, and he wore shorts and a T-shirt. Even though he'd been holed up in his condo for several days, he still looked handsome.

"Mr. Callaway," Bruce said. "What are you doing here?"

"Call me Lee. And your mom told me to come speak to you."

Bruce looked down at his bare feet. "Did she tell you what happened?"

"Yes, and she's worried about you."

Bruce bit his bottom lip.

"Can we talk?" Callaway said.

Bruce nodded and held the door for him.

Callaway found himself in an open-concept dining and living area. The condo was small, probably around five hundred square feet. But with the floor-to-ceiling windows, the space felt bigger. It was also sparingly furnished, which helped as well.

Callaway took a seat on a white leather sofa. Bruce sat across from him.

"Tell me what happened," Callaway said.

Bruce took a deep breath. "It was supposed to have been a great investment. A friend of mine told me about this company called Grannex Investments. They said they could give a return of ten to twenty percent."

Callaway cringed. He knew where this was going. Scammers promised outrageous returns—ones that were double what the market was offering—and people easily got suckered into them.

Bruce saw the look on Callaway's face. "I was skeptical at first. It sounded too good to be true."

"It usually is," Callaway said. "But, please continue."

"I checked the company online. They invested in apartment buildings throughout the country. Mostly in poorer neighborhoods where rent is cheap, but tenant turnover is very low. By buying into these undesirable areas, the cost of the buildings was very low, and with a little renovation, the units were back on the market in no time. It sounded counterintuitive. I mean, you want to build housing in up-and-coming neighborhoods, but then those houses cost a lot of money to build, and if the market changes, their values could plummet substantially, as they did during the Great Recession. So, this made sense. Get people into an apartment with little investment, and then collect rent for as long as possible and let the buildings appreciate in value."

"So, what went wrong?"

"At first, nothing. I didn't go all-in right away. Before handing over a single dime, I joined an online forum with other Grannex investors. I spoke to several people who had nothing but positive things to say about the company. So, I went in with a thousand dollars."

"How did you invest the money?" Callaway asked. "I mean, did you meet someone from Grannex?"

"No. It was done online. You created an account and then deposited the money via bitcoin."

Callaway cringed again. He wasn't up-to-date on all the latest technology, but even he knew digital currency was unregulated. Which meant it was hard to track where the money went.

"Okay, then what happened?" Callaway asked.

## EIGHTEEN

Bruce replied, "I kept an eye on the account. I could see my thousand dollars had increased by several hundred dollars in a short time. I then deposited ten thousand. The interest ballooned substantially in a matter of weeks. My profit ended up being close to six thousand dollars. I quickly withdrew that amount."

"So, you got six grand back?" Callaway asked.

"Yes."

"In bitcoins?"

"Yes. Which I was able to cash through an online cryptocurrency exchange."

"So, let me get this straight. You put in ten thousand, plus your initial thousand, for a total of eleven thousand, and you were able to pull out six thousand. Is that right?"

Bruce replied, "I know where you're going with this. It sounds like a Ponzi scheme."

"It does to me," Callaway said.

"But in my Grannex account, I could see my investment of eleven thousand there."

"Could you withdraw the eleven thousand?"

Bruce fell silent. "No. They said it was locked in."

"For how long?"

"They never said. But the account looked legit. I've had investment accounts with major banks, and this looked just like that."

"Then what did you do?" Callaway asked.

"Once I was able to pull out six grand, which I thought were profits, I then told my mom."

Callaway sat up on the edge of the sofa. "How much did she invest?"

Bruce fell silent.

"How much, Bruce?"

Bruce sighed. "Twenty-eight thousand."

Callaway's eyes widened. "Oh."

"Yeah, and I took out a line of credit and put in another twenty-five grand."

"So, you were in thirty-six grand, and she was in twenty-eight grand, for a grand total of sixty-four thousand."

"Minus the six grand I was able to pull out."

"Okay, for argument's sake, fifty-eight thousand."

"Yes."

Callaway sighed. "That's a lot of money."

"I know. And that's why I haven't been able to sleep for days, almost a week. I've even tried taking sleeping pills, but they won't help, either. My mind is racing all the time. I can't believe I could be so stupid."

"Can you still access the Grannex account?" Callaway asked.

"Yes."

"And is your money still showing up there?"

"Our entire investment plus profits."

"How much is the profit?"

"Thirty-three thousand."

"Are you able to take any of the profits out like you did before?"

Bruce shook his head. "I tried. Repeatedly. I even contacted their head office, but I got an email saying they were having, and I quote, 'withdrawal challenges,' because they were in the process of upgrading their systems. I asked when I could withdraw at least the profits—because I know my investments are locked in. They said they didn't have a date. But then I got another email advising me to invest a hundred thousand. Only then would I be able to withdraw my thirty-three thousand profit."

Callaway sighed again. "That's a textbook Ponzi scheme, Bruce. They take money from new investors to pay off old investors. In your case, they likely don't have new investors, and so they want *you* to invest more. Which they'll use to pay *you* back your own money. They know you are desperate and that in order to salvage your loss, you'll foolishly dig a deeper hole for yourself."

"I know."

"Did you go to the police?"

"I did," Bruce replied. "But they said they couldn't do anything because Grannex has broken no US laws."

"What?"

"They are actually registered in the Bahamas."

"Then how are they operating here?"

"They have an office in Bolton, but when I went there, it didn't exist."

Callaway fell back on the sofa and put his hand over his head. "We're dealing with international scammers. I'm not sure what I can do to help."

"That's what I told my mom," Bruce said. "But for some reason, she believes in you."

Callaway sat up straight. In all his encounters with his landlady, he never got the impression she thought anything of him. In fact, he figured Ms. Chen thought he was a loser. Why else would he avoid paying even the cheapest rent in the city?

"She's read about your cases in the newspaper," Bruce said. "She's even told her friends that she has a celebrity for a tenant."

Callaway suddenly felt a giant weight on his chest.

"But these scammers could be halfway across the world," Callaway said.

Bruce's shoulders slumped. "All I wanted was to help my mom. She's given everything to me. She's worked hard at the noodle shop, working fourteen-hour days just to save enough to send me to college. I was hoping the profits from these investments would help her to finally retire. Now I don't know if that'll ever be possible."

Bruce covered his face with his hands and began to sob.

Callaway wanted to reach out and console him, but he knew nothing he could say would get back all the money he'd lost.

"I'll see what I can do to get your money back," Callaway said.

"Thanks," Bruce whispered.

# NINETEEN

D&G Wholesale's office was located in the back of a warehouse in Torrens County. The office was small, with a single rectangular window and a wooden door. A large fan hung from the ceiling. It was turned on low to circulate air in the tiny space.

Holt and Fisher had found out that D&G was owned by two brothers, Doug and Gary Lomas. The brothers had started the business seven years ago. Doug worked for a chemical giant in Iowa, while Gary worked as a production accountant for a big firm in New York. Doug's experience had led him to believe that large companies were not only damaging the environment but also harming people through the use of artificial methods of growing foods. Consumers wanted bigger fruits and vegetables. They also wanted them cheap. The only way to possibly achieve that was to pump chemicals into the ground to speed up the process. This inevitably had side effects.

Doug wanted to change that, if only for his three children, who would one day have no choice but to consume these mutated fruits and vegetables. He had heard of alternatives—people cultivating their own gardens in their backyards, or farmers growing their crops the natural way. But he had to find a way to make it accessible for people living in Milton and the surrounding areas. By then, Gary was becoming disillusioned with his work as an accountant. He was also burnt out, spending close to seventy hours a week tethered to his desk.

Together they decided to start their own company. They purchased a large plot of land outside the city, built a large warehouse, and let local farmers bring their produce to sell on their property. Some farmers had trouble delivering the produce, and so they purchased a truck in order to bring those farmers' produce to the warehouse.

Trevor McGinty was one of their drivers.

Gary, who had stubble on his cheeks and unruly hair, said, "He showed up one day asking if we were looking to hire."

Doug, who was two years older than Gary and bald, said, "That very morning, our truck driver had quit because of a dispute."

"What kind of dispute?" Holt inquired.

"We paid the driver based on each delivery," Doug replied, "but he wanted to be paid based on distance. We were a young company. Gary and I were pumping in our own money to get the business up and running. We couldn't afford to pay based on miles driven, even though that was standard practice in the industry. It was something that was not feasible for us at the time. But then Trevor showed up and said he'd do it per trip. But he wanted to be paid in cash."

"Did he provide you with a social security number?" Fisher asked.

"We asked, but he said he couldn't remember it."

"Didn't you find that odd?" Holt asked.

"Of course we did," Doug replied. "Gary and I had a long conversation about it. For all we knew, he could be an illegal immigrant."

"Did he provide you with an ID?" Fisher asked.

"No, but he did give us a telephone number to call."

"And?"

"I called, and the person on the other end said Trevor lived there, but then they hung up."

Fisher looked at Holt. Doug had spoken to Gordon McGinty, who confirmed receiving a call about a job.

*But why didn't he just show them his driver's license?* she thought. The answer came to her right after the question popped into her head. The address on the driver's license was for a motel. If he'd given it to Doug or Gary, they would have known something was up. If they decided to run the telephone number Trevor had given through the phone directory, they would get the address of the real Trevor McGinty.

Gary said, "We were in a deep predicament when he showed up that day. We had farmers waiting on us to pick up their produce, and we had to stock up the warehouse for the late afternoon rush. We hired him on the spot and agreed to pay him in cash."

"How was he as an employee?" Fisher asked.

"Excellent," Doug replied. "He was always on time, polite to a fault, and he never haggled us over the amount we paid him. He liked the work, and the farmers liked him, too."

"So, why did he leave?" Holt asked.

"One day, while helping a farmer load up the truck, Trevor pulled his back. He took painkillers and rubbed creams on his back, but the pain got progressively worse."

*That explains the prescription meds and ointments on the table next to his bed*, Fisher thought.

"Eventually, he found it difficult to get out of bed," Doug said. "Sitting for long hours driving a truck was out of the question, so he had no choice but to quit."

"We were sad to see him go," Gary said. "He was a great help to us."

Holt said, "Did you ever get a sense that he might be using the truck for other purposes?"

"Like what?"

"Perhaps hauling drugs around the state?" Holt said.

Doug laughed. "That's absurd."

"Is it?" Holt said. "He wasn't charging you based on miles driven, so it would be easy for him to take the truck wherever he wanted."

Gary said, "We had installed a GPS in the truck to track the truck's movements. We didn't do it because we thought Trevor was involved in anything illegal; we did it because we needed to know where the truck was in real-time so that we could advise the farmers when Trevor was going to show up for the pickup."

Fisher said, "And Trevor was okay with the GPS in the truck?"

"Yes. He had no problem with it."

Fisher said, "Did Trevor hang out with anyone? Anyone we can speak to?"

Doug shook his head. "I'm sorry, I don't know."

Gary said, "He did hang around a bar in Milton."

"Yeah," Doug said, suddenly remembering. "We once took him out for drinks on his birthday, and he chose this bar on Chester Street. He said it was his favorite."

"Can you give us the name of this bar?" Fisher asked.

# TWENTY

The restaurant was in downtown Milton, surrounded by office towers occupied by big banks, insurance and investment firms, and oil and mining companies.

A bottle of wine at the restaurant could set you back hundreds of dollars, if not thousands. Dinner for two ran in the high five-figures. Everything about the restaurant screamed luxury, from the gold-plated cutlery, to the Egyptian drapes, to the diamond chandelier. Only the most exclusive and wealthy dined in such a place.

Howard Crenshaw was one of them. Dark Box had provided him with enough money to live a comfortable life. But there was another reason for his visit today, and it had nothing to do with enjoying a quiet meal.

Crenshaw was here to meet someone, and this someone was late.

He took another sip from the crystal glass. He was in no hurry. He had already consumed quail that was marinated to perfection, with an assortment of steamed vegetables covered in caviar on the side. The wine was to cleanse his palate after the meal.

He had glanced at his watch when a woman appeared at the entrance. The maître d approached her with a smile, and a moment later, he brought her over to Crenshaw's table.

Crenshaw stood up, smiled, and extended his hand.

Gabrielle Fuentes was short, with an olive complexion and brown hair. She was a little on the plump side, but that was the result of bearing three children. Her husband and children were still in Honduras. Gabrielle had come to the United States to work as a housekeeper for a wealthy family. Her employer was worth a hundred million dollars. He and his wife were on the boards of several charities, and the children went to prestigious private schools.

The man had tried to have his way with Gabrielle when his wife was out of town. The attack left Gabrielle battered and bruised. She had no choice but to seek refuge at a women's shelter.

Realizing the ramifications of his actions, the man hired Dark Box to resolve this matter. Rightly so, he feared the damage this scandal would have on his reputation. Not to mention what it would do to his marriage.

Crenshaw was able to convince Gabrielle to meet him, and he chose the restaurant. He wanted to dazzle Gabrielle but also get an advantage over her. She had never stepped foot in such an opulent setting. She was clearly out of her depth.

"Thank you for coming, Ms. Fuentes," he said graciously. "Please have a seat."

She did, clutching her battered purse over her chest and nervously looking around. Other patrons were glancing over at their table. They were wondering what *she* was doing in a place like this.

Crenshaw had to suppress a smile.

"Can I get you something to drink or eat?" he asked.

"No, thank you," Gabrielle replied. Her voice had a heavy accent.

Crenshaw waved the waiter over. "Bring a glass of this fine wine for the lady here," he said, holding up his crystal glass.

A moment later, the waiter returned and placed the glass in front of Gabrielle. Gingerly, she took a sip.

The glass of wine cost more than she made in an entire day. But the wine was to make her at ease. Get her to trust him. If she had any sense, she would have never agreed to meet him. But here she was.

"Ms. Fuentes," Crenshaw said, getting down to business. "I'm sorry for what you went through back at the… house." He was careful not to use the client's name. "It was an unfortunate incident. He is very sorry for what happened."

Gabrielle's face turned hard. "He hurt me," she said, careful not to raise her voice. But her anger was palpable.

"Again, he regrets what happened," Crenshaw said. "Now, we can't go back in the past and change what has happened, but we can move forward and change the future."

"What do you mean?" she asked.

"My client is willing to offer you a lot of money…"

"I don't want his money." She was seething. "I want him to pay for what he did to me. I will go to the police and tell them everything."

Crenshaw was very calm. "Yes, you can do that. It is your right. But what will you tell them?"

"I will tell them everything."

"My client—your current employer—is a very powerful and influential man. He will deny all accusations leveled against him."

"He can't deny the truth. He's an evil man. His wife must know who he is. What he is. I will tell her."

Crenshaw raised his eyebrow. This woman was no pushover. He didn't take pleasure in what he was about to do next, but she was not willing to reason with him.

He said, "You have a son and daughter in Honduras, yes?"

Gabrielle blinked but didn't say a word.

"Miguel and Sofia, right?"

Gabrielle was speechless.

"Miguel is six, and Sofia is four," Crenshaw continued. "They must really miss you, don't they? It must be hard on your husband, Jorge. He hasn't been able to find work ever since he got laid off at the bottling plant. So, your family relies on you to support them."

Gabrielle looked down at the table.

"Ms. Fuentes." Crenshaw leaned forward on his chair. "We know everything about your family. What time your kids go to school, where your mother lives, and how many times your brother has been in and out of prison for selling drugs."

Gabrielle's face was ashen.

"We are not people you want as enemies, Ms. Fuentes." His voice was calm but menacing. "We know people working for the cartels. It would be a shame if something were to happen to your mother or brother, not to mention your children."

Gabrielle hugged her purse tightly.

"If you listen to me, I promise you nothing will happen to anyone you love. In fact, if you agree to our terms, you can leave here a very rich woman," Crenshaw said. "All you have to do is sign a document and promise to leave the country and never come back."

She looked up at him. "Where will I go? The reason I left my family was so I could bring them to America and give them a better life."

"With the money you'll receive, you can give your family a better life in any country of your choosing."

She fell silent.

"The offer is on the table right now," he said, going for the kill. "You either take it or leave it. You have to make a decision *now*."

Gabrielle's shoulders slumped, and tears streaked down her cheeks. "Okay. Where do I sign?" she whispered.

The documents were already in Crenshaw's briefcase, along with a check. He never doubted for one second that he would leave the restaurant without a deal with Gabrielle.

He took a sip of his wine and grinned.

## TWENTY-ONE

Callaway was surprised when he received the call from Nina. She wouldn't tell him what it was about, but she wanted him to come to her school. Worried, he drove straight over.

He found her standing by the school entrance.

Sabrina "Nina" Callaway had dark hair like her mother, which reached down to her lower back. Her eyes were emerald green, like his, but she had her mother's smile. As she grew older, she was looking more like Patti, a fact he was most proud of. According to Callaway, Patti was the most beautiful woman in the world.

"Are you okay, baby?" he asked, rushing over to his daughter.

"I'm fine, Daddy," she replied.

"Are you hurt?" He scanned her face and hands. His heart was pounding, and his ears were ringing. His daughter meant the world to him. If anything were to happen to her, he didn't know how he'd go on with life.

"Nothing's happened to me," she replied. "I wanted to talk to you."

*Talk to me?* he thought. *I hope it's not a father-daughter talk.*

Callaway wasn't good with extolling words of wisdom. His entire life was a tsunami of mistakes. Plus, Patti was good at that stuff. She was the more responsible parent. She knew the right things to say and when. He would only confuse Nina.

"If you want to talk about a boy," he said, "I think you should talk to your mom."

"No, it's not about a boy," Nina said, rolling her eyes. "But it is important."

He checked his wristwatch. "It's lunch break, right? Do you want to go to a fast-food restaurant?"

She shook her head. "I already ate my lunch."

"Do you wanna talk in the car?"

"Follow me."

Nina grabbed his hand and led him around the side of the school, through the playground, and to the baseball diamond at the far end.

A girl was sitting at a picnic table. She had curly blonde hair, freckles on her cheeks, and the brightest blue eyes he had ever seen.

"This is Millie," Nina said. "She's in my class."

"Hi, Mr. Callaway," Millie said with a wave.

"Hi there," he replied.

"Please have a seat, Daddy," Nina said.

He was confused, but he did as he was told.

Nina sat next to Millie. Callaway was seated across from them.

"What's going on, kiddo?" he asked.

"Millie heard you talk in class at career day," Nina said.

Callaway didn't remember seeing her. Then again, he was petrified about making a fool of himself in front of Nina's classmates, so he didn't focus on each student.

"Millie wanted to talk to you about it."

"Okay," he said.

Millie said, "I loved your presentation. I thought it was awesome. It must be so cool to be a private investigator."

Callaway beamed.

*Well, at least I impressed one of Nina's classmates*, he thought.

"Thank you. That's very nice of you to say." He then said to Nina, "What did *you* want to talk to me about?"

Nina turned to Millie. "Go ahead. Tell him what you told me."

Millie fell silent and looked down at her hands.

"Tell me what?" Callaway asked.

"Mr. Callaway," Millie said. "I want to hire you for a case."

He blinked. "What case?"

"To find my mom."

## TWENTY-TWO

Callaway sat there for a few seconds. He couldn't believe a little girl wanted to hire him for a case. "Who's your mom?" he asked.

"Laura Sinclair," Millie answered.

"What happened to her?"

"She's gone."

"Gone where?"

"I don't know."

"What do you mean?"

Millie went silent, but then she blurted out, "They told me my mom is dead."

"Dead? How?"

"Murdered."

"By who?"

"My father."

Callaway blinked.

"Wait. Your father murdered your mother?"

"Yes, that's what my grandmother told me."

"Where does your grandmother live?"

"I live with her in Milton."

Callaway spoke his next words carefully. "And is your father alive?"

"Yes, he's in prison. But I haven't seen him since my mom died."

Callaway pinched the bridge of his nose. His mind was reeling. "Okay. If your mother is dead, then how can I find her?"

"I don't think she's dead."

"How can you be sure?"

Millie's eyes suddenly welled up. "I just know she's not gone."

Callaway felt for the girl. She was the same age as his daughter. He couldn't imagine going through a tragedy like this at such a young age. Children who grew up without their mothers and fathers felt like the universe had somehow betrayed them. They were robbed of the connection they were supposed to have with those who gave them life. It was one thing to have an absent parent. There was always hope that the parent would one day reappear in their lives and somehow mend or create a new relationship.

Callaway was fortunate to have that opportunity with Nina. He had abandoned her and Patti at a time when they needed him most. Nina was just a baby, and Patti was studying to become a nurse. He wasn't ready to be a husband or a father. He was figuring out his place in the world, and in some ways, he was *still* figuring it out. But deep down, he always knew he would find his way back to his daughter, and maybe even back into his ex-wife's life. And over the last few months, he had done just that.

But with a dead parent, the chance for a relationship was gone forever.

He stared at Millie, unsure of how to break it to her. She had lost her mom in the most vicious way, and her father was now locked up. She had no parent to turn to. Callaway was glad Millie had her grandmother to care for her, but her grandmother was no substitute for her mother. Millie's father had robbed not only the world of human life but also robbed his daughter of her mother's love.

Callaway gently said, "I know how much you want your mom back, but sometimes people are gone forever."

Millie reached into her backpack and pulled out several colorful envelopes. She laid them on the table.

"What are they?" Callaway asked, even though he had an idea.

"Each year, I get them on my birthday."

Callaway picked one up and looked inside. There was a handwritten inscription. "Happy Birthday, *cupcake,*" he read out loud. But the name of the sender was blank.

"My mom was the only one who called me *cupcake,*" Millie said.

"And you think your mom sent them?" he asked.

"Yes."

He flipped the envelope over and saw no postage stamp or return address.

*Someone had personally dropped these cards off,* he thought.

"I'm not sure how I can help you. I'm sorry."

"Please, Daddy," Nina pleaded. "You have to help her."

Millie pulled out a piggy bank that was shaped like a smiling panda and pushed it towards him.

"Kids still have those?" he asked, surprised.

"My dad gave it to me when I turned five. There's three hundred and forty dollars in there. I saved all the money I got for my birthdays."

Callaway fell silent.

"Please," Nina and Millie said in unison.

He sighed. "Fine. I'll look into your case, but I won't make any promises."

Both Nina and Millie smiled from ear to ear.

"And I won't take your money. I'll do it because you're Nina's classmate."

"Thank you, Mr. Callaway," Millie said.
"Thanks, Daddy," Nina said.
"Sure," he said.
*I'm such a softy*, he thought.

## TWENTY-THREE

Most of the shops in the neighborhood were pawn shops, cash-back stores, tattoo parlors, liquor stores, or boarded up completely.

According to Doug and Gary Lomas, they had celebrated Trevor McGinty's birthday at a bar in the middle of this neighborhood.

Why Trevor had chosen this bar over others, Fisher was not sure.

They entered the establishment. Right away, they were hit with a strong smell of cigarettes and body odor. It was also dark, which was probably necessary. Fisher could tell the place was grimy.

The bartender was a rough-looking man. He had a handlebar mustache and a long ponytail. His sleeves were cut off, exposing his flabby arms, which were covered in tattoos. A scar ran down the man's left cheek.

Fisher looked around and noted that even the bar's regulars were just as rough as the bartender. She was not scared of anyone. Her police training had equipped her with enough confidence to handle any situation. But she was still grateful to have Holt beside her right now.

If things got ugly, Holt could take down several people by himself.

She flashed her badge to the bartender and said, "We need to ask you a few questions."

"About what?" the bartender replied, unfazed by her credentials.

"A patron of your bar."

"He got a name?"

"Trevor McGinty."

The bartender thought for a moment. "Never heard of him."

Holt pulled out Trevor's driver's license and held it up. "Does this jog your memory?"

"I don't have my reading glasses with me," the bartender said, grinning. The regulars grinned, too.

"I'm glad you think it's funny," Holt said. "This man is dead. Shot right through the head. And someone roughed him up pretty good, too. You can answer our questions without being a smart ass, or we can come back with a bunch of cops and haul each and every one of you down to the station for questioning. I'm sure one of you knows something."

Holt's voice was loud, booming in the confined space.

"Dead, you say?" the bartender asked, straightening up.

"Bullet between his eyes," Holt answered.

He looked around. The regulars quickly turned to their drinks.

The bartender said, "Can I take a look at that again?"

Holt held up the driver's license.

"Yeah, he comes here sometimes."

"Did he talk much?"

"Not really. I tried starting a conversation with him, but he mostly kept to himself. One time, he came in with two other guys. They were nice fellas. Chatty. They bought everyone a drink. I think they were celebrating or something. Those guys tipped well, too."

"Did anything interesting happen the night they came in?" Holt asked.

"Whenever the guy came by himself, he always had one drink and left. But on that night, those guys got him a bit drunk. I think I heard him slip into an accent."

"An accent?" Holt said, confused.

"Yeah."

"What kind of accent."

"I don't know. It sounded… *Canadian*."

Holt glanced over at Fisher. They'd found a large amount of Canadian currency in Trevor's motel room.

"How can you be sure it was a Canadian accent?" Holt said.

"I have a cousin in Saskatoon. I've been there a couple of times. Nice place. Friendly people. But man, it gets mighty cold there in the winter. Your beard and eyebrows freeze up if you go out. One time I couldn't get my car started. It was so cold that my battery died. I ended up walking for three miles to the nearest gas station. I thought I'd lose my fingers and toes. Those guys who live up there are prepared for that kind of cold. I wasn't. Anyway, the people there tend to say, *eh*, a lot."

"Eh?" Holt repeated.

"Yeah, like, 'Whatcha doing there, *eh*?' 'How's it going, *eh*?' 'When're you coming back, *eh*?'"

"And he said, 'eh,' as well?" Holt asked.

"He did use that word a few times that night," the bartender said. "But then he caught himself, realized he was drunk, and shut up."

"When was the last time he was here?" Fisher asked.

"Last week."

"And did he sound agitated or upset?"

"No. He just came in like he normally did, ordered a beer, drank it quietly in the corner, and left."

## TWENTY-FOUR

Callaway returned to his office with a dark cloud over his head. He suddenly had two cases, and he wasn't sure how to tackle either of them.

The first was Ms. Chen's son. Bruce Chen had been suckered in by sophisticated scammers, and he'd lost a lot of money, most of it his mother's. The scammers were likely halfway around the world, so any chance of recovering the money was slim to none.

And then in the second case. Nina's classmate wanted him to find her mother. Callaway now remembered some of the details. He had caught it in the news. A husband had murdered his wife and was now in prison, serving a life sentence. It was a textbook case of domestic violence gone fatal. Callaway wasn't sure how he was going to change the outcome for Millie Sinclair.

*Why do I get cases that are impossible to solve?* he thought. And the payout from each was not going to be worth the trouble. He was not about to take a little girl's life savings. No way. Not a chance. And his landlady had always charged him the lowest rent in the city. There was no way he could charge her his usual fee.

"What is my usual fee anyway?" he wondered out loud.

Callaway never had a set rate for his services. He felt it deterred clients from hiring him. He let them tell him what the problem was, and if there was an urgency to resolving their problem, he trusted them to pay him his fair share.

Some clients were stingy and would haggle even after agreeing to an amount. But more often than not, his clients were grateful for having the problem go away, and they paid him extra, almost like a tip.

But there would be no extra fee for Millie Sinclair. Probably no fee at all. Nonetheless, he had agreed to look into her case, and that's what he was going to do.

On his laptop, he did a quick search about the case, and what he found began to jog his memory.

Laura Sinclair was actually *Doctor* Laura Sinclair. She ran her own clinic in Milton, and she had been married for fifteen years to Roger Sinclair, an engineer for a tech company. The couple was highly educated and accomplished, and they were also financially well off.

Why Roger Sinclair decided to kill his wife was always a mystery. One that had not been answered as far as Callaway was concerned.

He pulled up their images on the screen. Laura Sinclair had blonde hair, perfect teeth, and bright blue eyes. Millie was the spitting image of her mother. Roger Sinclair, on the other hand, had dark hair, a stubby nose, and his beard had begun to gray.

Callaway clicked on another link. It was an article from one of the newspapers. After strangling his wife, Roger Sinclair then set fire to the family home. By the time the firefighters arrived, the house was fully engulfed in flames. It took several hours for them to subdue the fire, and what was left afterward was a smoldering pile of rubble.

Roger Sinclair was taken into custody, where he confessed to torching the house.

He gave no reasoning for why he did it, but there was speculation that Roger Sinclair was having an affair, and his wife had found out. Fearing a messy divorce, he killed her. As Callaway scanned through other articles, he found even more theories. That Roger Sinclair had a gambling problem and was in so much debt, he killed his wife for the insurance money. That Roger Sinclair was jealous of his wife's success and felt threatened by her, so he had to get rid of her. Then there were theories that he had a drinking problem, had anger issues, or that he was gay.

None of it was ever brought up in court. And why would it? Roger Sinclair had confessed to the crime and had taken full responsibility for his actions. End of story. Case closed.

Callaway leaned back in his chair and stared up at the ceiling.

He was curious to know the real motive behind the murder. But more importantly, how was he going to find Millie's mother when her father was in prison for her death?

## TWENTY-FIVE

"What do we do now?" Fisher asked as they got back in the SUV. "We have no leads, nothing to work with."

"Not quite," Holt said. He pulled out a business card from his pocket and held it out for her.

Fisher took it. "The name of a pawn shop?" she said.

"I found it in the victim's back pocket."

"And you think it might be significant?"

"It may or may not be," Holt replied. "Why would he keep *this* business card and not someone else's?"

Fisher moved her thumb over the card. "It looks like it's been in his pocket for some time." She paused and then said, "Okay, let's go take a look."

She punched the address into the SUV's GPS.

"You won't believe this," she said.

"What?"

"The pawnshop is around the block from the bar we just came out of."

"I'm not surprised," Holt said. "It makes sense the victim would frequent a particular area or neighborhood."

In less than a minute, they pulled up to a store with a black sign on the front, iron bars on the windows, and a CCTV camera prominently displayed above the door. Everything to deter potential robbers.

They went inside. A bell chimed, announcing their arrival.

A heavyset man with wavy hair, wearing a shirt with the name Lucky on it, greeted them with a smile. "Are you looking to sell or buy?"

"Neither," Fisher said, flashing her badge.

Lucky's smile fell from his face. "If it's about stolen goods, I don't buy that kind of stuff."

"Then how do you buy stuff?" Holt asked.

"I examine the item the individual is trying to sell, and if we can come to an agreement on a price, I get them to write down their name, address, and telephone number on this ledger." He pulled out a heavy binder and placed it on the glass counter. "I also check their IDs to confirm who they say they are, and then we complete the transaction."

"How long do you hold on to their items?" Fisher asked.

"Two weeks. But most of the time, I can tell right away if someone is gonna come back for their stuff or not."

"How can you tell?"

"If someone brought in a wedding ring or family heirloom or their favorite guitar, for example, then I know pretty well they're gonna do everything to get it back."

"Did a Trevor McGinty ever sell you anything?" Fisher asked.

Lucky frowned. "That name doesn't sound familiar."

Holt pulled out the business card and placed it on the counter. "This was found in his possession."

Lucky shrugged. "I hand out cards wherever I go, so he could have gotten that anywhere."

"True," Fisher said, "but why your card and not someone else's?"

"You tell me."

Holt pulled out Trevor McGinty's driver's license and laid it on the counter. "Don't tell me you've never seen this man because we've been through this denial before with someone else, and believe me, he ended up telling us the truth."

Lucky stared at them. "Yeah, I've seen him," he finally admitted.

"Good," Holt said. "Now we're getting somewhere."

"Why did he come to the pawn shop?" Fisher asked.

"Like everyone else, he either wanted to buy or sell something."

"What did he sell you?"

"I don't know. I buy a lot of stuff."

Holt said, "Why don't you check your ledger?"

Lucky hesitated and then opened the binder. He scanned through it, moving his finger over each entry. "Actually, now that I look at this, he never sold me anything."

"If he didn't sell you anything, then that means *you* sold him something," Fisher said. "What did you sell him?"

Lucky fell silent.

"Was it drugs?" Holt asked.

Lucky put his arms up defensively. "I don't deal in that stuff. You can check my shop from top to bottom. You won't find any drugs, I promise."

"So why would he come to your shop?" Fisher asked.

"I don't know. Maybe to browse," Lucky replied with a shrug.

The doorbell chimed, and a customer entered the shop.

"Listen, I'm sorry I can't help you. But if you don't mind, I've got a business to run," Lucky said.

Seeing that they were making no progress, Holt and Fisher decided to leave.

## TWENTY-SIX

Callaway knocked on the door and waited. He was at a bungalow in the east end. It had a manicured lawn in the front and a recently paved driveway. He could smell the asphalt.

A woman appeared behind the door. She was a little stocky with brown hair and dark eyes, and she had on a light sweater.

"Can I help you?" she said.

"Valerie Turner?" he asked.

"Yes."

"My name is Lee Callaway. Can I ask you a few questions about Laura and Roger Sinclair?"

Valerie was Laura Sinclair's best friend. Callaway had gotten her name from an interview she'd done with a local newspaper after Laura was murdered. Once he had her name, it wasn't difficult to find her address online.

"I'm sorry," Valerie said, "but I don't want to talk about it."

"I understand." He pulled out his card and gave it to her.

"You're a private investigator?"

"Yes, and Millie Sinclair hired me to look into her mom's case."

Valerie smiled. "I'm not surprised she did. That little girl is as stubborn as her mother. If she gets something in her mind, she'll find a way to get it done."

"Has she told you that she believes her mom is still alive?"

Valerie nodded. "She has multiple times. I'm not sure if you know, but I'm her godmother, so I make sure to check up on her regularly," she said. "Do you want to come inside? I can put the kettle on."

"That would be nice."

He followed her inside and took a seat in the living room.

"My husband works for the city," she said. "He's very private. He doesn't like reporters, so I was worried you might be one."

"I'm not, I assure you."

She went into the kitchen. He heard a tap being turned on, and then something being placed on the stove. "Is tea, okay?"

"That'll be fine," he replied. "What do you do, Mrs. Turner?"

"I'm a social worker. I help at-risk teens stay out of trouble."

She returned with a tray holding two cups.

He took one. "Thank you."

She sat across from him and said, "I'm sorry Millie pulled you into this. I've tried to talk her out of it, but like I said, she's got a mind of her own."

"What can you tell me about her parents? How did they meet? Anything?"

She took a deep breath. "You wouldn't believe it, but they met on a cruise ship. This was before they went on to have successful careers. They were still college students. They needed the money, and they wanted to travel. Working on a cruise ship seemed like a good idea. They both worked at one of the restaurants on the ship. He worked behind the bar, and she worked as a waitress. They saw each other every day for almost three months. Eventually, they hit it off. When they got back to Milton and resumed their studies, they still kept in touch. And eventually, they got married."

"How would you describe their relationship?" Callaway asked.

"Rock solid."

He took a sip and waited for her to explain.

Valerie said, "They supported each other. They were also good friends, which is rare in a relationship. I've known Laura since grade school. When they got together, I was jealous because I thought Roger would take my best friend away from me." She paused. "Now that I think about it, he did take her away from me."

Callaway asked, "Were there any problems between them?"

"No. They loved each other madly. Roger couldn't stop fawning over her whenever I saw them, and Laura couldn't stop praising Roger. They also doted on Millie. She was everything to them. They were wonderful parents. Wonderful friends. Wonderful people." Valerie wiped tears from her eyes. "It was a shock when it happened."

"I'm sorry to bring up the past," Callaway said. "There was no indication of trouble in their house?"

"None whatsoever," she said. "Great careers. Great marriage. They had a perfect life."

Callaway realized his trip here was going to be a waste.

Valerie then said, "There was something that I thought was odd."

His ears perked up. "Like what?'

"Right before she was…" Callaway could tell she didn't want to say *murdered*. "She came to me one night and said that if anything were to happen to them, I should help her mom take care of Millie."

"She said *them* and not just her?"

"I think she was also referring to Roger."

"Did she say anything else?"

Valerie shook her head. "I wish she did. At least then I would know why this tragedy happened."

## TWENTY-SEVEN

Holt and Fisher were parked outside the pawnshop. They knew Lucky was hiding something. It was the way he kept sidetracking around why Trevor McGinty came to his shop. He couldn't tell them whether Trevor bought something from the shop or whether he sold something. This led them to another question: If Trevor was neither a seller or buyer, then what was he doing there? The simple answer was that Trevor knew Lucky, and Lucky was not entirely forthcoming with them.

With years on the job, Holt and Fisher had gained a sixth sense of who was telling the truth and who was not.

Their senses were on high alert whenever Lucky tried to dodge one of their questions.

They did, however, believe him when he said he didn't sell drugs from the pawnshop. The pawn business was rife with illegal activities. Stolen goods could easily be sold through the shop as legitimate items. Which, in a small way, made the pawnshop owners money launderers.

In order to avoid scrutiny, most shop owners stayed away from selling drugs. It was one thing to sell a stolen item without your knowledge. It was an entirely different thing to sell drugs to customers.

The sentences were far harsher for the latter.

Lucky could very well not know who Trevor McGinty was and why he had the pawn shop's business card in his pocket.

But what if Trevor didn't go to the pawnshop to meet Lucky? What if he went there to meet someone else? Someone who might know what happened to him.

This was all conjecture, but at the moment, they had nothing solid to work with. No one had seen anyone go in and out of Trevor's motel room at the time of the murder. No security cameras had caught it, either. The footage from Wayne's office was taken, and so was the footage from the camera in Trevor's room.

Holt and Fisher believed it was the same person who had taken them, and it further reinforced their belief that the murder was perpetrated by someone who knew what they were doing. Only a professional would know how to clean up the scene after committing a crime.

With little to work with, Holt and Fisher had no other choice but to wait outside the pawnshop for something to happen.

They didn't have to wait long. A man wearing a baseball cap with his hands in his pockets entered the shop. A moment later, he came out and began walking in the opposite direction.

"I've seen that man before," Fisher said.

"Where?" Holt asked.

"Outside the motel."

"What was he doing?"

"He was staring at me," Fisher replied. "When he saw me staring back, he just left. I didn't have time to follow him."

"Well," Holt said, starting the Volvo, "now we have time to follow him."

They drove up and saw the man cross the road. He then got into a maroon sedan. A moment later, the sedan pulled out of its parking spot, headed down the street, and turned right. Holt and Fisher did the same. They saw the sedan at the traffic light up ahead. Once it turned green, the sedan kept going straight, staying in the same lane.

Ten minutes later, the sedan turned left, went down another street, and then pulled into the parking lot of an apartment building. It went around to the back of the building, where the sedan disappeared in the building's underground garage.

Holt gripped the wheel tightly. "We lost him," he grumbled.

"Not quite," Fisher said. "While you were driving, I ran the license plate through the motor vehicle registry. I got a hit, and it's at this address."

"So, who is he?"

"His name is Guy Millson."

# TWENTY-EIGHT

Callaway rang the doorbell and waited. It was a split-level house with a beautiful garden in front, a high picket fence, and the garage door was painted a bright yellow.

A moment later, a woman answered the door. She had silver hair, wrinkled skin, and blue eyes. The eyes were similar to Millie and Laura Sinclair's. It made sense because the woman was Laura's mother and Millie's grandmother.

Diane Aldershot and her husband had lived in this house for over thirty-five years. They had raised their two children in this very house. The oldest, John, was a plastic surgeon in California. Their youngest child was Laura.

Her husband, Carl, had died of lung cancer ten years ago. He was a veterinarian, and Diane ran her husband's clinic as the administrator. After his death, she sold the clinic and retired. It was also Diane who had sold her daughter's practice after her death. The proceeds of that sale were put in a trust for Millie.

Diane had seen her share of tragedies, but she was a resilient woman who never let those tragedies get her down. Most people her age were enjoying retirement. Diane was raising a precocious nine-year-old all by herself.

"Mrs. Aldershot?" Callaway asked.

"You must be the private investigator," she replied, crossing her arms over her chest.

"Millie told you?" he asked.

"No. I just got off the phone with Valerie."

"Oh, right."

"How much did Millie agree to pay you?" Diane asked.

"It's pro bono."

"It always is at the beginning, but then you guys will start charging for extra work."

Callaway shook his head. "That's not how I do business, Mrs. Aldershot. Millie is in my daughter's class. She came to me with this case, not the other way around."

Diane stared at him, trying to see what his angle was.

"I'm only doing this because my daughter asked me to," Callaway said. "If you don't believe me, you should ask your granddaughter."

"I will once she gets home," Diane said.

"Now that I'm already here," Callaway said, "can I ask you a few questions?"

"You can. It's a free country. But I'm not obligated to answer them."

Callaway wasn't sure why she was so hostile to him.

Sensing what he was thinking, she said, "Listen, I'm not trying to be rude. My mother didn't raise me like that. But you can't go digging into what happened in the past."

"Your granddaughter believes—"

"I know what she believes. I hear it almost every day."

"Then you know why I have to look into this."

"And what do you expect to find? My daughter is gone, my son-in-law is in prison, and my granddaughter is without a father and a mother. There is nothing that can change that."

Callaway said, "Millie believes the birthday cards she receives each year are from her mother."

Diane stared at him. "She told you about them?"

"She did."

"I write those birthday cards and leave them in the mailbox."

Callaway's eyes narrowed. "Why would you do that?"

"I know it was wrong of me to do that," she said with a long sigh. "I was giving her hope that her mother might still be alive. But my emotions got the better of me. Millie was really upset on her birthday when her mom and dad were not there. I didn't know what to do, and so I made up a story that I'd found a birthday card her mom had left behind for her. And each year afterward, I did that same thing. I tell her I found another card."

"But Millie said only her mom called her *cupcake*."

"I know Laura called her *cupcake* whenever she was over at my house, so I just used that to personalize the cards. I regret doing it, but that doesn't mean my daughter is coming back and everything will be back to normal."

Callaway was silent.

Diane said, "Millie has lost both her parents. She's searching for answers as to why it happened. I'm afraid whatever you think you are doing will not help her."

"How can you be so sure? What if—"

She cut him off. "I know because I've had to console Millie after what happened. I don't want to console her again when you break it to her that her mother is really, truly gone."

Callaway said nothing.

"Please," Diane said. "Leave us alone, and let us grieve our loss."

She shut the door, leaving Callaway standing on the front porch.

# TWENTY-NINE

Guy Millson had a long rap sheet. He'd been in and out of prison at least five times. The first for writing fake checks, the second for scamming an elderly couple. But the last couple of times were for more serious offenses. Causing an injury due to drunk driving, assault with a deadly weapon, and once for robbery. The latter was particularly troublesome because Millson had threatened a man with a gun in order to steal his wallet.

The state's prison system was so overcrowded and underfunded that with good behavior, Millson was able to get out in six to eighteen months every time.

Millson was also three times divorced, and according to his records, he had six children.

"How can someone like him be married so many times?" Holt wondered out loud.

"What do you mean?" Fisher asked from the passenger seat.

They were parked outside the apartment building Millson had gone into. Fisher had her laptop open as she dug up more information on Millson.

They were not about to go in without fully knowing as much about him as possible.

They knew he was dangerous, but they also wanted to know anything that might help them link him to Trevor McGinty.

So far, Millson was only a person of interest. He hadn't committed any crime. For all they knew, Millson was a customer of Lucky's pawn shop.

But what was he doing at the motel on the day Trevor was murdered? On top of that, it couldn't be just a coincidence that Millson would show up at the pawnshop right after Holt and Fisher had left.

There was more to this than met the eye.

"Why are you curious that he's been married three times?" Fisher asked again, waiting for Holt's response.

"I mean, he's been in prison many times," Holt said. "What would women see in him that would make them want to be with him?"

"Maybe they see excitement."

Holt shook his head. "I don't see excitement. All I see is trouble."

"Is this about him being married three times or him having six children?" Fisher asked.

Holt looked away.

"I'm sorry," Fisher said. "That was a low blow."

A moment later, Holt replied, "You're right. I don't understand how people like him can father so many children when there are clearly many good parents out there who are childless."

Fisher knew he was referring to himself. Holt and his wife, Nancy, had gone through multiple miscarriages. When they couldn't have children of their own, they decided to adopt a boy from Ukraine. When the boy arrived in America, they thought their family was finally complete. But the boy didn't live past his first year in the country. He died of a rare form of cancer.

Angry and confused, Holt had gone to Ukraine to search for the boy's biological parents. They knew the boy was suffering. He'd been ill when Holt and Nancy had brought him over. They figured he was probably malnourished. Holt and Nancy believed that with love and the right treatment, the boy would be normal. But they had been mistaken.

Holt's trip to Ukraine revealed nothing. He was neither able to locate the boy's parents nor find the woman who ran the adoption agency they had used to bring the boy over. It was as if they had both vanished into thin air. Their objective was to make money—and to make the boy someone else's problem.

The entire ordeal had left Holt bitter. It also left him questioning humanity. How can someone treat another human being—one's own child for that matter—the way the boy had been treated? The only solace he could take away from all of this was that he had done everything in his power to help the boy and to provide him with comfort in the last days of his young life.

"Let's go talk to Millson," Holt said, looking at the apartment building.

## THIRTY

Callaway was surprised by Diane Aldershot's reaction. As Millie's grandmother, she'd understand why Millie would want answers to her mother's death. In Callaway's research, he'd not been able to find a reason for why Roger Sinclair had murdered his wife. Roger and Laura had life insurance. They were in high-earning professions. They were living a well-to-do lifestyle.

Prior to her death, Laura was an active traveler. She posted photos of their family trips on her blog. Photos of beautiful sunsets in Bali, Greece, and Egypt. Safari excursions in Tanzania. Backpacking trips through the backroads of France. A motorcycle journey through South America with her husband. Even scuba diving off the coast of Hawaii.

Some photos were taken before Millie was born, but many were with her. She was either strapped to Roger or Laura's chest with a baby harness or she was being pushed in a stroller. In each photo, Millie was smiling from ear to ear.

In fact, when Callaway went through Laura's online album, he couldn't help but feel a pain in his chest. The Sinclairs looked happy. Never once did they imagine that one day their happiness would be taken away—and by one of them.

On the day of Laura's murder, Roger had dropped Millie off at school. Instead of heading straight to work, which was what he normally did, he went back home. A neighbor confirmed seeing him pull up into the driveway. The neighbor even smiled and waved to him. The neighbor said Roger waved and smiled back. And then an hour later, the neighbor saw Roger get in his car and leave. The neighbor was working on his lawn, so he was certain of the timing.

Several hours later, the neighbor confirmed he saw the Sinclairs' house on fire. The neighbor rushed over to see what had happened, and he saw Roger standing in the driveway. Roger had a muted look on his face. The neighbor asked if anyone was inside, and Roger calmly told him Laura was. Roger made no effort to try to subdue the fire or go inside to save his wife.

When Roger was taken in for questioning, the police found tools and equipment in the trunk of his station wagon. They also found a fire-starter kit. Upon further investigation, they found a receipt from a hardware store in the car as well. On the morning of the fire, a few hours after dropping his daughter off at school, Roger had driven to the hardware store and purchased tools and equipment, including the fire-starter kit. The visit to the hardware store was around the time the neighbor had seen Roger leave the house.

The police believed Roger had dropped his daughter off at school, returned home, murdered his wife, then left the house to purchase supplies. Soon after, he lit the house on fire to destroy the evidence.

The police's theory was confirmed when Roger confessed to doing exactly that. He burned their house down with his wife still inside.

But Callaway could see giant holes in the story, even if the police didn't, or if they didn't care because they had their confession.

*Roger Sinclair was a smart man. He had a master's in computer science. He surely wouldn't be so careless as to murder his wife knowing full well that his neighbor was outside working on his lawn*, he thought. *And even if he did murder his wife, why would he drive to a hardware store in the middle of the day, pick up all the items that could be used to start a fire, and pay for them with his credit card? Any person with half a brain would know that credit cards can easily be linked back to the crime. And then, to top it off, Roger stood outside and watched his house burn down in front of him.*

Callaway blinked.

*It was as if he wanted to be caught.*

*But why? Why not make an effort to conceal the crime he had committed?*

When facing life behind bars, people did anything and everything to avoid getting caught.

Roger Sinclair didn't.

There was one theory that came close to explaining Roger's actions on that terrible day.

Roger and Laura may have had an argument on the morning of the murder. In a moment of passion, Roger may have struck and killed her. Then, in a state of panic, he drove to the hardware store to cover his tracks. He may not have had cash on him because most people these days didn't carry much hard currency. And instead of going to an ATM and leaving a trail there, he decided to just pay with his credit card.

*And the reason he stood outside his house as it burned may have had something to do with guilt. Maybe at that moment, Roger realized there was no way he could get away with this, and it was best for him to give up.*

Callaway leaned back in his chair and took a deep breath.

Regardless of Roger Sinclair's motives, the man was now stuck in a six-by-eight cell, and he would be there for the rest of his life.

## THIRTY-ONE

Holt was ready to get out of the Volvo to speak to Guy Millson when Fisher put her hand out to stop him. "Look," she said.

Up ahead, they saw the maroon sedan emerge from the building's underground parking garage.

"Should we stop him?" Holt asked.

"Let's see where he goes," Fisher replied.

Holt buckled up and pulled the Volvo behind the sedan. He kept a fair distance between the two vehicles. He doubted Millson was aware he was being followed, but Holt was not about to take any chances.

Even if he lost Millson in traffic, they knew where he lived. They could always come back and speak to him.

The sedan moved down the block and took a right at the light. The sedan drove two miles through several streets until it got on the highway.

The sedan spent the next ten miles in the same lane until it took the next exit.

"I think I know where he's going," Holt said.

"Where?" Fisher asked.

"You'll see in a second."

The sedan stopped at the traffic light. Holt and Fisher were three cars behind on the right. When it turned green, the sedan moved up and drove past a familiar location.

"That's the motel where Trevor McGinty was shot and killed," Fisher said.

"Indeed."

The yellow police tape no longer circled the motel property. There was no need for it anymore. Trevor's body had been removed. Holt and Fisher had conducted their preliminary examination, and the CSU team had thoroughly gone through the site. If there was any evidence left behind, there was nothing Holt and Fisher could do about it now. Trevor's room was still off-limits, however, and it would be for some time.

"If Millson is going to the motel," Fisher asked, "why did he drive past it?"

"We'll know in a minute," Holt replied.

The sedan turned left and then pulled up to the curb. A moment later, Millson got out. He adjusted his baseball cap, stuck his hands in the jacket pockets, and then began walking in the direction of the motel.

"So, that's why he drove past it," Fisher said as Holt parked the SUV.

Holt and Fisher got out and followed Millson.

Millson was half a block ahead, but they could see he had entered the motel's parking lot. They watched as he moved through the rows of parked cars and then up the stairs to the second level.

He stopped at McGinty's door. He looked around to see if the coast was clear. He then spent a couple of minutes fidgeting with the lock. A moment later, he ducked underneath the police tape that covered most of the door. Millson had to crouch low to get inside.

It was illegal to access a site that was secured by the police, but clearly, Millson was not concerned.

By now, Holt and Fisher were standing outside the door. They could see movement from a flashlight behind the drapes.

Whatever Millson was looking for, they could wait.

Less than ten minutes later, Millson appeared. He was carrying a black leather bag.

He stopped dead in his tracks.

"Guy Millson?" Fisher asked.

"Yes?"

Fisher and Holt showed him their badges.

Millson gulped.

"You're under arrest," Holt said.

## THIRTY-TWO

The evening was magical. It had started with dinner at a steakhouse, followed by a movie—a romantic comedy—chosen by Patti.

Patricia "Patti" Callaway had short, dark hair. Her brown eyes were great at detecting who was telling the truth and who was not. No lie got past them. Her lips were always curled into a smile, a trait that was reassuring. No matter how bad things were around her, she was able to find the best in it.

They were strolling down the street arm-in-arm.

Callaway's heart still skipped a beat whenever he saw her. She was the one that almost got away. No. That would not be entirely true. He had her once, and *he* let her get away. It was a miracle she had given him a second chance.

Callaway knew she could be with anyone. She was beautiful, intelligent, and had a heart of pure gold. There would be a long line of would-be suitors, but she had chosen him. Twice. A fact he did not take lightly.

Patti was a nurse at a local hospital. It required long hours, and the pay barely covered the expenses. But if you asked her, she wouldn't change a thing. She loved helping those in need.

She believed life was short and precious. There was nobility in spending your time making it better for those suffering.

Callaway used to subscribe to that belief, too—that life was short, and that's why you took care of number one. Meaning *him*.

He did things that brought him instant gratification. Drinking. Womanizing. Gambling. Only later did he realize that not only were those gratifications brief, they were also harmful.

The drinking impaired his ability to do his job properly. There were times when he would be intoxicated while following a client, and the next thing he knew, he couldn't remember who he was following. The womanizing left him feeling even lonelier. He would jump from one woman to another without having a meaningful connection. And the gambling was a no-brainer. He was broke most of the time.

Callaway had forsaken most of those vices. That didn't mean he was living a monk-like existence; he was just careful not to let his impulses get the best of him. And being with Patti helped with that.

She was a reminder of what he had lost—and what he could lose again if he didn't get his act together. He was working hard to steer clear of the road that led back to his old life.

"That was nice of you to take on Millie's case," Patti said. "Nina was so happy when she told me about it."

He smiled. "Sure."

"But I wouldn't have taken the case," she said.

His smile faded. "Huh? I thought you just said Nina was happy."

"She is, but what if you can't help her friend?"

They stopped and faced each other. He saw genuine concern in her eyes.

She said, "I read about the case after Nina mentioned it. It's sad and heartbreaking. Millie has been through a lot. But what will be even sadder and heartbreaking is if you tell that little girl that her father did indeed kill her mother."

Callaway fell silent.

Patti said, "Is there a chance that might not be true? That her father didn't do it?"

Callaway lowered his head. "I've found nothing to contradict that."

She put her hand on his cheek. "I know you want to help, Lee. I just don't want to see Nina upset. So, don't make any promises you can't keep. There is nothing worse than giving someone false hope."

Callaway felt like he couldn't breathe.

## THIRTY-THREE

Upon inspection, Holt and Fisher found that the bag Guy Millson was carrying out of Trevor McGinty's room contained half a dozen gold bars with an estimated value of sixty-eight thousand dollars.

Millson was now seated in a windowless room. There was no two-way mirror where someone on the other side could listen in. This room was intended to make a person feel confined. The interviewee had to feel like the walls were closing in on him after hours of interrogation.

Holt and Fisher hoped it wouldn't come to that. Millson would tell them what they needed to know. He was caught where he wasn't supposed to be—coming out of a dead man's room, carrying something belonging to the dead man.

"This doesn't look good for you, Mr. Millson," Fisher said, sitting opposite him. Holt stood in the corner. He would jump into the conversation when needed.

Millson looked down at his hands, which were not cuffed at the moment, but they could be if he didn't answer the detective's questions truthfully.

"I had nothing to do with what happened to Trevor," he pleaded.

"Why should we believe you?"

"I wouldn't hurt Trevor. He was my friend."

"Then what were you doing in his motel room?"

Millson fell silent.

"Let me rephrase that," Fisher said. "We know why you were there—to take the gold bars. The question is, how did you know about them?"

Millson was about to say something, but then reconsidered it. "Do I need a lawyer?" he asked.

"Do you?" Fisher said. "Is there something more serious than breaking and entering and stealing from a person who was the victim of murder?"

Millson stared at them. "Okay, I'll tell you everything. But I have no idea who did that to Trevor." Millson shook visibly. He hugged himself. "I met Trevor about fifteen years ago when he moved to Milton."

"Where did he move from?" Fisher asked.

"He never told me exactly, but I had a hunch."

"And that hunch was?"

"He came from Canada."

*That further explains the Canadian currency,* Fisher thought.

"Where in Canada?"

"He never said," Millson replied. "But if I had to take a guess, I'd say either Vancouver or Toronto."

"Is Trevor McGinty his real name?" Holt asked.

"It isn't?" Millson said, genuinely surprised.

Fisher said, "No, it isn't."

Millson's jaw dropped. "That's what he told me to call him. It was also on his driver's license."

"It's fake."

Millson looked like he'd been hit with a sledgehammer.

"Okay," Fisher said. "Tell us about the gold bars. How did your friend get them?"

"I helped him."

"Helped him how?"

"Through Lez."

"Who?"

"The pawnshop owner," Millson replied. "I've known Lez for a long time. And Lez knew people in the jewelry business, and he hooked Trevor up."

"How did Trevor get so much cash?" Holt asked.

"He told me he had sold his business a while back. He didn't want his ex-wife getting a penny from the sale, so he took the money and ran away."

"And you believed him?" Holt said.

"Why wouldn't I? Trevor was a good friend."

"Such a good friend," Fisher said, "that you decided to steal from him after his death?"

Millson looked away, deeply ashamed. "I'm not proud of what I did, but Trevor is gone. He has no use for the gold, but I…"

His words trailed off.

Fisher said, "We know about your gambling debts."

"And your six children," Holt added.

Millson looked up at Holt and lowered his head again. "The gold would have gone a long way in helping my kids."

"If you really cared about your kids," Holt said, "you'd get a job."

"I used to have a job," Millson said. "I used to work for a photography company, but then digital cameras came out, and no one made prints. Then I was laid off. Ever since then, I've been barely scraping by."

Fisher said, "Was Trevor involved in the sale or distribution of drugs?"

Millson frowned. "No, of course not."

"How can you be so sure?"

"If he was, he'd tell me."

"Why would he do that?"

"Because I would have joined him."

Silence fell over the room.

Holt said, "How did you know where the gold would be? We checked every corner of that room, and we didn't find it."

"I wasn't sure it'd be there, but I figured it was worth a try before the motel owner rented it out to someone else."

"And where was it?"

"It was stuffed in the air vent underneath the bed."

There was a pause.

Fisher said, "Where were you this morning?"

"I was staying at Covenant Place."

"What is that?"

"It's a homeless shelter for men," Millson said. "I missed out on paying my rent, and I was kicked out. That's why I needed the gold."

"And you had nothing to do with Trevor McGinty's death?" Holt asked firmly.

"If I did, why would I be so stupid to come back later for the gold?" Millson replied.

*Good point*, Fisher thought.

"Do you know anyone who'd want to hurt Trevor?" Fisher asked.

"I don't know."

"Did he have any enemies."

"Not that I know of."

"And why did he have a security system in his motel room?"

"I always assumed it was because of the gold."

"It wasn't," Fisher said. "We found a lot of cash in the room."

"How much cash we talking about?" Millson asked.

"Close to two hundred thousand dollars."

Millson's eyes widened. "Two hundred grand?" he said, stunned.

"Yes. In Canadian and US denominations."

Millson looked like he was about to have a heart attack.

# THIRTY-FOUR

The auditorium on the fourteenth floor of the ultra-luxury hotel was filled to capacity. There were shareholders, board members, people from upper management, and even a handful of trusted employees.

Denise Hollins sat behind a table at the front of the auditorium. Her hair was colored with blonde highlights, her nails were painted red, and her eyebrows had been plucked. After months in the gym with a trainer, she was able to fit into her favorite business suit.

People mistook Denise for a secretary, someone who was dolled up as eye candy for her male bosses, but that couldn't be further from the truth.

Denise had graduated from Columbia University with a degree in finance. She went on to complete her master's in business administration from Yale. She then joined her father's business and worked her way up from an administrative accountant to the CEO of Carta Aluminum.

Carta was the third-largest provider of automotive parts in the state. They built bumpers, door frames, engine radiators, and in some cases, even the frames. The company was worth billions.

It was a night of celebration. The company had beat quarterly earnings targets for six consecutive quarters—something it had never done before.

Denise believed luck played a big role in the company's success. No matter how great a leader was, sometimes things needed to fall into place for them to flourish.

The US economy had been chugging along at a rapid pace. Interest rates were low or near the bottom. People had jobs, and they could borrow money cheaply. And buying cars was at an all-time high.

As sales grew in the auto industry, the demand for materials to produce those goods grew as well.

But Denise knew the luck did not come from the monetary policy from the federal reserve or the historic low unemployment rate. The luck came from the political decisions made in Washington.

The president had decided to make China and Mexico his focus. He put in place restrictive tariffs and embargos on those two countries, which left the big car manufacturers scrambling to get cheap materials from local providers.

This was perfect timing for Carta Aluminum to assert themselves. They were now able to compete with the foreign corporations, who, for years, had undermined their costs to beat Carta.

Carta's vice president of operations spoke from the lectern. His words galvanized the people gathered in the room. There was excitement in the air. Carta had the potential to become one of the largest automotive suppliers in the state by the end of next year and perhaps could even become a force in the country. The possibilities were endless.

The shareholders saw nothing but high returns on their investments. And management saw nothing but more bonuses in their pockets.

Denise was the next and final speaker. Her speech was prepared well in advance, almost two weeks ago. She had read and memorized it. She knew where to raise her voice and where to lower it. She had to sound optimistic, but also cautious. As the leader, it was on her to steer the company with a steady hand. Shareholders wanted a good return on their investment, but they also wanted someone they could trust. Someone who wouldn't blow their investment away on unnecessary expenditures and fast expansion.

But Denise did not want to be here.

She felt none of the euphoria the other people were feeling. The company was doing great, better than she had expected, but her mood had nothing to do with how well the company was doing.

There was a personal storm brewing, one that none of these people had any idea about. But if what she knew came to light, it would destroy her. The scandal would be one for the ages. The company would survive, and someone else would quickly jump in to replace her, but the devastation would be too much for her personally.

The vice president of operations ended his speech and then turned to her. The crowd stood up and began chanting, "Denise! Denise!" They had waited all night to listen to her. She was the face of Carta Aluminum. She had taken the family-owned company to new heights. She would take them even further.

With her introductions over, she stood up, and the crowd applauded with excitement.

This was her moment to shine, to bask in the glory of everything *she* had accomplished. As a mother, wife, and daughter, she was an inspiration to all the women who looked up to her.

Instead of feeling strong and proud, she felt weak and hollow as she got to her feet, forcing a smile on her face and waving to the crowd.

## THIRTY-FIVE

The man wore a beige-colored striped suit with a brown leather belt and scuffed shoes. The suit had food stains on it. At least, that's what Callaway thought they were.

Callaway was at Sutton & Associates, a law firm fifty miles from Milton. Callaway had quickly come to realize there were no other associates—only Tim Sutton.

Sutton was a small, wiry man with graying hair and a bald spot. His skin was marked with sun spots, and he wore round spectacles.

The firm was located on the ground floor of a building that had seen better days. If you asked Callaway, the building should have been demolished a long time ago. None of the elevators were operational, even though the building had five levels. The carpet had not been cleaned in months, or perhaps years. An odd smell hung in the air. Worse yet, there was no ventilation, which made the space hot and stuffy.

Callaway was already sweating as he sat across from Sutton.

Sutton had represented Roger Sinclair in the murder of his wife. Callaway was flummoxed as to why Roger, an educated and accomplished man, would hire someone like Sutton when there were far more impressive law firms out there.

Maybe Roger knew his case was hopeless. Plus, he had already confessed. Why waste money on something that would not change the outcome?

Even so, it still left Callaway with a ton of questions.

Anyone facing the prospect of life in prison would do everything to fight back. Cold-blooded serial killers, who had little chance of winning, still dragged their cases through the courts, hoping that even one juror would believe them, and they'd have a hung jury.

They could also recant their confession at a later time. Roger hadn't done that. They could also appeal their sentence, another thing Roger hadn't done. They could, at the very least, show remorse for their actions, to convince the judge they deserved leniency. Roger accepted his fate without any fuss.

"You're a private investigator, huh?" Sutton said, staring at Callaway's business card.

"I am."

"Is there good money in it?"

"Sometimes."

"You know, I've thought about doing something else with my time. Maybe close down my firm. But I can't let my clients down. They're counting on me to provide justice for them."

"How many cases do you have ongoing right now?" Callaway asked. Sutton's desk was clear, and with no secretary—a rarity for lawyers, who hated doing their own paperwork—he doubted the man got much business.

"Enough to keep me busy," Sutton replied.

"I was going over Roger Sinclair's file," Callaway said.

Sutton cringed at the sound of Sinclair's name. "I advised him not to plead, but he wouldn't listen to me."

"Then why did he hire you if he didn't want your opinion?"

"The state still has the death penalty, and Roger's one condition was that he didn't want a death sentence. I was confident the prosecution would never consider it."

"Why not?"

"The murder had to be premeditated. As far as I could tell, there was nothing to indicate Roger was planning to kill his wife for some time."

"But he did kill his wife, didn't he?" Callaway said.

"That's what he confessed to."

"No, he didn't."

Sutton shifted in his seat. "I don't follow you."

"I read his confession, and he never once stated that he killed his wife. He confessed to starting the fire that destroyed the house."

"But he agreed that his wife was inside when he started the fire."

"No dead body was ever recovered from the wreckage."

"Did you see the photos? There was nothing left of the house. Everything on the property was burnt to a crisp," Sutton said, "so what's the difference if he confessed to killing his wife or not?"

"There is a difference," Callaway said. "One is that Roger Sinclair murdered his wife and then set the house on fire to hide his crimes. The other is that Roger Sinclair set the house on fire while his wife was still alive inside. Both are terrible acts, but one is far worse than the other."

Sutton stared at him in silence.

"Regardless," Sutton said with a dismissive wave of his hand, "Roger has never denied that his wife is dead. He has also taken full responsibility for starting the fire. He has accepted his fate *and* continues to serve his time for his actions. My hands were tied from the very beginning. There was nothing more I could have done to change the outcome of his sentence. Absolutely nothing."

Callaway wanted to respond, but he knew Sutton was right.

## THIRTY-SIX

Crenshaw leaned back in his leather chair and took a drag from the cigar. It was Cuban. Every year, Crenshaw took a week-long trip to Havana. It was not only to grab more cigars, but also to spend time with the local girls. Cuban women were beautiful, and they always satisfied his demands.

He took another puff.

His home office was close to a thousand square feet—a far cry from the office he had at Dark Box.

After spending all day at Dark Box, Crenshaw loved coming home. It was ten thousand square feet of glass and steel. It had marble floors, twenty-foot ceilings, and twelve-foot windows. The house was also surrounded by two acres of land, which meant he could have privacy while enjoying the view.

The home was built in nine months, and it cost a lot of money. Fortunately for Crenshaw, he had money to spare.

Business was good, and Crenshaw believed it would only get better. Over the years, the rich had seen their net worth grow exponentially. And because of that, these people had become more guarded. And they needed someone like Crenshaw to make sure nothing encroached on their way of life.

The rich had suddenly become targets. Targets of protestors who felt the rich were becoming richer on the backs of the poor. Targets of journalists who wanted to expose how the rich were making their money. Targets of government entities who wanted to find out if the rich were paying their share of taxes.

Everyone wanted a piece of them. And Crenshaw had no doubts about protecting them. That protection costs money—*lots* of money. And these people had the means to pay it.

Crenshaw was wearing a red silk robe he had purchased in Thailand, another country he enjoyed visiting on a regular basis. He wore cashmere pajamas, and on his feet were handcrafted loafers made from some of the finest materials available. When he was at home, he liked to dress comfortably.

The maid had left for the day. His personal chef would drop by to prepare dinner, but that wouldn't be for another couple of hours. He had the entire house to himself until then. He could drive to his favorite restaurant if he wanted to. But after his last visit to the doctor, he had to start eating healthy to control his cholesterol.

*I might take a dip in the pool*, he thought.

That brought a smile to his face.

His cell phone vibrated on the mahogany desk. He reached over and picked it up.

There was one message. He read it and frowned.

He typed a short response and placed the phone back on the desk.

He glanced over at the monitor up on the wall. The LCD screen showed images from a dozen cameras on the property.

A moment later, he saw a sedan pull up to the front gates. He recognized the license plate.

He pressed a button on his desk, and the gates opened.

He took a long drag from the cigar, got up from his desk, and walked over to the foyer. He opened the door.

A large man entered the house.

"I hope this is important, Kristoff," Crenshaw grumbled. "You know I don't like to be disturbed when I'm at home."

"We have a problem," Kristoff said.

Crenshaw stared at his chief security officer. The man was intimidating and ruthless—very good reasons why Crenshaw had hired him. Before taking the job, Kristoff had one condition: that Crenshaw also hire his partner, Andrei. Crenshaw didn't like spending the extra money, but he had thought, *Well, two killers are better than one.* Crenshaw had no issues with keeping hired guns on his payroll. They did things that others wouldn't. They also followed orders without asking too many questions. They knew the stakes were high. Powerful people paid good money to have Dark Box make their problems go away.

Kristoff and Andrei were rewarded handsomely. Their fee was non-negotiable, and Crenshaw wouldn't dare haggle them, either. He knew how valuable these two men were to his company. While the hackers at Dark Box worked behind computers, Kristoff and Andrei literally got their hands dirty.

Crenshaw knew Andrei was in the sedan. His partner rarely came into the house. He preferred to let Kristoff do all the talking.

"What's the problem?" Crenshaw asked.

"Someone is looking into the case," Kristoff replied.

"Is it the same case we are having trouble resolving?" Crenshaw asked.

"It is."

"Who is looking into it?"

"A private investigator."

"Does he have a name?"

"Lee Callaway."

Crenshaw's eyes narrowed. "Why now?"

"I don't know," Kristoff replied.

"Does it have something to do with what happened at the motel?"

Kristoff went silent.

Crenshaw said, "What you did complicated matters."

"I had no choice," Kristoff said through clenched teeth. "He saw me leave the room."

"He didn't see you commit a crime."

"He was recording me."

"So what?" Crenshaw said with a shrug. "You could've been a guest of the motel."

"He recorded me holding my gun."

Crenshaw's eyes widened. He understood. Anonymity was paramount in their line of work.

Now *they* had bigger problems to deal with.

"Keep an eye on this private investigator," Crenshaw said. "I want to know exactly what he's up to."

## THIRTY-SEVEN

After their talk with Guy Millson, Holt and Fisher had decided to contact someone at the Royal Canadian Mounted Police. It may have been for nothing, but it was worth a try. Millson believed Trevor McGinty had come from either Vancouver or Toronto.

Millson could be right. Trevor could have come from Canada, and he could have sold his business like he'd said and run off with the cash so that his ex-wife didn't get a share of it. It made sense that he would change his name so she couldn't find him.

But why would someone torture and kill him? It couldn't have been over a domestic dispute.

Sergeant Douglas Miller from the RCMP said over the phone, "I'm sorry for not getting back to you guys sooner, but I wanted to make sure of a couple of things before I did." Fisher and Holt had forwarded everything they had on the man who went by the name of Trevor McGinty to the RCMP. "It took some time matching up the photo you had sent us to the photos in our records, and I think I may have found a match."

"Okay, so who is he?" Fisher asked into the speaker-phone. Holt was next to her.

"Rene Tremblanc," Miller replied. "In 1987, Rene Tremblanc had shot and killed an armored truck driver in Winnipeg, Manitoba."

*So, it wasn't Vancouver or Toronto*, Fisher thought, *but still in Canada, nonetheless*.

"He had two other accomplices with him at the time of the incident," Miller said. "Ron Twoo, a Native Indian from a tribe in Northern Manitoba, and Dave Alden, who came to Winnipeg from Nova Scotia."

Fisher and Holt listened intently as Miller continued.

"Tremblanc was born and raised in Quebec City. He owned a local hardware store which he lost during his divorce from his ex-wife. He tried to sell the business before the divorce was finalized, but he failed."

*So, that part of his story was true*, Fisher thought. *People usually use real events to concoct a story around their past.*

"He then headed to Winnipeg to find work. There, he met Twoo and Alden. Twoo was known to the local police. He was caught multiple times stealing booze from the liquor stores. Alden had no priors. He was as clean-cut as they get. I think he got pulled into the scheme by Tremblanc. After the hit, all three had split up. They were supposed to meet up at some motel, but Tremblanc never showed up. We caught Twoo not long after, and Alden gave himself up. They didn't know Tremblanc's real name or even much about him. But they both confirmed in separate interrogations that Tremblanc was the one who had pulled the trigger. We put out a warrant for his arrest, but by that time, he had already fled the country."

"How much money was taken from the armored truck?" Fisher asked.

"Four hundred and sixty-five thousand dollars."

*That explained the Canadian currency*, Fisher thought.

Miller said, "We assumed he had gone to South America—maybe Brazil or Colombia. It's easy to launder that kind of money over there. We never thought he just crossed the border into the United States."

"Why not?" Holt said, sounding annoyed. "There is no way someone could carry that much cash on them while boarding a plane, so he had to have driven it into the States or Mexico."

Miller was not the least bit offended. "Moving money across borders is easy," he responded. "If you have the right connections or people you trust, you can simply hand over the cash to them, and they'll wire the money from their accounts."

"But McGinty was found with bundles of cash. It was the same currency he'd taken from the armored truck. He was just taking his sweet time converting it to US dollars so as not to raise any alarms," Holt said.

"We had a case of someone stealing a large sum of money from a bank," Miller said. "The person then flew out of the country. When he landed at his destination, his money was waiting for him."

"How'd he manage to do that?" Fisher asked.

"He mailed the cash through a shipping container. Most of the ports are understaffed. There are not enough Customs Officers to examine every shipment, and some officers are paid off, so it would be easy to get the money into another country."

"But that's not what McGinty did," Holt said. "He had to have driven through Customs with the cash in the trunk of his car."

"We now believe that's what happened," Miller conceded. "And you have to remember. This was over thirty years ago, pre-9/11. The rules were quite relaxed."

Fisher asked, "How did you know Trevor McGinty was, in fact, Rene Tremblanc?"

"We have still images from the surveillance camera at the time of the armored truck robbery," Miller replied. "It's grainy, but it looks a lot like the person on the driver's license you sent us."

There was a beat of silence.

Miller asked, "Do you guys know who could have killed Rene Tremblanc?"

"We're still working on all leads," Fisher replied. "But do you know where Ron Twoo and Dave Alden are? They were involved in the robbery with Tremblanc, and from what you just told us, Tremblanc betrayed them when he ran away with the stolen money. If anyone has a reason to murder him for revenge, these two would."

"I don't think it was either of them," Holt said.

Fisher looked up at him. "Why do you say that?"

"We found the money in the motel."

He was right, she knew. If either Twoo or Alden had tortured and murdered McGinty, they would have taken the money with them.

Fisher kicked herself for opening her mouth.

Miller said, "I should add that Twoo died of alcohol poisoning ten years ago, and Alden is in prison for fraud. He won't be out for another year."

There was silence on the line.

Miller then said, "When you guys are done with your investigation, it would be nice if we could bring Rene Tremblanc's body back to Canada. He is still a Canadian citizen. And also, we would appreciate it if you could send back the stolen money to the RCMP. The money from the armored truck belonged to several banks in Winnipeg. I'm sure they'll appreciate having their property returned to them."

"That will not be a problem," Fisher said.

## THIRTY-EIGHT

Callaway ended the call and rubbed his temples. It was from his landlady. Normally, he avoided answering her calls. It was always about unpaid rent, but now she was his client. Even though no money had been exchanged, Callaway had agreed to take her case on.

Callaway believed in good customer service. Word of mouth was crucial in his line of work. If people trusted you, they were willing to recommend you to their family and friends. In order to build that trust, he had to make himself available to his clients at all times.

Ms. Chen told him that Bruce was acting even more erratic. He hadn't gone to work in days, and his supervisor was calling regularly. Bruce loved his job, so his behavior was concerning to all.

Bruce was suffering from guilt and depression, Callaway believed. He felt guilty for advising his mom to invest in a scam, and he was depressed that the money was now gone.

Callaway knew the only way Bruce would feel better was if he and his mom got their money back.

Callaway sighed and decided to start from the beginning.

On his laptop, he loaded the website for Grannex Investments. The website was professional. There were no pop-ups flashing on the screen, demanding people to invest right away and become rich. Nothing like those late-night infomercials where if the customer called in the next minute, they not only received an additional product, they also didn't have to pay for shipping. It was all done to create FOMO: fear of missing out. People felt pressured to call right away, or else they could lose out on the deal of a lifetime.

Nothing like that was on Grannex's website. They made no wild claims on any of their main webpages, except when you went to their review sections. One investor stated he had doubled his money in ten days. Another investor said he was getting returns of as high as sixty-five percent—a percentage that was impossible to achieve in today's market, but for the unsavvy investor, it was enough to convince them to jump in.

Some investors talked about quitting their jobs and spending more time with their spouses and children, all because of the returns from Grannex. A good portion of working people in the United States hated their jobs. And this claim spoke directly to their hearts. The scammers were shrewd to know what emotional strings to pull.

As Callaway went through the reviews, he saw a pattern. The more outlandish the claims, the more likely people believed them.

*The reviewers are likely not even real*, he thought. *John D., Claire B., Mr. & Mrs. Jones.* And to make them look and sound real, the scammers made some of them out to be doctors, retired professionals, or even military vets. Who wouldn't trust a doctor or someone who had served their country?

Callaway then went to the last webpage, one that listed the bios of Grannex's staff. Jim Morris was the company's managing director. He was born in Montana on January 14, 1965. He graduated from University of Providence.

As a private investigator, Callaway had access to certain databases. He punched in the information, and there were no records of anyone born in Montana with that name in that year.

He then checked the next staff member. Janis Chaplin was the CEO. She was born in Tennessee on July 29, 1971. She previously worked on Wall Street before founding Grannex Investments. She had started the Grannex Foundation, which had donated millions of dollars to fight homelessness in the state of New York.

Callaway did a quick online search and found that no Grannex Foundation was registered as a charitable organization.

The last staff member was Grannex's managing partner. Curtis Cobane was born in Nebraska on October 21, 1977. He had experience working in Silicon Valley and brought vast amounts of technical knowledge and experience to Grannex Investments.

Callaway paused and read the names of the staff members again. He grinned and shook his head. Jim Morris was Jim Morrison. Janis Chaplin was Janis Joplin. And Curtis Cobane was Kurt Cobain. All were once musicians, and all had died at the age of twenty-seven.

*Someone loves rock music*, Callaway thought.

He did another quick online search and found that all the photos for Jim Morris, Janis Chaplin, and Curtis Cobane were stock images.

Nothing on the website was real. It was all fake. There was no Grannex Investments—only a website to convince unsuspecting people to fork over their life savings for unrealistic returns.

Bruce Chen had done just that.

# THIRTY-NINE

Fisher decided to head home. There was nothing more she could do for the day. They knew Trevor McGinty was not who they thought he was. He was, in fact, Rene Tremblanc from Montreal, Canada.

He was also a killer—someone who had shot and killed an armored truck driver who was only doing his job. Fisher had taken a deeper look into the truck driver. Could any member of his family have wanted revenge for what Tremblanc had done?

The driver's name was Chad Kennedy. He was twenty-three years old, and he had been on the job only a few months. It explained why Chad had decided to pull his weapon out when Tremblanc, Twoo, and Alden jumped him. A more experienced driver would have analyzed the situation and realized the odds were against him.

Twoo and Alden later confessed under interrogation that neither of them was carrying a weapon; only Tremblanc was. But Chad didn't know that. He thought he could defend himself and protect the money he was hired to keep safe.

A senior driver would have known that no money or job was worth being shot and killed.

Tremblanc did shoot and kill Chad, and he lived a peaceful existence for three decades until someone ended his life brutally.

A part of her thought Tremblanc got what he deserved. Chad was not married, nor did he have any children. But he did leave behind his parents and three siblings. Fisher couldn't imagine what his parents must have gone through having to bury their child.

But Fisher couldn't let what Tremblanc did in the past affect her investigation. Tremblanc's killer was out there, and it would be another injustice if he wasn't punished the way Tremblanc hadn't been for thirty years.

Fisher was glad the RCMP would provide closure to Chad's family. Fisher wasn't sure if Chad's parents were still alive, but hopefully, his siblings were.

Fisher parked her SUV in her apartment building's basement garage and took the elevator up to the sixth floor. Her building was old and constantly in need of repairs. The windows in most of the units were not insulated. The hot water did not always work properly. Sometimes Fisher would end up taking a cold shower before heading out to work. The building's roof had recently been repaired, but that was only because the building management had no choice. Further delay would have resulted in a bigger expense. The hallway carpets were earmarked to be replaced this month, but with the budget gone to fixing the roof, there was no telling when the carpets would be replaced.

Fisher could move out if she wanted to, but rent in Milton had still not come down, nor had the prices of houses for sale. She was hoping to save enough for a down payment. Until then, she would have to suck it up and deal with the problems in her building.

Fortunately, her job required long hours, so she was mostly in her apartment to sleep or get a change of clothes.

She entered her unit. The apartment was painted in bright colors, something she had done upon moving in. It was a one-bedroom, but the previous tenants had enclosed the balcony, giving her an extra room. She used it as either an office or a meditation room.

Fisher was about to take her coat off when she sensed something was not right. There was light coming from underneath the bedroom door. Fisher always turned all the lights off before leaving the apartment because management charged her for the use of electricity.

She removed her weapon from its holster and took a glance inside the kitchen on the left. She then proceeded down the hall. The living room was as she had left it. The magazine she was reading was still open on the coffee table.

She tiptoed to the bedroom and pressed her ear to the door. She heard movement inside.

*Someone's in my apartment!* she thought.

She took a deep breath, aimed the gun in front of her, and then burst through the door.

"Don't shoot," a voice said.

Lance McConnell was standing next to the bed. He was tall, with deep blue eyes and a prominent chin. His blonde hair, which was usually hidden underneath his police cap, was now neatly combed.

She looked at him and then at the bed. There was a message written in rose petals.

WILL YOU MARRY ME?

She turned to Lance. He was grinning. He then got down on one knee.

"Detective Dana Fisher," he said. "Will you make me the happiest man on earth and be my wife?"

Fisher stared at him, turned around, and left the apartment.

## FORTY

Callaway checked his watch for the umpteenth time. He was sitting on a park bench in a quiet neighborhood. The park was halfway across town from where his office was, so the drive was not trivial. But he had to come.

After going through Grannex's website in detail, Callaway had scoured the social media sites for any links to Grannex. He found one, a social media page set up by a woman named Tammy Rosetto.

When Callaway searched for her, he was surprised to find that a person by that name lived in Milton. He contacted her, and after some discussion, he was even more surprised when she agreed to meet him—but only at this particular location.

The park was eerily empty. It was surrounded by residential homes. There was even a kids' playground at the far end. No kids were playing there at the moment.

*This was a mistake*, he thought. *Someone's playing a sick joke on me.*

He got up to leave when he saw a woman walking in his direction. The woman was slightly overweight. Her hair was colored pink, and she had on sneakers, jeans, and a light sweater.

"Mr. Callaway?" she said.

"You must be Tammy," he said.

They didn't shake hands.

"Let's get this over with," she said, and she sat down on the bench.

He sat next to her, but with enough space between them.

Tammy looked around nervously. Then she crossed her arms over her.

"Is everything okay?" he asked.

"It's not," she replied. "You're not the first person to contact me about Grannex. I've got two young kids. I can't have people showing up at my house asking me what happened to their money. One time I had to call the police because the person wouldn't get off my property."

"People have lost their life savings because of Grannex," Callaway said, "including my client, whose mom may also lose her business because of Grannex."

Tammy put her face in her hands. "I wish I knew what happened to everyone's money, but I don't."

"How did you get involved with Grannex?"

"I'm a single mom. I'm self-employed. I help companies run their social media pages. Someone from Grannex contacted me."

"Did he give you a name?" Callaway asked.

"Jim Morris."

*There's that fake name again*, Callaway thought.

"We emailed back and forth," she said. "We agreed on a fee. I would set up a page for Grannex and also moderate it."

"How were you paid?"

"That's the thing," Tammy said, shaking her head. "I was told I would be given an account with Grannex, and all my fees would be converted into investments. I could access the account any time I wanted. After one month, my fee of two thousand dollars had doubled. After three months, I had almost fourteen thousand dollars in the account. I never bothered to pull any of the money out because I could see the money growing."

"How were you able to pay your bills if you didn't take any money out?" Callaway asked.

"I live in my mom's basement," Tammy replied. "After my ex-husband ran off, my mom took me in. I pay her whatever I can. She doesn't have a mortgage, so she doesn't ask for much." Tammy paused, and her eyes turned moist. "I really thought the money was growing. I really thought people at Grannex had a magic wand or some special skills to get such high returns. I really wanted that money for my two girls, to give them a better life."

"But that money doesn't exist, does it?" Callaway said.

She wiped her eyes and shook her head. "I started getting nasty emails from people. They said they couldn't withdraw their money. Freaked out, I tried to withdraw the money from my account, and I couldn't. I contacted Grannex, and they told me they were having a system error, that I'd be able to access the money soon."

*Those were the same lies told to Bruce,* Callaway thought.

"I checked out the page you ran for Grannex," Callaway said. "It had screenshots of large withdrawals from people's accounts to show that they were making money with Grannex."

"All supplied by Grannex," she said. "They would send stuff over to me, and I would post it. I also posted screenshots of *my* account to show how my money was growing—which in reality, it was not. I think that's why Grannex hired me. They wanted someone who was naïve enough to believe they were making money and to convince others of it, too. And I did. But I swear, I didn't know it was a lie. I was scammed as well."

Callaway sensed genuine pain and fear in her voice.

"Why did you agree to meet me?" he asked. "I could be an investor looking to hurt you for your part in the scheme."

"I searched for you online while we were speaking on the phone," she said. "You're a good person. You've helped a lot of people. I knew you were not going to hurt me, especially if I told you my side of the story."

Callaway stared at her and then stood up. "You're right. I only hurt those who deserve it."

He walked away.

## FORTY-ONE

Crenshaw was not a man who scared easily, but he was scared now. He was in the back seat of his Rolls Royce as his driver drove him to his destination.

He was expecting the call, but he never expected the tone of the man's voice on the other end.

Crenshaw was used to dealing with powerful people, and almost all of them were men. They were masters of their industry and worth hundreds of millions of dollars. They liked to have things done their way and to have people at their beck and call, including Crenshaw.

But his relationship with the men was not one-sided. They hired him to dig up *their* skeletons and bury them. They never dared threaten him. They knew what leverage he had on them.

This client was different.

Crenshaw had failed him. He had not been able to bury the problem completely, and now the client was in danger. If he went down, Crenshaw would surely go down with him. The client had a lot of money and power, and he could ruin Crenshaw and destroy Dark Box.

Crenshaw would not let that happen. He would do everything he could to resolve the problem and get back in the good graces of his client.

The Rolls moved down an empty road and then entered a dirt path. The wheels crunched the dirt and gravel as it drove farther up. Crenshaw looked out the window and saw nothing but trees and bushes.

The Rolls slowed in an area deep in the forest. It then parked next to a Bentley. The windows of the Bentley were tinted, but Crenshaw knew the client was inside.

He got out of the Rolls, walked over, and got inside the Bentley.

Wilbur Graft had silver hair, a thick silver mustache, and steely eyes. His gold cane was next to him, and he had a diamond ring on his pinky finger. Even though he was over seventy years old, the man was still intimidating.

"I thought you said the matter was taken care of," Graft growled. Graft was never one for pleasantries. He got right down to the point.

"We thought it was…" Crenshaw stammered.

"But?"

"It's a little more complicated than we anticipated."

"I paid a king's ransom for you to make this problem go away."

"We did make it go away, but now the problem has come back."

Graft grunted disapprovingly.

Crenshaw wanted to tell him that it was because of Dark Box that he was not in prison. The man's crimes were unforgivable. They were not only unethical but also illegal. It was Dark Box that had buried his crimes for this long.

But Crenshaw couldn't say this to the man. People like him didn't dispense with gratitude. They bought people with their money, and they used their money to make their troubles disappear.

"I assure you," Crenshaw finally said, "we are working on this as we speak."

"You better," Graft growled. "I'm not going to spend the later years of my life dealing with the law. I've worked too long and too hard to start worrying about anything in life. Do whatever you have to and resolve this situation. I don't care how you do it, but just do it."

There was a heavy silence in the Bentley. Crenshaw wasn't sure if he should break it or wait for Graft to do it.

Graft then said in a low growl, "What about my most *recent* problem?"

"We're working on it."

"Do it fast. The board is going to vote in a couple of months. I want a new CEO in place when they do. Understood?"

"Yes, sir," Crenshaw replied.

"We are done here," Graft said with a wave of his hand.

Crenshaw quietly exited the Bentley and walked back to his Rolls Royce.

# FORTY-TWO

Callaway parked his Dodge Charger in front of a bar and turned the engine off. He was making every effort to steer clear of bars, casinos, and any other place that could suck him back into his old habits.

His impulses always got the best of him. He had very little self-control. If he started with one drink, before the night ended, he'd had enough to be thrown out of the bar. Whenever he went inside a casino, he would vow not to spend more than he could afford, but by the time he left, he not only had burned through the money he had on him but also owed money to the casino. As a frequent customer, the casino wouldn't hesitate in extending him credit. But finding ways to pay that credit off was not easy. He would take on jobs that he wouldn't normally take.

Once, he was hired by a man to follow a woman whom Callaway thought was his wife or girlfriend. Only later did he realize the man was a pimp and wanted Callaway to make sure his girl wasn't doing jobs on the side without him knowing. Needless to say, Callaway returned the man's money and warned him never to come back. He had debated a long time whether to inform the police about the man, which he eventually did. The man had hired Callaway to do a job, and as his client, he was afforded a certain amount of confidentiality. But the man hadn't been entirely truthful. Had he told Callaway why he wanted the woman followed, Callaway would have turned him down right then and there. No amount of money would compel him to let a man abuse a woman. Callaway had a daughter, and that woman was someone's daughter as well. The police descended on the man. The last Callaway heard, the man was in prison for intimidation and human trafficking.

Callaway stared at the neon sign above the bar. He hesitated, but he knew he couldn't turn back. He had come here for a reason.

He looked around the dark bar and spotted her in a booth in the back.

Dana Fisher had a tall glass of beer in front of her. He could tell she hadn't touched it. Callaway had once gone out on a date with Fisher. She was the one who had told him long ago that he still harbored feelings for his ex-wife. Callaway didn't believe her, but she turned out to be right.

Most people in the police department wanted nothing to do with private investigators. They didn't respect what private eyes did. They weren't real cops, so why even have them?

Fisher was different. She knew how hard Callaway worked for his clients.

He sat down across from her.

"Thanks for coming," she said.

"I came the moment you called."

Fisher said, "I was going to order you a drink, but I know you're…"

Callaway put his hands up. "That's fine. I'm not thirsty."

She looked down at her glass. She took a deep breath and said, "Lance proposed to me."

A smile spread across Callaway's face. "That's great news. Congratulations. I'm happy for you."

"I didn't say yes."

His smile faded. "Oh."

"I don't know what to do," she said. "And I didn't know who else to call at this time of the day. So, I need your help."

"I could suddenly use a drink now." He waved the bartender over and ordered a root beer. After it came, he took a sip from the bottle and asked Fisher, "Do you want to get married?"

She shrugged. "I like the thought of having a wedding. I mean, what girl doesn't, but…"

"But what?"

"It's just that… it suddenly feels overwhelming."

Callaway paused and then asked, "Do you love Lance?"

"I mean, it's the longest I've been in a relationship."

"But do you *love* him?"

Fisher thought for a moment. "I do."

"But love isn't enough to sustain a marriage," he said.

She looked up at him. "It isn't?"

"Listen, I'm probably not the right guy to talk to about marriage. I walked away from mine. It's one of my biggest regrets. When I think back, I had no reason to leave. I was madly in love with Patti, but you know what? I wasn't ready to be married. Marriage is more than saying, 'I love you.' It's about sacrifice, commitment, going through good and bad days. Marriage is hard work. I applaud those people who can make it work a long time. Heck, there should be a medal for couples who can find a reason to be together for decades. No matter what Patti did when we were married, I wasn't happy. I thought my marriage was a burden. Now I want nothing more than to be married again—and to the same person." He paused and then said, "You'll know better than anyone when *you* are ready. No one can tell you otherwise."

Fisher stared at him. "That's some deep stuff."

Callaway's eyes widened. "I know. Sometimes I even scare myself."

Fisher smiled. "Thanks, Lee."

# FORTY-THREE

Holt sat at his desk, staring at the laptop. Instead of reading what was on the screen, his mind was elsewhere. He was thinking about the case.

Whenever Holt was on a new case, he became obsessed with it. Nothing else mattered. Except his wife, Nancy. She was the one person who could pull him away from an investigation. She was his rock. Without her, his life would be meaningless.

The job was a distraction from all the tragedies he had gone through. Losing his parents at a young age, with his older sister taking on a maternal role. Then Nancy having so many miscarriages. If those things weren't bad enough, he also lost his adopted son to cancer. Then, as if to pour salt in his wounds, he lost his nephew to murder. Holt was close to his nephew. The boy could have become a professional basketball player, but his life was brutally cut short.

If it weren't for Nancy, Holt would've put a gun to his head by now and ended his misery. But he couldn't be selfish and leave Nancy on her own. She needed him as much as he needed her. Both had suffered together, but Nancy had suffered more so. It couldn't have been easy having to go through those miscarriages. The physical pain healed with time, but the emotional pain lasted a lifetime.

The what-ifs always followed Holt around like ghosts from his past. What if he and Nancy had been blessed with one child? That child would have changed their lives in so many ways. He or she would have given them a purpose. To see that child grow up, learn, and become an adult. They would've shared all the milestones with that child. The first time he or she walked, said "mama" or "dada," or went to kindergarten, high school, and then maybe college. And if luck was still on their side, and they lived long enough, Holt and Nancy would see that child get married and have children of their own.

Holt felt like he had been robbed of those opportunities, but he knew regret would only get him so far. If he let it consume him, he wouldn't get out of bed in the morning.

His work gave him a sense of purpose. He wanted to provide closure to those who had lost someone, as well.

Unfortunately, no one was grieving Rene Tremblanc, aka Trevor McGinty. He had no family, and no one to visit him at his funeral. Holt doubted that even his friend, Guy Millson, would show up to pay his respects. Millson was upset that Trevor had so much money, but didn't share any with him.

The money was ill-gotten gains. Trevor knew that, and he made sure to keep his past hidden, even after three decades on the run.

Holt wasn't one to cast aspersions on anyone, but Trevor got what he deserved. He was a killer—no doubt about that.

Holt still had a job to do, however, and he would do everything in his power to find the person responsible for Trevor's death.

He opened the case file and began to go through the photos of the crime scene.

One photo caught his attention. It was of the front window. He leaned closer and examined the picture in detail.

He grabbed his jacket and left the Milton PD.

# FORTY-FOUR

The metal door clanged behind him, and the lock snapped shut. In an instant, Callaway felt like he was suffocating. He was inside a windowless room at the state penitentiary.

He had to call twenty-four hours in advance to schedule this meeting. Once he arrived at the prison, he had to sign in, be searched, and then go through several layers of security before entering the room.

He sat down on a metal chair behind a metal table. Both the chair and table were bolted to the floor. There was nothing else in the room. This was done for a specific reason: nothing could be used as a weapon.

He took a deep breath to regain his composure.

The door opened with a loud creak. A man entered wearing an orange jumpsuit. Behind him was a uniformed guard. The guard escorted the man to the table, pushed him down on the chair, and then fastened his handcuffs to the table.

The guard left the room.

Callaway stared at the man before him. He had unruly hair. His beard was long, covering his neck, and it had streaks of gray. He was rail-thin, mute evidence that he had not become accustomed to prison food. Everything about the man made him look like he was ill, but his eyes told a different story.

They were full of energy, and they now bore into the visitor seated across from him.

"Thank you for seeing me, Mr. Sinclair," Callaway said.

Roger Sinclair did not smile, nor did he exchange pleasantries.

Instead, he said, "On the phone, you said you were looking into my wife's case?"

"Your wife's case is linked to your case, so in essence, I'm also looking into *your* case."

"Why?"

"You wouldn't believe it, but your daughter, Millie, hired me."

Hearing his daughter's name, Roger's face softened. "You met Millie?"

"I did."

"How?"

"She's in my daughter's class. I did a talk at her school, and I guess Millie liked what she heard."

Roger paused and then asked, "You're a private investigator?"

"I am."

"And what do you hope to accomplish in your investigation?"

"Millie thinks her mom is still alive," Callaway replied.

"She's not."

"Is she dead?" Callaway asked.

Roger stared at him. "You're not my lawyer, so I don't have to answer any of your questions."

"Speaking of your lawyer," Callaway said, "I spoke to him. He said you didn't take his advice. You pleaded guilty the moment you stood up in front of the judge."

"I didn't want to drag my family through a long trial," Roger said. "Millie had already lost her mother. I didn't want kids in her school talking further about what happened."

"I get it. You wanted to spare Millie the pain of having to listen to all the sordid details that come out in any trial," Callaway said. "But this was about your freedom. Isn't that worth giving it a shot?"

Roger fell silent. He then leaned closer, the handcuffs rattling before him. "You need to stop doing what you're doing," he said. "This doesn't concern you."

Callaway stared at him. "I'm a little confused, Mr. Sinclair. If I were in your position, I would be grateful that someone was looking into my case. Someone who could perhaps exonerate me and get me out of this place. I can't imagine you enjoy being locked up in a six-by-ten cell."

Roger looked away.

Callaway then said softly, "Help me understand what's going on. That's the only way I can help you."

"How can *you* help me, Mr. Callaway?" Roger asked, meeting his eyes.

"For one thing, tell me why you never confessed to killing your wife, only to setting your house on fire."

"Whether I killed my wife, or she died in the flames… it's all semantics. What matters is that she is gone. And I am responsible for what happened to her."

Callaway suddenly felt a headache coming on. Roger was being elusive. He was hiding something, and Callaway could clearly sense it.

"Wouldn't you want to be with your daughter?" Callaway asked. "As a father of a little girl myself, I would do anything to hold my daughter, to be there for her, to tell her everything will be all right."

For a moment, Callaway saw genuine pain cross Roger's face. But the pain disappeared as quickly as it had appeared.

"You have no idea what's going on," Roger said, raising his voice. "By sticking your nose where it doesn't belong, you are putting everyone's life at risk. Especially Millie's. If I were you, I would go back and forgot about this case. Millie's just a child. And as her father, I have to make sure no harm comes to her."

"Who wants to hurt her, Mr. Sinclair?" Callaway asked.

Instead of answering his question, Roger yelled, "Guard!"

The door opened, and the guard rushed in.

"We are done here." Roger glared at Callaway. As he was being led away, he stopped and said, his voice suddenly low, "If you see Millie, tell her I love her. I always will."

Roger was escorted out of the room, leaving Callaway even more confused than when he first came in.

## FORTY-FIVE

Wayne Lemont was seated behind the main desk when Holt walked into the motel.

"I'm glad you're here," Wayne said.

"You are?" Holt said, confused.

"Yes. I wanted to ask you about room ten."

"What about it?" Holt asked.

"I wanted to know when I can put it back on the market," Wayne replied. "I'm losing money each day it's empty."

Holt paused and then said, "Did Rene Tremblanc pay for the entire month?"

Wayne blinked. "Who?"

"Trevor McGinty," Holt said, correcting himself.

"Yeah, Trevor paid at the beginning of each month."

"There's still a week left for the month, isn't there?"

Wayne scoffed. "Come on, man. Trevor's dead. You can't expect me to wait for the rest of the month."

Wayne wanted to squeeze additional money out of the room. It didn't matter that the room still had most of the victim's belongings. If Holt had to take a guess, the moment the room was accessible to the public, Wayne would go through the room and try to sell whatever items that could net him extra money.

*People are dispensable*, Holt thought.

169

One minute, you were a living, breathing organism with friends, family, and co-workers, and the next minute, you were buried six feet underground with people trying to take your possessions. It was as if you were just a visitor, and the moment you left, you were forgotten.

*In some ways, we are all visitors on this earth,* Holt thought. *We come, we live, and then we are gone.*

*Most of us will be forgotten, except by those close to us. Those lucky few will forever be remembered for what they did.*

Holt always wondered who would remember him when he was gone. Definitely, Nancy, if she was still alive. Fisher, for sure. And maybe a handful of others, until they became preoccupied with life.

*Why am I ruminating over my existence?* he thought.

He knew the answer.

The anniversary of the death of his adopted son was approaching. It was always a difficult time at the Holt residence. Nancy would go eerily quiet, and she would not be herself. She would stop eating. She would avoid getting out of bed. She wouldn't do anything that brought her joy: watching TV, sewing, or even going out to shop.

Holt would have to make sure she didn't fall apart completely, or worse, try to hurt herself. He would stay with her until she got over her melancholy. In order for him to do that, he had to solve this case as soon as possible.

He suddenly felt the weight on his shoulders.

"Detective?"

Wayne's voice snapped him out of his reverie.

"Yes?" Holt said, blinking.

"Do you expect me to wait until the end of the month to access *my* room?"

"I do," Holt said. "No one is allowed into the crime scene until *we* say so. Is that understood?"

Wayne stared at him. He clearly was not happy with Holt's answer. Holt didn't care. Helping Wayne Lemont make more money was not his priority, finding Trevor McGinty's killer was.

"Can I have the key to the room?" Holt asked.

"Yes," Wayne replied and handed him a key.

Holt left Wayne's office and made his way to the second level of the motel.

He walked up to the desk next to the front window. In the corner, there was an electronic device. He picked it up.

It was a modem.

There was a large sign outside Wayne's office announcing that they now had internet service. Businesses like motels couldn't compete if they didn't provide free Wi-Fi. People wanted to be connected 24/7. Holt believed that Wayne had somehow found a way to pass the extra expense to the customer.

*If the motel had Wi-Fi*, Holt thought, *then why would Trevor McGinty pay for his own internet service?*

Maybe the motel's service was spotty or weak. Maybe Trevor needed extra bandwidth. He didn't look like a gamer, nor did he have a smart TV for streaming movies.

Whatever the reason, it had something to do with the missing laptop.

There was a sticker on the back of the modem. Holt made a note of the service provider and then left.

## FORTY-SIX

Denise Hollins sat in her office with the lights off. At the moment, she preferred darkness to light. She wanted to hide from the world, from what was waiting for her.

Two framed photos sat on her desk. One was taken on her wedding day. Brett Hollins was a former pro hockey player. He played for six years on four different teams. But after one concussion, Brett decided to change his life. No matter how much he loved hockey, he didn't want to damage his body permanently. Brett was wise enough to know his health was paramount to his quality of life.

The decision was also easier because Denise, whom he'd married a year prior to hanging his skates up, came from a family worth hundreds of millions of dollars. Money was no longer an issue. Brett had other options in life. He became a minor league hockey coach. He loved teaching young athletes how to play the sport the right way.

Denise had met Brett at a charity event hosted by Carta Aluminum. He was tall, handsome, and strong. But there was a vulnerability to him that she found attractive. Guests at the event could bid for the chance to have dinner with a variety of sports athletes—football players, basketball players, baseball players. But Denise had her eye on Brett.

When he came on the stage, Denise blew away the competition with the first bid. It turned out to be the only bid.

They went to dinner three weeks after the auction. It had to be scheduled when Brett's team was back in town. The dinner was supposed to be only an hour; it turned into three. There was an instant attraction, but more than that, they found they had a lot in common, which was odd considering she came from wealth, and he came from humble beginnings. But they both wanted commitment and a sense of security in their relationship. Brett's parents had divorced when he was young. His father had walked out on his family, leaving Brett's mother to take care of him and his siblings. And even though Denise's parents were still together, her father's philandering had an impact on Denise growing up. Both Brett and Denise suffered as a consequence of their parents' actions.

Brett became a troublemaker, always getting into fights. Denise became a wild child, moving from one bad relationship to another. They didn't want that for their children. They wanted to create a stable family nucleus, one that would provide a healthy environment for their offspring.

Denise picked up the second photo on her desk. Jake and Jillian were smiling at the camera. Jake was four, and Jillian was two. Brett had planned to teach Jake to play hockey, and Denise would teach Jillian about the family business. Whether the children became successful like their parents was beside the point. What mattered was that they always knew their parents loved them and were there for them.

But now, that picture of a happy family could be shattered into a million pieces.

Her cell phone blinked. She didn't want to touch it, but she did. It could be a message from her husband.

It wasn't. It was a message she had been dreading for days.

The first text message was an introduction from someone she had never heard of, telling her they knew what she had done and that they had proof of it.

The second message included that proof. It also informed her that she should expect another message from them. This would include instructions for her to follow.

That message now filled the entire screen of her cell phone.

Denise couldn't get herself to read it. Instead, she covered her face and cried into her hands.

## FORTY-SEVEN

Callaway rushed to the hospital the moment he got the call. He took the elevator up to the fourth floor, down a winding hall, and then to the intensive care unit.

He found Ms. Chen sitting outside a room. She was being consoled by an older Asian man. Callaway recognized him as Ms. Chen's younger brother. He sometimes worked in the noodle shop's kitchen. He spoke very little English, but he was always polite to Callaway. He would smile and bow his head whenever he saw him.

"How did it happen?" Callaway asked.

Ms. Chen wiped her eyes with a handkerchief. "His girlfriend called me. He had swallowed a bottle of pain medicine, washing it down with alcohol."

Callaway turned to the room. Through the window, he saw Bruce Chen lying on the bed, hooked up to half a dozen tubes and monitors. There was an oxygen mask over his face. A pretty girl was sitting in a chair next to the bed. She had a somber look on her face.

"Why?" Callaway asked. "Why would he do that?"

"Because of the money," Ms. Chen replied.

"How do you know?"

She pulled out a piece of paper from her coat pocket and held it out for Callaway.

He took the paper. The note was handwritten in blue ink, and it was easy to see that it was a suicide note.

Bruce blamed himself for what had happened. He felt he had let his mother down. He knew how much pain the loss of the money had caused her. She worked her whole life to take care of him while he wore the best clothes and played with the best toys. She worked fourteen-hour days at the noodle shop. Bruce wanted to do for her what she had done for him. He wanted her to take it easy in her old age, work less, and enjoy more of her time. And the only way for that to happen was to invest her money and let it grow. He thought he had found the perfect investment. But he was naïve and careless to get caught up in the scam. He should have known better. He should have asked more questions. His greed got the best of him. He understood his mother would now have to work longer to recoup the money. Or worse, she would have to sell her business to cover her losses. And he couldn't watch her do either of those things. He had brought shame to his family. He was a disappointment. He had let her down. And because he couldn't deal with her seeing him as a failure, he had decided to end his life. It was the only way he could stop the guilt from tormenting him.

Callaway looked up from the letter. He was speechless.

Ms. Chen said, with tears in her eyes, "I don't care about the money. I don't care about the noodle shop. I only care that my son is okay."

Callaway wished he could tell her something that would ease her pain, that he had found the people behind the scam and that these people would be punished for taking Bruce and her money. Or better yet, they would repay the money they had stolen from them. But that would be a lie. The task he had been given was monumental. The culprits were most likely hundreds of miles away. Worse, they were likely having a laugh at what they had been able to pull off. They had suckered people into believing they were reaping high returns from their investments while they, the scammers, were spending the money for their pleasure.

Callaway knew he was not responsible for what happened to Bruce, but he couldn't shake the feeling that he could have done more to help him.

## FORTY-EIGHT

Holt and Fisher were in a room on the fourth floor of a glass building. Fisher had not told Holt that Lance had proposed to her and that she turned him down. She knew what Holt's answer would be. Holt was a big advocate of marriage. He believed if two people wanted to live together, they should make a commitment in writing.

Fisher thought that was a bit outdated. Most people living common-law were just as happy as those officially married. Some were even more committed than most married couples.

But she knew where Holt was coming from. Holt and Nancy had been through a lot during their marriage, and Holt believed, rightly or wrongly, that if he had not stood in front of his family and friends and made a vow to Nancy, their relationship might have crumbled from the weight of their tragedies.

Once, during the lowest moments of his life, he had confessed to Fisher that he once considered leaving Nancy and trying to have children with someone else. But he quickly came to his senses. The only reason he wanted to be a father was because of Nancy. She made him a better person, and if she couldn't have children, then he wouldn't, either. They would share the joys of parenthood together, not separately.

Holt wasn't religious, Fisher knew, but he believed in a higher being. And that higher being, according to scriptures, promoted marriage.

Fisher had her own reasons for not wanting to be married, and she wasn't ready to discuss them with Holt. Not right then, at least.

When she had arrived at the Milton PD in the morning, Holt had filled her in on what he'd found in Trevor/Rene's motel room. They decided to visit his internet provider and see if it led them anywhere.

"Do you think we'll find anything here?" she asked.

"It's worth a try," he replied.

A moment later, a man entered the room. "I'm sorry for keeping you waiting, detectives. I'm Ken Johnson, Head of Corporate Affairs." Ken wore a plain blue shirt, black pants, and black dress shoes. His tie had a Christmas tree on it. Realizing they were staring at it, he said, "I was in a rush to catch my train, and I picked the wrong tie."

"We need a customer's internet history," Holt said.

"Do you guys have a warrant?" Ken asked, looking at them both.

"We don't, but the customer is dead."

"I'm sorry to hear that, but our policy is still the same when it comes to customer privacy."

"He was murdered," Holt said. He then placed photos of the crime scene one by one in front of Ken. Holt hated using this tactic; it was underhanded, but it was effective. It also saved valuable time, and time was crucial in any new investigation. The detectives would have to prepare their request, which needed to be reviewed by their supervisor, then wait for a judge to approve it. Hours or days could go by before they had the warrant in their hands, and by then, the case could go cold.

The images were gruesome, and Ken averted his eyes several times. "How far back do you need the internet history?"

"We just need it for one day."

"What day is that?"

"The day Trevor McGinty was murdered."

## FORTY-NINE

Denise Hollins had met him at a convention in Florida. He was tall with jet black hair and tanned skin. He smiled easily and often, revealing his exceptionally white teeth.

His name was Jared Stevens. He worked as a commercial real estate broker. While Denise was in town for the annual automakers' convention, Jared was there for the property developers' convention.

She ran into him in the elevator. Her event was on the top floor of the hotel, while his was one floor below. She always thought their encounter was a coincidence, but now she thought otherwise.

There was so much about him that was suspicious. The way he singled her out, even though there were others in the elevator. He made a comment about the tag on her jacket, something about how he wished he could join her convention rather than have to listen to some of the speeches in his. She didn't remember the exact words he'd said, but it made her laugh. He got off on the same level as her. She wanted to get coffee from the hotel's only coffee shop. He asked if he could tag along. He needed the caffeine to stop him from falling asleep.

Their talk, which should have lasted until they got their respective coffees, ended up being close to an hour. She found him to be smart, receptive, and he hung on to every word she said.

In hindsight, he was too… *perfect*.

He asked if she would meet him for drinks later. She told him she was married. He was married, too. She could see the wedding ring on his finger. It was the first thing she had noticed about him. He told her that he and his wife had just renewed their vows in the Turks and Caicos for their tenth wedding anniversary. Their son was the ring bearer, and their daughter was the bridesmaid.

*He has a boy and a girl just like me*, Denise had thought at that time. It was another coincidence she did not pick up on. She was too enamored with him.

*It's only drinks*, she had told herself. She was happily married, and so was he.

Against her better judgment, she agreed.

Later that day, once the convention had wrapped up, they met at the hotel bar. They talked, laughed, and had a few drinks.

She wasn't sure how, but she ended up going to his room, which happened to be in the same hotel.

Another coincidence she had missed!

But nothing happened between them. They talked some more, about married life, about having demanding careers while still trying to juggle family life. Innocent stuff. He never once made a move on her. If he had, she would have stormed out. Instead, he was a real gentleman. He ordered room service. They had a nice meal. And an hour later, she left.

When she got back to Milton, she forgot about her time with Jared Stevens.

Until now, when she received an encrypted email in her personal account. The individual who had contacted her had also sent her photos.

There were images of her having drinks with Jared at the bar, images of her walking with Jared to his room, and images of her leaving his room.

The pictures left the convincing impression that she'd had an affair.

She never took Jared Stevens's telephone number because she didn't intend to ever contact him. She couldn't call and ask him what was going on.

But there was no point in searching him out. She'd been set up.

Jared Stevens—if that was his real name— was the male version of the honeytrap. He was there to seduce her or make it appear like he had seduced her.

And she had fallen for it—hook, line, and sinker.

In the last encrypted email, the blackmailers had made a demand.

They wanted her to resign from her position as CEO of Carta Aluminum, and they wanted her to submit her resignation before Carta's next board of governor's meeting. If she failed to comply, they would send copies of the photos to her husband, as well as to every stakeholder of Carta, which included the board members, upper management, and shareholders.

It wouldn't take long for those images to make their way to the public. Once they got out, no matter how hard she tried to explain herself, no one would listen to her.

Her marriage would be over. Her career would be over. Her reputation would forever be tarnished.

And this did not include the devastation it would inflict on her husband and her two children. The very people who made life worth living.

# FIFTY

Callaway returned to his office, angry and heartbroken. Bruce Chen had tried to end his life. If it hadn't been for his girlfriend, he surely would have died.

Ms. Chen told Callaway that Bruce was planning to propose to his long-time girlfriend, and he had it all planned out. He was going to take her to the Grand Canyon—a trip they had been discussing for some time. When the sun was coming down, and the moment was just perfect, he would get down on one knee and ask her to marry him. Bruce had even taken his mother to a jewelry shop to look for engagement rings.

When Callaway saw Bruce hooked up to tubes and monitors, he thought of Nina. His daughter was still young, and she was protected, but one day she would have to face the world on her own. Callaway and Patti would no longer be participants in her daily life, but spectators. They wouldn't know who she was associating with, or whether those people could be trusted or not.

They would try to be cool parents, make Nina feel like she could tell them anything. But as her parents, there would always be a fine line in their relationship. They would always have their secrets, and she would always have hers.

Callaway hoped Nina would be surrounded by people who genuinely cared for her. Her friends, classmates, and later on, colleagues.

Bruce, by all accounts, had people who were concerned for his well-being. But even that wasn't enough. He got pulled into a scheme that was too good to be true, and he was paying a heavy price for it.

There were some who would argue that Bruce got what he deserved, that he had no one to blame for his predicament but himself. He was foolish, or perhaps greedy, to think someone would give him an impossible rate of return.

Callaway would argue that even the smartest or most prudent people could be conned when the other person's only objective was to deceive. Their lies were so well laid out that it was hard to decipher whether to believe them or not.

Bruce was careful. He didn't invest all his money right away. He took his time. It was only when he saw his returns that he put more money into the scheme. This was akin to a poker game, where the professionals would let the amateur win the first few hands, and when the stakes were high, and the pot was big, they would take the amateur for every penny.

Bruce was taken by professionals, people who knew the game and had rigged it to their advantage.

Callaway had to find a way to get to them. But how was he going to do that?

He had an idea.

*Might be for nothing*, he thought, *but it's worth a shot.*

He pulled out his cell phone and sent a short text message. He prayed the person on the other end would read it and respond.

# FIFTY-ONE

Trevor McGinty's internet history on the day he was murdered showed that he went on a couple of news sites, watched some online videos, and checked his emails. Trevor wasn't a big internet user, so that begged the question of why he had an additional Wi-Fi modem when the motel's internet would have sufficed.

The answer was simple.

Trevor needed the bandwidth to upload data to another site, a company that made compact digital cameras—ones you could place on a car's dashboard, for instance—and let the user upload the recorded data onto a cloud network. The user then had seven days to either save the data or let the system copy new data over it.

Because Trevor was murdered only a few days ago, Holt and Fisher were confident the data would still be available for viewing. They were also fortunate to discover that the company's headquarters was in a city right next to Milton, which is where they were now.

Unlike others they had spoken to, the owner was more than willing to cooperate. His only demand was that the public never know how the police got access to the video. If word got out that his company was *not* protecting customers' privacy, he would be ruined. And as a new and upcoming enterprise, they couldn't weather the bad publicity.

Holt and Fisher agreed. They didn't have a warrant. Whatever they found on the footage would not be admissible in court anyway.

They were taken to a small room, where they sat in front of a large LCD monitor.

The owner set everything up and then left.

The angle of the camera faced the outside of Trevor's motel room. They fast-forwarded through the first several hours. They saw Trevor leave his room and then return some time later. He was carrying grocery bags.

More hours went by, and Holt and Fisher had a feeling this would be a waste of time. Then they saw a woman enter the room down the hall. There was no one in that room when Fisher had gone to speak to the tenant. The woman was wearing a hoodie, slacks, and white runners. They couldn't clearly make out her face from this angle, but Wayne had told them her name was Karla Johnson. She had her head down as she entered her room and disappeared behind the closed door.

Holt was about to fast-forward the footage when Fisher stopped him.

A burly man appeared from the left side of the screen. He was wearing a trench coat and sported a buzz haircut. He kept walking until he stopped in front of the woman's room. He looked around and then began to fiddle with the door. Thirty seconds later, the man looked around once again and then removed something from the back of his coat. The way he held it told Holt and Fisher that it was a gun.

He then entered the room and disappeared inside.

Less than a minute later, the man came out. He was about to leave but then stopped. The sun was at such an angle that the light shaded his face, but Holt and Fisher could tell the man was staring in the direction of Trevor's room.

Still holding the weapon in his hand, the man walked in the direction he had come from.

A couple of minutes went by. Fisher was about to fast-forward the footage when Holt stopped her this time.

A shadow came on the screen, followed by the same man with the gun. This time, he had his right hand covering his face. He clearly knew he was being recorded. The man stood in front of Trevor's door for a moment and then went inside.

Several minutes passed. Nothing happened.

Then the screen went blank.

## FIFTY-TWO

After sending the text message, Callaway waited anxiously, but he didn't have to wait long before he got a reply. The person on the other end wanted more details. This person wasn't big on pleasantries. Their conversations were short and to the point. Callaway knew this, and he was not about to engage in small talk. He needed her help. He felt like she was his last resort.

She told him to send the details through a secure email address, which she had provided in the text message.

Callaway spent the next twenty minutes, typing up everything he knew about Bruce's case. It wasn't much, though. Bruce had been taken in by someone online, someone he had never met or spoken to. And worse, he had paid them in Bitcoin. The cryptocurrency was used by criminals for a reason. It was hard to track, so there was no way for the authorities to link the money to the scammers.

But if there was one person who could help in this situation, it was her. She was *the* best computer hacker he knew. On numerous occasions, she had bailed him out of a tough spot. She could be relied upon to send him something useful. She always did.

Once he hit the Send button, he leaned back in his chair and put his hands behind his head. There was nothing more for him to do but wait.

He heard something. He sat up straight and listened.

There were footsteps. *Several* of them, in fact. And they were coming from the metal stairs outside his office.

His back tensed, and his senses heightened. It wasn't normal for him to get many visitors all at once.

He reached for his desk drawer. His weapon was locked inside. But then he stopped himself.

His office door was locked. It would take great force for someone to break it down. By then, Callaway could arm himself.

*Why am I overreacting?* he thought.

He pulled out his cell phone and swiped an app open that was linked to the camera outside his office. The black and white image came up on his screen. He could see the metal landing right outside his door.

He was waiting with bated breath when he saw Patti appear on the small screen. Right behind her were Nina and Millie.

He jumped up from his chair and opened the door.

"Hi there," Patti said with a smile.

Callaway couldn't remember if Patti had ever visited his office before. He doubted she was interested in seeing where he worked. Plus, he never had an office worth showing to anyone. Most of the places he rented were in rough, seedy neighborhoods, where the rent was cheap, and the crowd was sketchy.

His previous office was underneath a massage parlor. He got some of his strangest and weirdest cases while at that office.

"Hi, Daddy," Nina said with a wave.

"Hi, Mr. Callaway," Millie said.

Nina turned to Millie. "This is where my dad works."

Millie looked around in awe. "Wow, it's just like the movies. It's very clandestine."

*Millie's got a good vocabulary*, he thought, impressed by the way she knew how to use that word, but he would never call his office "clandestine." His office was a dump, plain and simple.

"What are you guys doing here?" Callaway asked.

"Millie wanted to talk to you about her case," Patti replied. "And Nina wanted to tag along."

"Okay, but I could have come to the house, you know."

"They wanted to take the bus to see you," Patti said. "I thought it might be better if I drove them over instead."

Callaway glanced back at his office. He suddenly felt insecure and embarrassed. It wasn't every day that his daughter and his ex-wife showed up at his place of work.

"Why don't we go someplace more comfortable to talk?" he suggested.

# FIFTY-THREE

Crenshaw was inside his office at Dark Box when there was a knock at the door. He buzzed it open.

Kristoff came in, followed by Andrei.

Ever since his meeting with Wilbur Graft, Crenshaw was on edge. He didn't like disappointing his clients. These clients thought they were above God, but Crenshaw had a way of knocking them down to his level. They needed him more than he needed them.

There weren't that many firms out there that were willing to break the law. Some firms that worked in the shadows boldly stated they did everything to protect their client, but when push came to shove, most were not willing to back this claim up.

*No one wants to go to jail*, Crenshaw thought.

Money was useless when you were locked up in a cell, surrounded by hardened criminals who wouldn't hesitate to slit your throat over a pack of cigarettes.

What made Dark Box more dangerous was that they didn't have a moral compass. They were willing to do anything and everything for a price. They didn't even bother justifying why they did it.

If a client wanted a matter resolved, they made sure it was done to the client's satisfaction.

That didn't happen with Graft. His problem did not go away; it was merely delayed.

Crenshaw never believed the stories he had read in the papers. He always knew there was more to it than met the eye, but without proof, he couldn't take any action. Plus, if the problem seemed like it was buried, then who was he to try to dig it up?

Digging deeper, though, required more effort and more money. Graft was a very wealthy man, but wealthy people didn't stay wealthy without some penny-pinching. Asking Graft for additional funds was out of the question. Graft was right. He had paid Dark Box a hefty sum.

Dark Box had used a blunt instrument to resolve the problem. Cut the cancer out to save the patient. What the problem required was a more surgical procedure, because even though the cancer was gone, or so they had thought, it still had roots in the body and could potentially kill the patient.

Graft was the patient, and he had hired Dark Box to perform the operation. And they had failed miserably.

Crenshaw was now under Graft's thumb. Until the job was done, he would have to acquiesce to Graft's every whim.

"What's the update?" Crenshaw asked Kristoff.

"The motel owner just informed me that the cops were back at the motel," Kristoff replied.

"Why?"

"They took something from the dead man's room."

Dark Box had informants everywhere. They kept a sizeable budget for just that purpose. Information was the most powerful asset they had. They could use it against their enemies and the enemies of their client.

Some called it bribery. Dark Box called it incentive. It gave people a reason to speak to them. It also gave people a reason to keep that information away from the police.

The motel owner had tipped them about a new guest. She had come in the middle of the night. She paid with cash and refused to take her dark glasses off. The motel owner thought she was a fugitive. He figured he would make extra cash by contacting Dark Box. After he described her to them, they knew the woman was far more valuable than the few hundred bucks they would pay him. She was the key to all their troubles.

Crenshaw had sent Kristoff to check it out. Not only did Kristoff fail to bring her in—dead or alive—he also made matters more complicated by getting the police involved.

"Do you know what the detective took from the room?" Crenshaw asked.

Kristoff shook his head. "The motel owner isn't sure, either," he replied.

Crenshaw was not pleased. "I thought you took everything incriminating out of that room."

"I did."

There was silence in the room.

Crenshaw pondered all the scenarios before him. He didn't like the outcome of each one.

He then leaned over his desk and glared at Kristoff. "Whatever this detective took from the room, we have to find out what it is. The longer this investigation continues, the closer it could get to us," he said. "This was your problem. Fix it. Understood?"

Kristoff stared at him. "Understood," he replied.

## FIFTY-FOUR

Callaway had thought about taking Patti, Nina, and Millie to the noodle shop, but it was closed for the first time in thirty years. Ms. Chen was at the hospital. She wouldn't leave until Bruce regained consciousness. And even then, Callaway wasn't sure when she'd come back to the shop.

Ms. Chen had given a better part of her life to the business. She was there every single day. She would open the shop and close it.

She did it to give her son a better life. She taught him hard work and sacrifice. Callaway had seen him at the shop making deliveries when their delivery guys failed to show up.

Ms. Chen was devoted to the shop and to her son, but she did not want Bruce to take over the family business. As an immigrant, she had no choice. Without an American education, there were not many opportunities for her. She had to create her opportunity. The shop became the only way for her to put a roof over their heads.

Bruce would make something of himself, she believed. He would live the American dream. Work on Wall Street. Be the head of a Fortune 500 company. Anything his heart desired. And if he worked hard like she had done all these years, there was nothing stopping him.

All those hopes and dreams Ms. Chen had for her son came crashing down in a moment of mental anguish. Bruce was depressed and in pain, and he thought the only way out was to end his life.

On the way to his office, Callaway had always passed by an ice cream shop. He didn't have a sweet tooth, so he never bothered to go in and take a look. He decided now would be a good time to do that.

Patti ordered a banana and mango shake, Millie and Nina both got waffles with ice cream, and Callaway opted for a hot chocolate.

When they were all seated, Millie turned to him. "Mr. Callaway, do you know where my mom is?" she asked eagerly.

Callaway wanted to tell her the truth, that her mom was dead and that her father had killed her, but he didn't want to break her heart. Instead, he said, "I'm still working on it. I don't want to say anything until I have completed my investigation."

If Millie was hoping for a more satisfactory answer, she didn't let on. Callaway got the sense the girl was far more mature than her age—something he always said about his own daughter. Nina had to grow up fast because Patti couldn't be there for her all the time, so she became self-reliant.

Millie had it even worse. She couldn't rely on either of her parents. One was dead and the other was locked up forever. Sure, she had her grandmother, but her grandmother couldn't replace her parents. No one could.

"You know," Callaway said, trying to cheer Millie up, "I met your dad."

Millie's eyes lit up. "You did?"

"Yep. And he asked about you."

"He did?"

"Absolutely. He misses you a lot."

Millie looked down at her plate. "My dad won't let me visit. He says he doesn't want me to see him like that."

"You speak to your dad often?" Callaway asked.

"Not on the phone," she said. "But he sends me letters each week."

Callaway's brow furrowed. "And your grandmother lets you read them?"

"Sure, she does. She even lets me write to him."

Callaway was stunned.

Why would Diane Aldershot let her son-in-law communicate with her granddaughter? Especially if her son-in-law had murdered her daughter?

*It just doesn't make sense*, he thought.

## FIFTY-FIVE

Holt and Fisher viewed the footage from Trevor McGinty's security camera several more times, in slow motion and in great detail, but they couldn't get a clear image of the burly man who had gone into Trevor's room.

Unlike the movies, the authorities didn't have the technology to enhance a blurry image. Images consisted of thousands of pixels. Enlarging the image only enlarged the individual pixels, making the image even blurrier.

Fisher said, "I think I know what might have transpired before we lost visual."

"What do you mean?" Holt asked.

"It's only a theory, though," Fisher said.

"It's all we've got, so let me hear it."

"I believe Trevor was never the target."

Holt's brow furrowed. "Okay."

"I think the woman across the hall was," Fisher continued. "In the video, we saw her go into her room. A couple of minutes later, we saw the man enter her room."

"Do you think he was following her?" Holt asked.

"I do."

"But then what happened to her?"

"What do you mean?" Fisher said.

"The man had a weapon… we're sure of that," Holt said. "And we saw him go inside her room, so where is her body?"

Fisher pondered the question. "Good point."

"Were there any signs of a struggle when you checked the room?" Holt asked.

Fisher shook her head. "Nothing."

"What about blood?"

"I would have seen it if there was."

Holt rubbed his chin. "And we know the man came out of the room alone, so what about the woman? She couldn't have vanished into thin air."

They were silent.

"Let's go back to Trevor," Fisher said. "We can't lose track of the fact that he's dead, and we have to solve *his* murder."

"Sure," Holt agreed. "You said Trevor was not the target, right?"

"I did."

"So, why would this man kill Trevor if he wasn't there for him?"

Fisher was quiet for a moment. She tried to work out all the scenarios in her head. She discarded some and focused on others. She then stopped on one.

"The security camera," she said.

"What?" Holt said, confused.

"The security camera outside Trevor's motel room. You told me you interviewed one of Trevor's neighbors…"

"Yeah, Freddie Iseman. What about him?"

"He told you that whenever he walked past Trevor's room, he could see the red camera light blinking, which meant the camera was recording."

"That's what Freddie told me."

"What if this man came out of the room across from Trevor's and saw the red light blinking?"

Holt's eyes widened. "That explains why he paused outside the woman's room and stared in the direction of Trevor's room."

"He wanted to confirm what he was seeing."

"Right," Holt agreed. "And when he went to Trevor's room, he made a concerted effort to hide his face. He didn't want to be recorded."

"Exactly. Trevor wasn't killed because he had a lot of cash on him, or else the money would be gone by now; he was killed because this person thought Trevor had recorded him going into a room with a weapon in his hand."

"You know what this means, don't you?" Holt said.

"What?"

"We have to find this woman."

"Karla Johnson."

"Yes," Holt said with a nod. "We find her, and we find the man who killed Trevor McGinty."

## FIFTY-SIX

Denise wore a large sweatshirt—which belonged to her husband—gray track pants, and teal sneakers. She had on a baseball cap and dark sunglasses. She hoped the attire was enough to disguise who she was. Not that anyone passing by would notice her.

She wasn't a celebrity or a well-known person. As the head of Carta Aluminum, she was on the covers of a few business magazines, but the readership wasn't so substantial that she couldn't walk down the street without someone hounding her for autographs.

Denise was far more concerned about the people who were blackmailing her. They weren't asking for money. They were asking for something she had worked so hard to achieve. These people wanted her to give up her position at Carta, and Denise wasn't going to go down without a fight.

Carta Aluminum was started by her father. Her brother wanted no part of it. He never worked an honest day in his life. All he cared about was that the trust money kept flowing so he could spend it on girls, booze, and having a good time.

Denise wanted to make something of herself. She wanted to make a difference, and what better way than to use Carta to do just that.

She worked her way up from the bottom. It was the proudest day of her life when her father handed her the reins to the company. It meant he could trust her, and Denise did not want to disappoint him.

Her father was a man of convictions. He was also strong-headed. If he got something in his head, it was hard to talk him out of it. His father had a lot of side ventures which were not part of Carta, but Carta funded them.

Ever since he was a boy, he loved planes. His dream was to one day own his own airline. With the company now in Denise's control, her father decided to buy a local carrier and turn it into one of the largest in the country.

Unfortunately, all of this cost money. He went from owning three planes to now over a dozen. He also purchased a large plot of land and was in the process of building an airport where these planes would be based.

For a long time, Denise let him indulge in his hobbies, but now they were hemorrhaging money, and Carta was footing the bill. The board was not pleased with this, but they were appointed by her father, so their loyalty lay with him.

Denise was working hard to slowly win them over.

She was able to cap the amount of money going into her father's ventures. She also placed restrictions on how that money would be used. Naturally, this did not bode well with her father. He accused her of treason. It was still his company, he believed, and as such, he should be allowed to use the funds as he wished. But Denise did not relent. Her father was in his seventies, and his only concern was getting his airline business up and running. Her concern was the viability of Carta Aluminum.

Carta's shareholders were not fully aware of the internal drama. The family was still in control of the company. The shareholders knew a portion of the money would be allocated to Carta's founder as part of a retirement arrangement. They just did not know how much was being sucked out.

As long as the board approved it, the shareholders were not privy to the details.

Denise never believed that her father would stoop so low as to try to blackmail her. But her suspicions were confirmed when the blackmailer wanted her position at Carta. She, however, had no proof he was behind it. Even if she confronted him, he would merely deny it.

But then, out of the blue, Denise had received a telephone call. The caller had information about her father. Denise was skeptical at first, but what the caller told her was not something just any person would know. The caller knew specific details, some of which even Denise was not fully aware of. As the head of Carta, there was so much she was in the dark about. For good reason, she later realized, as she began looking into it.

Two days ago, the caller informed her that they should meet. Denise jumped at the opportunity. They agreed to meet at the food court of a large shopping mall.

Denise had found a seat at a table in the corner, and she waited for this person to appear.

She watched as people milled around the mall. She didn't know what the caller looked like, but the caller told her exactly what Denise should wear.

The disguise was for the caller to notice, and to elude anyone who might be following her.

*I hope I didn't overdo it*, Denise thought, adjusting her baseball cap.

An hour went by, and no one approached her.

Her cell phone buzzed. The telephone number was blocked.

She answered. "Who is this?"

A robotic voice said, "It's not safe. You have to leave."

The call abruptly ended.

Denise stared at her phone and then quickly left the mall.

## FIFTY-SEVEN

After his talk with Millie, Callaway was determined to find out what happened to Laura Sinclair. Many things were not adding up, so he decided to start from the beginning.

Laura was a doctor. Her former clinic was in a plaza. The sign on the front read, *Family Health.* All insurance was acceptable. No patient was turned away.

The interior was cozy, but with enough chairs to seat a dozen people or so. The walls were painted light gray, and there were posters of people smiling and looking healthy. The clinic had an inviting feeling.

Callaway made his way to the receptionist. The girl behind the desk had never heard of Laura Sinclair. She had only been at the clinic for less than a year.

The new owner's name was Dr. Sohail Reza, and he was currently with a patient, Callaway was told. He would wait for the doctor, Callaway replied in return.

He grabbed a magazine and sat in the corner of the waiting area. Over the course of an hour, several people went in and out of the clinic. When his turn came, the receptionist waved him in.

"Room number four down the hall," she said.

The room had an examination table, a computer in the corner, and a stool. A few minutes later, a man entered the room.

He had tanned skin, a grayish beard, and he was completely bald. He wore a white lab coat and had a stethoscope around his neck.

"Hi there, I'm Dr. Sohail Reza," he said with an easy smile and a quick handshake.

"Lee Callaway," Callaway replied.

Dr. Reza moved to the computer and then frowned. "What was your name again?"

"Lee Callaway."

"You're not in the system. Did you register with the receptionist?"

"I told her I was a friend of yours."

Dr. Reza blinked, unsure. "Why would you say that?"

"Did you know a Dr. Laura Sinclair?" Callaway said.

Dr. Reza's eyes narrowed. He stood up and shut the door. He turned to Callaway. "Who are you? And what do you want?" His voice was now hard.

"I'm not here to cause trouble," Callaway said. He held his card out, and Dr. Reza took it.

"You're a private investigator?" Dr. Reza said.

"I am."

"And who hired you?"

"Dr. Sinclair's daughter."

"Millie?"

"You know her?"

Dr. Reza shut his eyes and took a deep breath. He then walked over and sat on the stool.

"I knew Dr. Sinclair. I knew her well."

"How well?"

"She hired me at the clinic as an assistant while I completed my equivalences."

"Equivalences?"

"As you can tell by my accent, I'm not a born American. I came to the United States from Iran. Although I was a doctor in Tehran, the only way I could practice in the US was to obtain a medical license. And the process is quite rigorous. You need to acquire the right visa, pass the United States Medical Licensing Exam, then become certified by the Education Commission for Foreign Medical Graduates. But that's not the end of it. Once you are accredited by a US residency program, you have to pass the licensing exam. It can take years and a lot of money. Dr. Sinclair was kind enough to help me through the entire process."

"How would you describe her?" Callaway asked.

Dr. Reza broke into a smile. "A wonderful woman. Kind. Generous. A very good person.'"

"And as a doctor?"

"One of the best." Dr. Reza's voice quivered with emotion. "She cared for each and every patient that walked through those doors. I know I shouldn't say this, but she even treated patients who had no insurance. The sign at the front window is not just for show. She didn't turn anyone away, and I've continued that tradition."

"And how did you take over the clinic?"

"Dr. Sinclair's family wanted to sell the clinic. After what happened, there was no one else to keep it running. I borrowed money from the bank, and I bought the practice."

"Prior to her death," Callaway said, "did you notice anything off about her?"

"Off?" he said, confused.

"Troubling."

Dr. Reza fell silent. He then said, "What is your objective, Mr. Callaway? I mean, what are you hoping to achieve?"

"I want to find out what happened to Dr. Sinclair."

"You didn't read the newspapers?"

"I know they say that her husband, Roger, killed her. But I don't believe them."

"And why don't you believe them?"

"I get the feeling people aren't being forthcoming with me. The more I look into the case. The more questions pop up."

"Maybe you shouldn't look into it," Dr. Reza said.

"That's exactly what I'm talking about," Callaway said. "I feel like everyone who is or was involved with Laura Sinclair is comfortable with the story that's been told to the press."

"But isn't that the truth?"

"I'm not sure it is."

There was a pause.

Dr. Reza stood up. "I'm sorry I can't be much help to you, Mr. Callaway. Dr. Sinclair helped me come to this wonderful country. I owe her everything. Every day I am reminded of her when I come to the clinic. I pray I can fulfill my duty as a practitioner as well as she did. Now, I have actual patients to attend to."

He held the door for Callaway.

"Thank you for your time, doctor," Callaway said, and he left.

## FIFTY-EIGHT

Holt and Fisher decided to go back to the motel. They wanted to speak to Wayne Lemont and learn more about the woman who had moved in across from Trevor.

Who was Karla Johnson? And why was someone after her?

Whoever it was, they clearly wanted to harm her.

What puzzled them was what happened to the woman. Did the man shoot her and, perhaps, kill her? If so, where was her body?

Maybe the man returned later and cleaned the scene? They didn't believe this scenario. Why would he do that when he had also murdered Trevor? Why not clean the other crime scene as well?

It wasn't so easy to clean an area of blood and DNA. An experienced investigator would have caught something, and Fisher saw nothing of concern when she went through Karla Johnson's room.

They entered Wayne Lemont's office. They found a man waiting by the front desk. The man was wearing casual attire, and he was holding a hand-carry and a backpack.

There was a bell on the counter. Holt rang it.

"I already did that," the man said. "But no one's here."

"How long have you been waiting?" Fisher asked.

"Over half an hour," the man replied. "I need a cheap place to stay, and this is the cheapest I can find at the moment."

"Where're you coming from?"

"Newark," he said. "I was renting a place with a buddy, but he and I got into a fight. He accused me of sleeping with his girlfriend."

"Did you?"

"Did I what?"

"Sleep with his girlfriend?"

He shrugged. "Yeah, but she initiated it. I mean, they were already thinking of splitting up, so I think what I did only sped up the process, you know?"

Fisher wasn't sure why she bothered asking. It was none of her business what the man did. She pulled out her cell phone, dialed a number, and waited.

A second later, they heard a ringtone. Fisher looked at Holt. He walked around the front desk, searched, and then held Wayne Lemont's cell phone up.

Fisher ended the call. "It's strange he would've left his cell phone behind," she said.

"Maybe he was in a hurry," Holt said.

"Let's see if he's upstairs," Fisher said.

"Can I join you guys?" the man asked. "I need a room badly."

"Official police business," Fisher replied, flashing her badge. "But if we see the owner, we'll tell him someone's waiting for him in his office."

They left the office and walked through the motel's parking lot. They took the stairs up to the second level.

The yellow police tape was still visible on Trevor McGinty's room. They decided to go across the hall. They hoped Karla Johnson's room had not been rented out, but knowing how desperate Wayne was to rent Trevor's, they doubted that it hadn't been rented yet.

They knocked on the door and waited.

No response.

They knocked again.

Still no response.

Fisher tried the door handle. It was unlocked.

"Should we go in?" she asked Holt.

"If it's empty, then why not?"

They went inside. Fisher saw that nothing had been moved since the last time she'd been here. The bed had still not been made, and a bag filled with clothes still lay next to the bed.

Fisher moved to the bathroom.

She opened the door and froze.

"Holt!" she called out. "I found him."

He came and stood next to her.

In the middle of the bathroom was Wayne Lemont. He was sitting on a chair, and his hands and feet were tied to it.

There was a dark hole in the middle of his forehead.

## FIFTY-NINE

Callaway drove back from the clinic with a cloud over his head. His meeting with Dr. Reza had left him even more confused.

Whenever he broached the subject of her death, the responses of those close to Laura Sinclair left him baffled. It was as if they preferred to leave the matter as it was.

Diane Aldershot didn't want to talk about her daughter's death, which was understandable. It was a terrible reminder of what she had lost. But she also didn't want Callaway to look into it.

*Strange.*

Same thing with Roger Sinclair. The man was rotting in prison, but even he didn't want the case to be re-opened.

*What was he hiding?*

And now, Dr. Reza. When Callaway asked about Laura Sinclair, Dr. Reza advised Callaway to stop looking into the case.

*Why?*

Maybe the truth was more complicated than he thought. Maybe there was more to it than he was seeing. Maybe there was a completely different piece to the puzzle.

*What if I'm seeing the puzzle from the wrong angle?* he thought. *What if this case isn't about Roger Sinclair murdering his wife?*

*Then what's it about?*

He racked his brain for answers, but nothing came to him.

"Why does it always have to be so hard?" he wondered out loud. "Why do I get myself into these kinds of cases?"

Callaway wasn't getting paid a dime for his services. He was doing it as a courtesy to make his daughter happy. It wasn't every day that Nina came to him for something. He'd let her down all her life, and he didn't want to let her down now.

But what did he expect to achieve when he took on Millie's case? Surely he didn't think he could bring her mother back and overturn her father's conviction.

That's not how things happened in real life. There were rarely any happy endings.

He sighed. Eventually, he would have to break Millie's heart. He would have to tell her he didn't find anything.

His cell phone buzzed. He checked it and saw a text message. He quickly turned the Dodge Charger around.

He hurried back to his office and got behind his laptop. He opened the email he had just received but found that it was password-protected. A question had popped up on the screen, prompting him to enter the answer.

IN WHICH CITY DID WE FIRST MEET?

Callaway thought for a moment and then typed.

FAIRVIEW.

The email opened.

Callaway leaned back in his chair. A smile crossed his face.

He had gone to Fairview while on another case. A woman had seemingly vanished into thin air, and her family wanted to find out what happened to her.

It was in Fairview that Callaway had met Echo Rose.

Echo was not only a great hacker, but she also had a good moral compass. If someone was in need, she would go out of her way to help them. It didn't matter what law she broke, as long as it was for a good cause. Callaway had leaned on her expertise multiple times.

Echo worked as a reporter for *Above the Fold*. Through her line of work, she always found herself in some sort of deep trouble. She was like Lee in many ways. They both put their lives on the line for the greater good. They wanted to get to the bottom of the truth.

He clicked on the email attachment and saw a dozen files.

Echo had dug up a mountain of information, and it was up to him to go through it all.

He took a deep breath and clicked on the first file.

## SIXTY

Wayne Lemont had been tortured. There were bruises on his cheeks and a welt under his left eye. There was also a cut on his upper lip. His hands and feet were held to the chair with zip ties.

"This is exactly how we found Trevor McGinty," Fisher said, looking solemn.

Holt nodded and then got down on his haunches.

"What're you looking for?" Fisher asked.

"A shell casing," Holt replied. "Wayne was shot once, so there should only be one empty shell."

Holt looked underneath the bathroom sink, behind the toilet, and then stood up. "It's not here."

"The killer took it like he did from Trevor's room," Fisher said.

"He's a professional," Holt said. "I have no doubt about it now."

"We could tell from the footage that we are dealing with someone who knows what they are doing."

Holt narrowed his eyes. "We have to circulate his photo to the media. We have a killer roaming the streets of Milton."

Fisher shook her head. "I don't think that's a good idea."

"Why not?" Holt asked.

She could tell Holt was irked by Wayne's death. He was blaming himself. If they had caught Trevor's killer sooner, maybe Wayne would still be alive. But she didn't subscribe to that belief. There was no indication that Wayne was in danger. If he was, they would have protected him. Why the killer chose to go after Wayne now, they'd have to figure out.

"If we post the killer's photo to the public," she said, "it'll only create a panic. And it would encourage the killer to disappear, further putting us at a disadvantage. Plus..." Her words trailed off.

"Plus what?" Holt asked.

"The footage is grainy. The killer was too far away when Trevor's camera caught him coming out of the room. And when he got close to the camera, the killer shielded his face. What image would we show to the public anyway? Even *we* don't know what he looks like."

She could see Holt mulling this over. Holt was prone to letting his emotions get the best of him. He was a great detective, relentless and determined, but his determination had turned narrow during previous investigations. He would get so focused on one suspect or one piece of evidence that they would end up wasting valuable time looking into it. It was important for Fisher to keep him from getting distracted.

He grunted and shook his head.

She said, "We have a bigger question to answer."

"What's that?"

"How did Karla Johnson disappear from this room?"

"Are we even sure she disappeared?" Holt asked.

"If she didn't, we would have found her in the same position as Trevor and Wayne."

"Good point," Holt said. "So, how did she leave this room anyway? I mean, we saw her go inside, followed by the man with the gun, but we never saw her come out."

Fisher pointed. "That window. It was open when I first came to speak to Karla Johnson, but it's closed now."

Holt shrugged. "Maybe Wayne closed it."

"Or maybe his killer closed it," Fisher said.

Holt's eyes widened. "I see, so no one heard him scream while he was battered and bruised."

"Exactly." Fisher moved past Wayne's body and got inside the bathtub. She then pushed the window open and took a look outside. She stood there for a moment. She then said, "I think I know how Karla disappeared."

"How?" Holt asked.

Instead of answering him, she hurried out of the room, went down the stairs to the ground level, and walked to the back of the motel. She pushed through shrubs and bushes and then stopped next to a wall. She looked up and then turned to Holt, who had been following right behind.

"That's Karla Johnson's room," she said, pointing up.

"How can you be sure?" Holt asked.

"None of the other rooms' windows are open except for the window I just opened."

"Okay."

She then gripped a pipe attached to the outside wall next to the window. It spanned from the ground all the way up to the roof.

"The window is large enough for a small person to fit through," Fisher said. "I believe Karla Johnson climbed out of the window and then climbed down via the pipe."

Holt thought for a moment. "I'm not sure..."

"How else do you explain how she left her room without going through the front door?"

Holt was silent.

She looked down, searching for something. She then knelt and pointed to the ground. "That looks like a shoeprint."

Holt knelt beside her. "You're right. It does," he said.

Fisher stood up. "We know she came down this way. The next question is... where did she go?"

## SIXTY-ONE

Fisher checked the back of the motel. There were no security cameras, and why would there be?

The back of the motel was surrounded by buildings and a wooden fence. There was nothing valuable that required extra cameras. And the way that Wayne ran the motel, he wouldn't have spent an extra dime if he didn't have to.

She decided to go back to Wayne's office.

The man with the backpack and hand-carry was still there.

"You find the owner?" he asked.

"We did."

"And?"

"You're better off finding another motel," she said. "This motel is closed for business."

The man grumbled, cursed, and then left.

Fisher looked around the office for anything that might stick out. She then spotted a door in the back. It was a small room the size of a walk-in closet. There were shelves with boxes and other items on them. She picked up one box and took a peek inside.

She found tiny cameras, listening devices, and various kinds of recording devices.

*Why would Wayne have these?* she wondered. She then remembered her conversation with a tenant from the motel—Madison Dier. She mentioned that Wayne gave her the creeps, like he knew something about her but wouldn't say.

*He was spying on her*, Fisher thought.

Wayne was probably a voyeur. He got off on spying on unsuspecting guests.

*But where did he store the footage?* she wondered.

She returned the box from where she'd found it and left the small room. She saw an old computer monitor on the front desk. Upon further inspection, she noticed the base of the computer was missing, which contained the motherboard and hard drive. Wires hung over the edge of the desk.

Wayne's killer had taken it. That was the only reasonable explanation.

But why did the killer torture and kill Wayne? What did Wayne know?

Fisher then began going through all the items underneath Wayne's desk. She found the motel's registration ledger and then searched for unit number nine, which was the one across from Trevor McGinty. She found it and frowned.

The name on unit nine was not Karla Johnson but Danielle Perkins.

Fisher was confused.

She spotted a binder next to the ledger. This one contained photocopies of documents. She flipped through the pages until she found what she was looking for.

The driver's license for Danielle Perkins showed a woman with cropped blonde hair, sunken cheeks, and dark eyes. It said she was five-five and weighed a hundred and ten pounds. It was about the right height and weight for the woman they'd seen on Trevor McGinty's camera footage.

Fisher's eyes narrowed.

If the woman across from Trevor was Danielle Perkins, then why did Wayne tell them her name was Karla Johnson?

Why would he lie to them?

# THE UNKNOWN WOMAN

## SIXTY-TWO

Grannex Investments was registered in the Bahamas, but according to Echo Rose, the website was hosted from a server in Serbia. Even then, there was no guarantee that Grannex was actually in Serbia. The owners of the website would be smart to use a VPN, or virtual private network. A VPN would allow them to shield the origins of their website in case someone wanted to access it and shut it down.

Then there was the matter of how Grannex was receiving payments. There was no money trail. Investors weren't wire transferring funds or paying by credit or debit. They were using bitcoins, which were nearly impossible to trace. Bitcoin was not administered by the banks or a governing body. There were no physical bitcoins. There were only balances kept on a ledger in the cloud.

Telephone scammers encouraged their victims to send them payments via gift cards. It wasn't unusual for victims to purchase gift cards in the thousands of dollars. This was a red flag that the call was a scam. Scammers knew it would be impossible to trace the gift cards back to them.

Echo had tried to weave her way through all the added security Grannex had enabled, but because everything was in the cloud, it was a monumental task to locate their network.

However, Echo was able to find other victims, and some were in the city, but many others were all over the world. It didn't help that Tammy Rosetto had set up and maintained a social media page for Grannex. This site gave them credibility. It also helped them reel in more victims.

Echo had tried to deconstruct Grannex's network, but without other victims coming forward, it was not easy to get a full picture of how big Grannex was. With time, maybe she could have dug up more, but this was all she could get so far.

She did find one person who had tried hard to warn Grannex's investors. He lived in England, and Callaway decided to give him a call.

It was late in Manchester, but Alistair Forley still picked up. Callaway introduced himself and told him why he was calling.

Forley let out a long, exasperated sigh. "I tried to contact your local authorities, but it seems like no one wants to do anything about Grannex. They just don't have the jurisdiction to investigate them."

"Did you lose money with Grannex?" Callaway asked.

"I didn't, but my sister did. She lost everything. She tried to recruit me, but I'm a journalist, and I've seen dozens of these types of schemes," Forley replied. "They make it sound like they are doing *you* a favor by letting you invest with them. In reality, they are stealing your money."

"Why doesn't the media just expose them?" Callaway asked.

"My guess is they're not a big operation."

"Big operation?" Callaway said, surprised. "They just stole sixty thousand from my client and his mother."

"That's a penny in the bucket when you compare it to some other schemes out there," Forley replied. "I was looking into a company that dealt with cryptocurrency."

"That's what Grannex accepted as payment."

"This company had created its own version of bitcoin and recruited marketers from all over the world. They also held large events in countries like Hungary, Spain, and Portugal. They never held an event in the United States, mind you. But some of their recruiters were bringing in a million dollars a month from investors. They sold it like a revolution, like they were going to change the world. No more cash. No more need for different currencies. Just one coin."

"So, what was the problem with them?" Callaway asked.

"The cryptocurrency they were purported to be selling didn't exist. There was no block-chain. No ledger of any transactions. And they were smart to target investors who weren't savvy with that technology."

"And what happened to this company?"

"I tried to expose them, but the backlash was vicious. They attacked me in every which way, but I was able to increase awareness about what they were doing. Unfortunately, they are still going, but they're not thriving like they once were."

"Is that why you spoke up against Grannex?"

"Both are Ponzi schemes. Both target people by making wild claims."

Callaway fell silent for a moment. He then asked, "How do I get my client's money back?"

"I don't think you can," Forley replied.

Callaway's heart sank. He wasn't expecting that response.

Forley then said, "Listen, I'm not sure if this'll help, but during my investigation into Grannex, I got into heated discussions with a couple of fervent Grannex supporters. I think one of them lives in Bellview County."

"It's not far from where I am," Callaway said.

"Maybe you can see what they know."

"What's their name?"

## SIXTY-THREE

She watched from a distance, hidden by an oak tree across the road.

Several police cruisers were now in the motel's parking lot. Yellow police tape circled the property. There was another murder, and this time it was the motel owner.

She never wanted this to happen. She never thought her coming back would result in two deaths. She didn't even know how *they* had found her.

It was the motel owner, she now believed. He had informed them. There was something sketchy about him the moment she saw him. It was the way he looked at her. His eyes, always prying.

It was a mistake staying at this motel, but she had done her homework before she decided to walk through the doors. The owner didn't ask too many questions, and he preferred payment in cash. Both were prerequisites for her picking a place to stay.

Plus, when she provided her ID—something all hotels and motels now demanded to see—the owner didn't examine it in detail. Even if he did, he wouldn't have spotted that it was a fake.

She should have walked out the moment the alarm began ringing in her head. The motel owner couldn't be trusted, her internal voice had told her. But she was only going to stay for a night, maybe two at most.

She knew the longer she was in Milton, the more dangerous it would become—for her and for those she loved.

*I should have never returned*, she thought. *But I was tired of running*.

How could she be running when no one was looking for her? As far as anyone was concerned, she didn't exist. Not anymore.

But someone was looking for her now.

When she last spoke to her only connection from her past life, she was told a private investigator was asking questions about her. She couldn't talk long on the phone. She feared someone was listening in on her calls, so she always used an untraceable number. And she made sure their conversations were cryptic. She would act like she was calling about duct cleaning, or like she was taking a survey, or even as if she was selling a product. The person on the other end was now familiar with the calls. Together they had created their own language.

It was necessary to keep this charade going. It was the only way to protect everyone involved.

When she found out the private investigator was snooping around, she became concerned. Everything they had worked so hard to create could all be destroyed.

However, she didn't come back because of the private investigator. His appearing out of nowhere to dig up the past was nothing more than a coincidence.

She came back because she thought she'd found a way to regain her old life. She had found an ally, a woman, someone with the means to help her.

She was supposed to meet this woman at a mall food court. She was going to tell her everything, and she was confident this woman would be receptive. When she went, she saw *them*. They were sitting at a table not far from her contact.

At first, she thought this woman was working with them, luring her to her demise. But this woman was under attack as well. *They* were following to see what she was up to, and if she had shown up, both of their lives would have been in danger.

She had no choice but to cancel the meeting.

She hated doing it, but going ahead with the meeting was not worth the risk. She could try to contact this woman again, but would she trust her? She had already left her hanging.

She had promised to expose everything that was going on. The lies. The betrayal. The deception. She was going to reveal it all.

With *them* close by, her task had suddenly become monumental.

She was running out of options. She didn't know who she could turn to. She felt even lonelier than before.

## SIXTY-FOUR

Fisher couldn't understand why Wayne had lied to them.

The woman in room eight was not Karla Johnson. According to her driver's license, she was Danielle Perkins.

Who was Danielle Perkins? And why was someone after her?

Fisher would have to look into it when she got back to the station. She wanted to know who Karla Johnson was, if only to satisfy her curiosity. Wayne had given them that name. There had to be a reason for this.

Wayne's cell phone was still in the office. Fisher decided to take a look. Maybe she could find a clue. Unfortunately, it was password-protected.

She then had an idea. Most cell phones had fingerprint sensors. Maybe she could use Wayne's finger to unlock it.

She left the office and made her way back to unit eight.

On her way over, she spotted two people coming out of one of the units. They were carrying their bags.

"Excuse me," Fisher said, catching their attention. "You can't leave. We still haven't interviewed everyone at the motel."

"Who are you?" the man asked. He had on a jacket, jeans, and construction boots.

Fisher flashed her badge. "I'm the detective investigating what happened in room eight."

The woman had on a dress, a light jacket, and heels. She said, "We just heard, and we're scared."

"Did you hear anything?" Fisher asked.

"I was at the gym all morning," the man said. "When I came back, I saw the police cruisers."

"How long have you been staying at the motel?"

"Too long," he said with a sigh.

The woman said, "I was here before I met Chris."

"Yeah, I was living in upstate New York. I met Debbie at a party."

"You're from New York as well?" Fisher asked Debbie.

Debbie nodded. "I lived around the block from Chris."

"So, what made you guys come to Milton? It's not a must-see destination for many people."

Chris said, "I had a construction business in New York, but it went belly-up. And if you've been to New York, you know it's not a cheap place to live. My buddy worked for a construction company in Milton, and he offered me a job."

"So, how did you end up at the motel?"

"The funding ran out on the project we were working on, so I was out of a job again. Next thing I knew, I couldn't pay my rent, and we were evicted."

Fisher turned to Debbie. "What about you? How did you end up in Milton?"

"Once I finished school, I decided to join Chris. I did temp work, but that wasn't enough to cover our expenses."

"Did you know Wayne well?" Fisher asked.

Chris looked down at his boots. "Yeah, well enough."

Debbie said, "Chris got into it with Wayne once."

"About what?"

Debbie fell silent.

"You can tell me," Fisher said. "I promise it won't come back to haunt you."

"I had found cameras in our unit," Debbie said. "In the fire alarm, under a light fixture inside an air vent." She shivered visibly and hugged herself. "I told Chris, and he confronted Wayne. Wayne swore he didn't know anything about it. He blamed the previous tenant."

"Did you believe him?" Fisher asked.

"No, of course not," Chris replied. "I told him I was going to report him to the police."

"And did you?"

Chris looked away. "He offered us free rent for a year if we didn't tell anyone."

Debbie said, "He also promised to delete all records of us and promised never to do it again."

"And you took him up on the offer?" Fisher asked, knowing full well they did.

"We had no choice," Debbie replied. "We were broke. Where else could we go? Everything is super expensive in Milton."

*Tell me about it*, Fisher thought.

"So, you guys didn't hear or see anything unusual?"

Debbie said, "I was putting out the garbage when I saw Wayne talking to a guy down the hall."

"What guy?"

"I'd never seen him before."

"What did he look like?"

"Big guy... huge. Mean-looking. Wearing a trench coat."

*That's the guy we saw on Trevor McGinty's security camera*, Fisher thought.

"Did you know what they were talking about?"

Debbie shook her head. "I was too far away. Plus, after the camera incident in our room, I avoided Wayne. And to be honest, he avoided us, too. But when I think about it, the big guy didn't look happy with Wayne."

## SIXTY-FIVE

Kristoff had to kill Wayne Lemont. He had no other choice.

After Kristoff's meeting with Crenshaw, he and Andrei decided to go have a word with Lemont.

They found Lemont in his office, seated behind the front desk, his eyes glued to his computer screen. Lemont was always spying on his tenants. The man was sick. He had installed cameras throughout the property. He even had a camera in a current tenant's room. She was an actress, Lemont had told them, bragging. She was past her prime, but she was still a looker. Lemont had offered to sell Kristoff some of her intimate footage. That's what Lemont had been doing as a side hustle. He would sell private photos and videos to people over the internet. His biggest clients were from Asia. Most were Japanese businessmen who worked long, hard hours and were willing to pay money for his collection.

Lemont also had cameras in room eight, the room Kristoff had gone into to take care of the problem that had suddenly reared its ugly head. But the woman had escaped through the bathroom window.

Andrei was in the parking lot, but the woman somehow slipped by him as well.

Kristoff was not pleased with Andrei, but he wouldn't show his displeasure to him. Andrei was a comrade from his home country, and the only person Kristoff could truly trust. He couldn't blame Andrei for losing the woman. She was resourceful. She had eluded them for this long. Not an easy feat.

Kristoff and Andrei had gone to Lemont to find out what the detective had taken out of Trevor McGinty's room. Crenshaw was concerned the police would eventually find something that could incriminate him or Dark Box. He wanted Kristoff to make sure that didn't happen.

Lemont swore he had no idea. The detective was by himself when he went into the room. Kristoff believed him, and that should have been the end of it until...

Kristoff gritted his teeth.

Lemont decided to make demands. He wanted more money from Kristoff. He had footage of Kristoff entering and leaving the woman's room.

Earlier, Lemont had assured him that all footage of him was destroyed. In fact, he had gone so far as to show him deleting it from his hard drive. Kristoff realized later that it was a charade. Lemont had already made a backup.

Lemont's biggest mistake was underestimating who he was dealing with. He figured he could blackmail Kristoff.

*He should've learned his lesson after what I did to Trevor McGinty*, Kristoff thought.

Kristoff took him up to room eight on a pretense. He told him he wanted to check something in the room. He then revealed his weapon, tied Lemont to a chair, and proceeded to teach him a lesson.

When Lemont told him where he had kept the backup of the footage, Kristoff put a bullet in his head. He was certain Lemont wasn't lying then. There was genuine fear in the man's eyes.

Kristoff would have preferred to dump the body elsewhere—a remote location perhaps. Far away from the motel, for sure. Two deaths in one place would definitely raise alarms. The police would become even more vigilant in finding the killers. But there were people milling around the motel. It would be impossible for him and Andrei to drag Lemont's body from the room and take it to their vehicle without getting caught.

He had decided to come back later and remove it in darkness. He just never expected that the detectives would show up before then.

Regardless, what was done was done. There was nothing he could do about it.

The only thing that mattered was that he now had the video files of him setting foot in the motel.

## SIXTY-SIX

Alistair Forley was kind enough to speak to him from England, and Callaway was going to follow any leads that came his way.

He still didn't know who exactly was behind the Grannex Investments scam. Without a name or face, Callaway couldn't get Bruce's money back—if that was even possible anymore. The money was likely gone for good. But if he could somehow shine a light on the scam, and maybe even get the authorities involved, perhaps it might be enough retribution for the Chen family. It might also prevent others from being suckered in like Bruce.

Forley had given him a name. Rick Wallen did indeed live in Bellview County. Wallen was active on the social page that was once run by Tammy Rosetto. He always posed as an investor who'd had success with Grannex Investments. Like Tammy, he posted screenshots of his accounts, the amount of money he'd made each month, and his rate of return on his investments. However, his screenshots also included large withdrawals from his account.

As Callaway dug up more on Rick Wallen, he got the sense Wallen was not just someone posing as an investor. He might actually be working for Grannex.

On Wallen's personal media account, there were photos of him posing in front of a luxury car or in some exotic travel destination. He had blondish hair that was shaved from the sides. He wore a tight polo shirt that exposed his muscular, tattooed arms.

Wallen came across as a con artist. He even loved posting quotes on his photos.

*Live life to the fullest.*
*Never have any regrets.*
*Haters will always hate.*

He referred to himself as an entrepreneur, a lifestyle guru, and a philanthropist.

There was no mention of Grannex Investments on his personal page. However, Callaway was able to dig up messages between him and other Grannex investors. They accused him of running a scam. He pleaded that he didn't know anything about it, that he was duped by Grannex just like them. They asked how he was able to withdraw money from his account when many of them couldn't. He refused to answer those questions, and when they pushed, he would get nasty with them, calling them terrible names and insulting their appearances.

Even if Wallen was not behind the scheme, he was perhaps a recruiter. Someone who facilitated the scam.

When new investors signed up to create an account, they had to enter the person who referred them to Grannex. That person would get a referral fee for bringing the new client in.

Wallen was most likely scouring the social media page Tammy had created. He would then pick out individuals who showed interest in what Grannex had to offer. From there, he would contact them, and even if they were on the fence about signing up with Grannex, he would find a way to reel them in.

Callaway knew he had to go speak to Rick Wallen. He was the only link he had between Grannex and the money lost by Bruce and his mother.

## SIXTY-SEVEN

The medical examiner would arrive soon to take Wayne Lemont's body to the morgue for an autopsy. Until then, he stayed where he was.

Fisher used Wayne's thumb to unlock the cell phone she'd found in his office. The cell phone screen came to life.

"What're you looking for?" Holt asked.

Fisher had already filled him in on what she'd found in the motel's ledgers. The guest in room eight was not Karla Johnson, but Danielle Perkins.

She said, "I want to know where Wayne got the name Karla Johnson. He couldn't have plucked it out of thin air when we inquired about her. I believe both Wayne and Trevor's murders had something to do with the woman in this room. I'll bet my badge on it."

Holt thought for a moment. "When Wayne lied to us about this woman, was it to protect her or her killer?"

Fisher hadn't thought of that. "If I had to guess, I would say the latter. This woman had shown up the night before, and the next morning a man appears at her door with a loaded gun. It seems to me that Wayne had tipped him off."

"Why would he do that?"

Fisher shrugged. "I don't know, maybe for money. Wayne was always looking for ways to make extra cash. Also, a couple down the hall said they saw Wayne talking to a large man earlier."

Holt raised an eyebrow. "Same man we saw in the security footage?"

"That'd be my guess."

Holt mulled it over. "Going back to the woman, she wasn't a person of interest. We already ran her name through our system, and it came back empty."

"We ran the name Karla Johnson," Fisher said. "We need to check for Danielle Perkins once we get back to the station."

"Good point," Holt conceded.

Fisher scrolled through Wayne's contact list and then smiled. He held up the phone for Holt to see.

There was an entry for KARLA J.

Fisher speed-dialed the number and put it on speaker.

The phone rang and then a female voice came on the line. "Wayne, you gotta stop calling me."

"Are you Karla Johnson?" Fisher asked.

"Who's this?" the woman replied.

"This is Detective Dana Fisher. I'm afraid there was an incident with Wayne."

"What kind of incident?"

"Wayne is dead."

There was silence.

"How?" the woman finally asked.

"He was murdered."

"Oh my god!" the woman shrieked.

"Are you Karla Johnson?" Fisher asked again.

"I am."

"And how do you know Wayne?"

"He used to be my boyfriend."

"How long were you in a relationship?"

"We broke up six months ago."

"Can I ask why?"

"I used to be a guest at his motel. That's where we met. He was always nice to me, so we started going out. He even gave me a discount on my rent. But then…"

She fell quiet.

"You found out he was spying on you."

"How did you know?" she said, surprised.

"He was spying on everyone."

"I felt violated," Karla said. "He promised he wouldn't do it anymore, but I didn't believe him. I packed up my bags and left."

Fisher said, "But he still tried to contact you?"

"He wanted us to get back together, but I didn't trust him."

"Is there anything you can tell us that might explain who would want to kill him?"

"I don't know. I mean, he had his foot in a lot of stuff."

"Like what?"

"He tried importing and selling cigarettes, but the people he got involved with were dangerous."

"How dangerous?"

"Bikers. And they didn't like anyone getting on their turf. They showed up at the motel one day, a dozen of them on bikes, and that scared the shit out of Wayne. He then thought about making his own booze, but that required a lot of work, which he wasn't willing to do. He was always looking to make a fast buck. If Wayne could snitch on someone and get paid for it, he'd do it."

"Snitch on who?" Fisher asked.

"Not the cops, for sure. He didn't go near the police. He didn't want them digging up all the illegal stuff he was doing." She paused and then said, "One time, though, he took me to a fancy restaurant. I asked him how he was paying for it. He said he gave valuable information to someone, and they gave him a nice reward for it. He wouldn't tell me what that information was, but he seemed proud of it."

"Do you know who he gave it to?"

"He mentioned a name..." Karla fell silent. "It was something like... black box... or maybe even dark box."

"Dark box?" Fisher said, confused.

"Something like that. But that's all I know."

## SIXTY-EIGHT

Crenshaw saw the news, and he was not pleased. A second person was dead at the motel. Crenshaw knew who was behind it, but he never authorized the killing.

Crenshaw ran a tight ship. While he had a lot of people on computers digging up information for Dark Box, there were only a handful of people who were involved in the day-to-day operations. Kristoff and Andrei were two of those people.

They made sure nothing led back to Dark Box, and they were pretty good at it. Dark Box's survival depended on it.

Now, Crenshaw wasn't so sure. The police would be even more vigilant. They might think they had a serial killer on the loose.

If they had any idea what Dark Box had done, how many lives it had tragically ended, they would be terrified. Kristoff and Andrei were the blunt instruments used by Dark Box. They were professionals. They knew how to keep the media from sniffing around.

This was different. Crenshaw could feel it in his bones. Mistakes were made, and they could come back to bite them.

He had already summoned Kristoff and Andrei to his office. He wanted to have a word with them. Andrei rarely spoke; Kristoff did the talking for both of them. Crenshaw was fine with that, just as long as they both understood the stakes.

The door opened, and Kristoff came in, followed by Andrei.

"I had no choice," Kristoff said immediately.

Crenshaw put his fingers together. "Do explain," he said.

"He was trying to blackmail me."

"How much did he want?"

"I didn't bother to ask."

This was one thing they both differed on. Crenshaw believed everyone had a price, and he was willing to pay to avoid complications. On the other hand, Kristoff believed all problems could be resolved with brute force.

Crenshaw knew that arguing with Kristoff would be a waste of time. What was done was done. He had his reasons for doing what he'd done, even if Crenshaw strongly disagreed with it.

"Has the problem been contained, though?" Crenshaw asked.

Kristoff nodded. "The owner had a hard drive with footage of me at the motel. Andrei and I destroyed this footage."

"Where is it?"

"At the bottom of Lake Erie."

"You should have dumped the body with the hard drive," Crenshaw said.

"We didn't have time. There were others there."

Crenshaw's eyes narrowed. "There were witnesses?"

"It happened so fast. We didn't have time to plan it."

Crenshaw placed his fingers on his temples. He then looked up. "Can they identify you?"

Kristoff fell silent.

Crenshaw didn't like the response, but he would let it go for now.

"What about our other problem?" Crenshaw asked. "The one with the private investigator?"

"He looks like he's distracted with another case," Kristoff replied.

Crenshaw raised an eyebrow. "He hasn't made progress on the case of particular interest to us?"

"He looks like a dog chasing his tail."

Crenshaw smiled at the sound of that. At least there was something he didn't have to be concerned about. In fact, the news was music to his ears.

## SIXTY-NINE

Callaway wasn't expecting the call. It had come out of the blue. But it was a call he couldn't ignore.

The caller gave him specific instructions, and if Callaway followed them, only then could they meet.

Callaway felt like he was in some spy movie. He drove around the city for half an hour, turning left, then right, going up a narrow street, then through a gas station. He then got onto the main road. He drove for another ten minutes and then took the next exit.

He was in another part of the city, one that was farther from his office. Callaway knew Milton like the back of his hand, but even so, there were parts of the city he rarely went to. Not that they were shady or dangerous, he just never had a reason to go there.

Callaway spotted the sign up ahead. He took a hard right and entered the parking lot of a large department store. People were pushing shopping carts or loading their trunks with purchases. He drove around the lot until he found a spot. He parked and then pulled out his cell phone.

He dialed the number and said, "I'm here. Where are you?"

"I'm in the silver Mercedes next to the handicap parking," the voice replied.

He got out and walked down a row of parked cars until he spotted the Mercedes.

He got in the passenger seat and said, "Was all that really necessary?"

"I'm afraid it was, Mr. Callaway," Dr. Reza replied.

"Really? I mean, I think I saw half of Milton just now."

"Are you certain you were not followed?" Dr. Reza asked.

"I'm certain," Callaway replied. "I'm a private investigator, you know. I do a lot of following in my line of work. I know when I have a tail or not."

Dr. Reza nodded. His shoulders relaxed.

He said, "After what happened with Dr. Sinclair, I felt like I was being watched."

Callaway's brow furrowed. "Watched? By whom?"

"I don't know. I would see a black sedan outside the clinic. And when I would go to see who it was, they'd drive away. Patients would come in with no illness and ask me odd questions about Dr. Sinclair. Where was she? Did I know what *really* happened to her?" Dr. Reza fell silent. He stared at his fingers. "One time, I caught a student, whom I'd recently hired, in my office. I confronted him, and he confessed that someone had paid him to go through our records."

"Do you know who paid him?" Callaway asked.

"He didn't know."

"What was this student looking for?"

"He wouldn't tell me."

"Okay, so what am I doing here?" Callaway said.

Dr. Reza paused to collect his thoughts. "There was something I didn't mention to you at the clinic. The week before the fire at her house, Dr. Sinclair was particularly stressed and anxious. She didn't seem herself. I could tell something was troubling her. I asked her if everything was okay, and she said that it was a personal matter. As it was none of my business, I wasn't going to push her on it, but then she said something that surprised me."

"What did she say?"

"She asked if I would be interested in taking over the clinic," Dr. Reza said. "I was shocked. She loved her job. She loved her patients. She had put everything into the clinic. And until she mentioned it, I had never imagined that she would ever leave."

"Leave?"

"Yes."

Callaway was confused.

"What do you mean?"

Dr. Reza fell silent. He bit his lip and then said, "I don't know if I should say this, but I think she was planning to leave the country."

"Why?"

"I think she was going to leave her husband and take her daughter with her."

Callaway mulled this over. It didn't make sense. As far as he could tell, Laura and Roger Sinclair had a great relationship. But then again, Roger was charged and convicted of killing Laura.

"Do you know where she planned to take her daughter?"

"I don't know, but I saw travel brochures on her desk."

"Do you know what Dr. Sinclair's relationship was with her husband?" Callaway asked.

He shook his head. "I never asked her."

"Did she ever talk about her daughter?"

Dr. Reza smiled. "She loved Millie. She would always talk about her when we were alone."

"Do you have any children, doctor?" Callaway asked.

"My wife and I couldn't have any of our own, but we were fortunate enough to adopt one."

Callaway looked out the Mercedes' window. He wasn't sure if anything Dr. Reza had told him would help him solve the mystery.

*Why did Roger Sinclair murder his wife?*

Dr. Reza said, "The reason I called you, Mr. Callaway, is because a day prior to her... um... anyway, I went to her office to speak to her, but she had already left for the day. I saw that her computer was on. I went to turn it off, and I saw articles on her screen."

"What kind of articles?"

"Articles on a patient of Dr. Sinclair's."

"What happened to this patient?"

"I don't know. She had been at the clinic multiple times. Sometimes even after the clinic was closed."

"Was that normal?"

He shook his head. "Dr. Sinclair would make exceptions for her."

"Okay."

"What was strange was that after I took over the clinic, I was going through the patient inventory, and her file was no longer there. No physical or digital copy, as if someone had destroyed the hard copy and wiped the system clean."

"Do you think Dr. Sinclair destroyed her records?"

"Who else could do it except for her?"

"Did you ask any of your assistants or the secretary?"

"I did, and they have no idea."

Callaway paused. "Why are you telling me this?"

"I know you are trying to find out the truth, and I want to help."

"I don't know how this helps me."

"Dr. Sinclair talked a lot about this patient with me."

"What was wrong with this patient?"

Dr. Reza fell silent. "I would rather not get into that. Even though she was not my patient, and Dr. Sinclair is no longer here, I have to respect doctor-patient confidentiality."

Callaway thought for a moment. "I'm not sure what this has to do with Roger Sinclair murdering his wife."

"Please take a look. It might be something. Or it might be nothing."

Callaway sighed. "All right, what's this patient's name?"

## SEVENTY

Roger Sinclair sat on the bed in his cell, staring at a photo of his wife and daughter. He had tears in his eyes. His heart broke each time he looked at the photo. For a long time, he considered tearing it up. It was a cruel reminder of a past life. A life that was full of joy and laughter. A life brimming with hope and immense possibility. A life he had worked so hard to cultivate.

But then, in a very short amount of time, it was all gone.

He would never get to hold Millie's hand again. Hug her and tell her everything will be all right. Smile at her graduation. Walk her down the aisle on her wedding day. Or even hold his first grandchild.

He was given life with no chance of parole. He would die in prison. Old and decrepit. The world never knowing the truth of why he did what he did.

That weight was far heavier than what he had actually done. It was on him like the shackles on his hands and feet, choking him until he could no longer breathe.

But he knew the reason. He did it for *her*.

He moved his finger over his daughter's smiling face. All of it was for her. The sacrifice. The pain. The torture.

He had to keep her safe.

They had thought about going to the police, but the threat was real and imminent. They knew how dangerous their enemy was. How desperate they were. How far they were willing to go. Because they had seen what their enemy could do.

They didn't know who they could trust. It felt as if everyone around them worked for the enemy. Perhaps even the police.

The enemy had the means and the desire for violence. They couldn't compete with that. He was an engineer. He spent most of his days solving complex problems, and this problem was the most complex he had ever tried to solve.

He had examined all options on the table. Disappear. Leave the country. But how long would they have to run?

The enemy had tentacles everywhere, maybe even more in some third world countries.

Maybe they could go into witness protection. That was only possible if they could prove what they knew, which they couldn't. No one would believe them. No one would take their case on.

Even if they could get a lawyer, there was no guarantee they'd make it to trial. The enemy would do everything in their power to shut them down.

They would be exposed. They would be living their lives not knowing when the end would come.

Would it happen when they started their cars? Or when one of them walked their daughter home from school? Or when they went to visit their parents? Or went on a vacation?

When?

The unknown would torment them for the remainder of their lives.

They had considered faking a suicide, but that would have left a lot of unanswered questions.

They were left with no choice but one.

Remove him and his wife from the equation for the sake of their daughter.

He paid a high price for it, but so did his wife.

Now they would never be a family again. That hope was gone when he lit the fire that burned their entire lives to ashes.

He placed the photo on his chest and hugged it.

He began to sob.

## SEVENTY-ONE

Holt and Fisher did an online search but couldn't find anything on Dark Box. The only things that came up were physical boxes that were colored black.

Maybe Karla Johnson was mistaken. Maybe she hadn't heard right. She wasn't even sure what this *Dark Box* even did.

Were they a corporation? If so, what did they sell? Where was their headquarters?

Holt and Fisher then decided to go check out the address on the driver's license for Danielle Perkins.

The drive was less than forty minutes, but the moment they got close to their destination, they got the sense that something was not right.

For one thing, the area they were in was mostly commercial or industrial. There were factories, warehouses, distribution centers—they even passed by a utility station. The last residential neighborhood was several miles back.

They pulled into what looked like an office building.

"This is the address according to the driver's license," Fisher said.

"We should have known it was a fake," Holt grumbled. "Why would this person go to a motel when their address was in Milton?"

Fisher stared at the driver's license in her hand. "Who is she?" she said, more to herself than Holt. "Why would she go through the trouble to get a fake ID?"

"I don't know," Holt growled. "But this case is getting weirder and weirder."

"What do you mean?"

"We came to the motel to investigate Trevor McGinty's murder, only to discover that he was not who everyone thought he was. He was actually a fugitive from Canada named Rene Tremblanc. And then we found out that a person across from Trevor may have been targeted. We asked Wayne Lemont about her, and he gave us a false name. When we go back to the motel, we find him dead, too. And on top of that, this woman in the room across from Trevor's was also using a fake ID. Maybe she's a fugitive from Canada as well."

Fisher could tell he was frustrated. Everything about this case was frustrating. They felt like whenever they took one step forward, they took two steps back.

Instead of getting answers, they had more questions.

Was Trevor killed because he was at the wrong place at the wrong time? Was Wayne killed because he knew too much? Who was the big man in the middle of all of this? And how was this woman linked to everything that had transpired at Motel 86?

They felt that if they didn't find her, they couldn't solve this case. Two murders would end up as cold cases, and one killer would get to roam free.

"Maybe we dust the room for her prints," Holt said. "We might get a match."

Fisher shook her head. "Have you seen the rooms? Wayne never cleaned them. I wouldn't be surprised if the sheets had bed bugs. If her prints are there, it would be among dozens of people who had rented the room before her. We could end up spending weeks or months trying to cross out people who could or could not be her."

Holt grunted and looked away.

Fisher said, "It would be nice if we knew where she got this fake driver's license. I mean, you can't just walk into any store and get one."

Holt turned to her. "I may know a guy who might be able to help us."

## SEVENTY-TWO

*Tara Sandhu.*

That was the name Dr. Reza had given Callaway.

He returned to his office and quickly did a search on her. What he found puzzled him.

Tara's mother had reported her missing three years ago. Tara was only twenty-four at the time of her disappearance. She had an olive complexion, hazel eyes, and dark hair.

Tara's father, George Sandhu, had come to the United States from Guyana almost thirty years ago. He met Tara's mother, Olivia Giesel, in college when they both studied at the Arkansas Baptist College. When they decided to get married, Tara's grandparents were not too thrilled about it. They felt the marriage wouldn't last. And thirty years ago, interracial marriages were still frowned upon in some parts of the country.

Tara's mother and father eloped in Las Vegas without her parents' permission. They moved to Rockford, Illinois. George worked as an electrician for a local company and then went on to start his own business. During this time, Olivia became pregnant with their first child. They ended up having three children. Thomas first, followed by Terrence, and then came Tara. As the only girl, her parents doted on her. But unlike her older siblings, Tara was rebellious and a troublemaker. She broke curfew multiple times. She even ran away twice when her parents refused to let her date boys much older than her. Olivia blamed the people Tara hung around with. She was smoking pot at the age of fourteen, drinking at the age of fifteen, and even dabbling in hard drugs before she turned seventeen.

Somehow, Tara managed to get through high school and even got into a college in Chicago. But before graduation, she was expelled from school for getting into a relationship with one of her professors. The professor had to resign.

She then made her way to Milton. She joined a temp agency and worked for a variety of companies as a secretary. She was at a law firm, an insurance company, and a real estate brokerage firm. But the work was only for a few months at a time. She was either replacing an employee who was on maternity leave or she was there for operational requirements because the company needed extra manpower to meet demands.

According to her mother, Tara seemed happy. Even with the uncertainty of her employment, she still felt secure and in control of her life. Something she never felt growing up.

Tara's parents had divorced when Tara was not even a teenager. She had to shuttle between two parents until she was eighteen. That was why she had acted out. Her brothers, on the other hand, found a way to deal with a broken home. One ended up working as a manager for a tire manufacturer, and the other worked as a real estate agent.

Callaway found this information through a variety of interviews Olivia had done with reporters. Olivia believed something worse had happened to her daughter. And by talking about her and putting a face to her name, somehow her daughter would not become a statistic of all the people that had gone missing in the country.

Olivia was adamant that Tara would not disappear without telling anyone. She had a lot going for her—a new job she enjoyed, and even a new man in her life. Tara never mentioned the man's name to her mother, but she assured her that soon she would have good news for her.

She thought Tara was engaged and that a wedding date was on the horizon, but she was never able to find out who her daughter was engaged to. Olivia believed this man knew what had happened to her daughter, but so far, her search for this man had been in vain.

No one in Tara's inner circle had heard of this man. She never mentioned his name to any of her friends. In fact, her best friend said the year before her disappearance, Tara had started to distance herself from everyone. She refused to meet them in person, but she always responded to each message she received.

She would tell her worried friends that she was fine, that she was just busy with work, but she always promised to meet them one day. She would also drop hints along the way. She would post photos of engagement rings, resorts, massive houses, and even baby carriages.

Her friends didn't know what to make of them, but as long as she was staying in touch, they were happy for her.

When the replies stopped coming, they contacted Tara's mother.

Olivia still held out hope that one day her daughter would walk through the door and give her a hug. She was, after all, her baby girl.

Callaway shut his eyes tight. He wasn't sure how Tara Sandhu fit into all of this. He wasn't even sure why Dr. Reza had given him her name.

There was no connection to Laura Sinclair except that Tara was once her patient.

He then did a quick search online.

*The last place Tara Sandhu was employed at was... Carta Aluminum,* he thought.

## SEVENTY-THREE

Holt and Fisher parked in front of a nondescript house. There was a minivan parked in the driveway. A basketball net was just above the garage. A child's bicycle lay next to the front steps.

"Are you sure he lives here?" Fisher asked.

"He does. Trust me," Holt replied.

They walked up to the front door and rang the bell.

A moment later, the door swung open. A man wearing a tank top, shorts, and socks stood before them. He had several tattoos on his flabby arms, and he wore a gold chain around his neck.

"J.J.," Holt said. "How are you?"

J.J. stared at him and swallowed. "Officer Holt," he said nervously.

"Detective Holt now."

"What can I do for you?" J.J. asked. "I'm watching my kids right now."

"This won't take long," Holt replied. "Unless you want us to speak to you inside."

J.J. shook his head. "The kids are watching cartoons, so we can talk out here."

He came out onto the porch and shut the door behind him.

"I heard you got married," Holt said. "Where's your wife?"

"She's at the salon."

Holt pointed to Fisher. "This is my partner, Detective Fisher. And this is J.J. Turner."

"Hi," J.J. said sheepishly.

"Did you know," Holt said matter-of-factly, "that when I was a uniform officer, I brought J.J. in for cashing fake checks. When I searched his apartment, I found equipment for making fake IDs, even passports."

"That was a long time ago," J.J. said.

"It was," Holt agreed. "Because back then, you weren't even married. How many kids do you have?"

"Two."

"How old are they?"

"One is four and the other is turning two soon."

"Good to see that you have turned your life around. What do you do now?" Holt asked.

"I work for a printing company."

"And your wife?"

"She's at home with the kids."

"Then that begs the question: how does one afford this house and the car in the driveway on a single income?"

J.J. shrugged. "We get by fine."

Holt then leaned closer, his face inches from J.J.'s. "I know you're still hustling on the side, J.J., and I want to know what it is."

J.J. shook his head. "I'm clean, I swear."

"If my partner and I went inside and tossed your house, are you sure we wouldn't find anything incriminating? Nothing in the basement, perhaps?"

J.J. bit his lip. They could see he was considering his options.

"Listen," Holt said. "You tell us what you've been up to, and we'll walk away."

"Just like that?" J.J. said.

"Just like that. And no one needs to know we were even here."

J.J. looked down at his socks. "Okay, fine. I have a lab in my basement. I create false IDs for clients."

"Why am I not surprised," Holt said. "And where do you meet your clients? At your house?"

J.J. twisted his face. "Of course not. I don't let anyone come to my house. I got little kids, and my wife doesn't know what I do."

"So, how do they find you?"

"I have a website. They fill out a form, make the payment, and then I mail them the documents they ordered."

Holt pulled out Danielle Perkins' driver's license. "Did this woman pay you to make her this ID?"

J.J. stared at it, but said nothing.

"Come on, J.J. You give us what we want, and we get back in our car and leave you alone. Unless…"

J.J. sighed. "Yeah, I made her that card."

"And she filled out the forms and made the payment online?"

"She filled out the forms, but she didn't want to pay using a credit card or any other online payment system. She mailed me cash."

"And to what address did you send her the ID?"

"Hers was a bit different."

"How so?"

"She didn't want me to mail it. She paid extra for me to drive to a park and leave the envelope underneath a park bench."

"When was this?"

"A week or so ago."

"And you never saw the woman pick up the envelope?"

"No, man. I did as I was instructed, and I got the hell out of there."

Holt frowned. If they were hoping for some kind of lead, then they had just hit a brick wall. J.J. didn't know who this woman was, and he most certainly didn't know where they could find her.

Fisher asked, "Do you still have the envelope?"

"I told you, I dropped it at the park," J.J. replied.

"No, the envelope with the cash she sent you."

J.J. thought for a moment. "I might still have it. Why?"

"We want it."

## SEVENTY-FOUR

Denise Hollins was in her office with the blinds down. She had a dozen emails and phone calls to return, but her heart wasn't in it. As the head of a billion-dollar company, Denise could not ignore those calls and emails for long. People relied on her to make important decisions. Carta Aluminum was a big machine, one that didn't require her to micromanage it, but still, she had to be the one running the ship. Without her signing off on key matters, those decisions would then be left to her vice president of operations.

Denise had a feeling that her father would be more than pleased to make him the CEO of Carta.

William Hoffman was much younger than her father, but he held the same values. He was old school. He liked running things his way. And, more importantly, he was loyal to her father.

If her father demanded more funds to be taken out of Carta for his airline business, Bill Hoffman would gladly approve it. Bill was a company man, and the only reason he survived this long at Carta was that he never said no to her father.

Bill should have been in charge of Carta. He had worked his way up to becoming the next CEO. But, at the time, her father wanted someone from the family to run it. It wasn't that he didn't trust Bill. On the contrary, her father figured it would be easier to get his way by appointing one of his children.

As his daughter, Denise would never go against his wishes. And she didn't want to, but her father's actions were reckless. He was not thinking about the company anymore. He was thinking about himself. He had given everything to the company, and it was time to get some back. In short, her father thought the company was his personal piggybank. He made withdrawals on a whim, and he used those funds however he liked.

Denise was concerned about the employees. Each decision she made could impact them more. If the company lost half of its value, Denise and her family would manage fine. But those thousands of employees who relied on Carta for their survival might not be so lucky.

She wasn't always like this. She didn't spend much time being altruistic. Growing up, she wanted to be like her father—motivated by wealth and power. But when she saw how his actions impacted her mother, she decided she was not going to emulate him.

Her mother had a sweet soul. She wasn't as cold as her father. She cared about other people's well-being. Something her father rarely thought about. How these two stayed married for so long was always a mystery to her. While her father was busy fornicating with other women, her mother was dying a slow death. Denise later realized that her mother needed him more than he needed her. She was not strong enough to leave him. He had made her reliant on him, and he used that to his advantage. He cheated on his wife repeatedly, knowing full well that she was not going anywhere. He was a cruel man, and Denise had vowed to cut him out of Carta completely when the time was right.

Now, she would never be able to do that.

The clock was ticking. Soon, she would have no choice but to resign. Her husband and two kids were more important than some feud with her father.

She stood up from her desk and walked over to the window. She pulled the blinds up and blinked as the sunlight flooded into the room.

When her eyes adjusted, she looked down at the streets below. From the top floor of her office, she could see the city in all its glamour and beauty. Whenever she felt like everything was falling apart around her, she would stare out at the city and know that there was a whole world out there, and that everything would be okay.

She saw people crossing the street, riding their bikes, or walking on the sidewalk. Her eyes stopped at the hotdog stand in the corner. Normally, Denise ate lunch at one of those fancy restaurants in the downtown core, but sometimes she would run across and pick up a hotdog. It reminded her of her childhood, of innocent times, when her father would take her and her siblings to a baseball game, and they would gorge on hotdogs.

Suddenly, she felt the urge to have one.

She left the office and took her private elevator down to the lobby.

She got out of the elevator and made her way past the security desk. She heard the guard say, "I'm sorry, but I don't see the name Tara Sandhu at Carta Aluminum."

Denise stopped in her tracks.

She turned and saw a man talking to the guard. He had a look of danger to him. Denise had dated enough guys like him in high school to know he was trouble. But there was something else about him. Not only was he tall and handsome, but he also came across as someone who had been tamed by the trials of life.

"Can I help you?" she said, walking over to him.

"Yeah," he said. "I was looking to speak to someone about a former employee."

"What was this employee's name?" Denise said, if only to confirm that she'd heard it right the first time.

"Tara Sandhu."

"And you are?" Denise asked.

"Lee Callaway." He held his business card out for her.

She took it. "You're a private investigator?"

"I am."

"And why are you looking for this person?"

"She's actually missing, but I wanted to find out more about her."

Denise stared at him. "You know what? I can ask our human resources department, and if they pull anything up, I'll give you a call." She waved his card in the air.

"That sounds good," he said with a grin. "Thank you."

She watched him leave the building.

A moment later, she left the building, too. She made her way to the hotdog stand across the street, but she was no longer hungry.

She pulled out her cell phone and quickly began typing a text message.

## SEVENTY-FIVE

Holt and Fisher sent the envelope J.J. Turner had given them to the forensics lab. They wanted to see if they could lift fingerprints or DNA from it. Maybe then they would know who this woman really was. The lab assured them a quick turnaround, which was only done under extreme circumstances.

Holt and Fisher decided to run the name Danielle Perkins through the system.

There was a Danielle Perkins in Idaho. She was eighty-two and collecting social security. Another Danielle Perkins lived in New Jersey. She was nineteen and a student at Seton Hall. The third Danielle Perkins was in Dallas. She was forty and worked as a nurse at a hospital. When they looked into her, they saw that this Danielle Perkins was black, which did not fit the description of the woman in the video.

There was a reason the woman in unit eight had chosen this name. There were several dozen Danielle Perkins in the country, and it would require a lot of manpower, not to mention cooperation from various local authorities, to find out if any of them were somehow linked to this woman.

While they waited for the results, Holt decided to check up on Nancy. He'd been working long hours. Fisher insisted he go.

With him gone, she took the opportunity to call Lance. After she turned down his proposal, she hadn't had a chance to talk to him about it. He was gone when she returned to her apartment after her talk with Callaway.

She knew he was heartbroken. She could have said yes just to make him happy, but she wanted to be honest with him. Their relationship would not survive if they chose to placate each other just so the other's feelings were not hurt. Eventually, somewhere down the line, a big fight would end the engagement.

Fisher didn't want that. She cared about him. Above all, she respected him.

She decided to call him. After a few rings, it went to voicemail. She didn't know whether he was on duty or he was avoiding her. Regardless, she said, "Hey babe, it's me. I'm sorry for what happened the other day. I shouldn't have left you like that in my apartment. I should have stayed so that we could talk about it. To be honest, the proposal blindsided me, and I suddenly got scared." She paused to let this sink in. "I like the way things are, and I thought if we got serious, then maybe things might not be the same. Me... or you... I don't know... both of us might demand more from the relationship. I'm just not ready for that. Not right now anyway. Please call me when you get this message. We have a lot to talk about. A lot to sort out before we can take the next step. A big step. One that I hope will last a lifetime. Again, please call me, babe. Nothing has changed the way I feel about you. Okay? I hope you'll give me a chance to explain myself. I love you."

She hung up. She didn't know if what she said made any sense, but everything she said came from the heart.

She sighed and put the phone away.

## SEVENTY-SIX

Kristoff and Andrei were at a bar in a seedy part of town. Andrei rarely spoke up, and when he did, it was to let him know he was displeased about something.

Even though Crenshaw was their boss, Andrei didn't like how he spoke to Kristoff. In Russia, Andrei would have cut his tongue out by now, but Kristoff was more cool-headed. He knew those methods did not work in America. If word got out that they had done that to their superior, no one would hire them. They would be fearful of what they might do to them.

It was not like that in Russia. If a subordinate killed his boss, the boss's enemies would seek to hire him. It was a risky and, as some would call it, irrational decision. Who is to stop the subordinate from killing his new boss? But there was a reason for this: they would rather have someone like him on their side than their enemy's.

Before hiring him, the new boss would find out the motive for the betrayal. Did his previous employer not pay him well? Did the previous employer insult him in some way? There had to be a rhyme and reason for the killing.

Murdering one's boss was not a trivial task. It was a dangerous power move, one that could have serious ramifications for the subordinate. Others, loyal to their dead boss, would come after the subordinate. Some would try to exert their control over whatever criminal enterprise the boss was involved in, but even if they were able to take over, there was no guarantee other criminal organizations would be willing to work with them. Business was built on trust and loyalty. It could all fall apart in one single act. An act that could seem like a betrayal.

Kristoff was not prepared to take such drastic actions against Crenshaw. His boss was not a killer, which made him weak in Kristoff's eyes. Kristoff doubted if the man had ever even fired a gun. The bosses in Russia had earned their stripes. Some had spent years in the gulag for serious crimes, such as murder. They knew what it took to gain power, and they were willing to resort to just about anything to keep it.

Crenshaw was a businessman, first and foremost. He used Kristoff and Andrei to get the job done. In some ways, Kristoff preferred this approach. It made him and Andrei far more valuable to Crenshaw. He needed them more than they needed him. He never haggled with them over their fee. And after this problem was taken care of, Kristoff believed they were in line for a raise.

Kristoff had learned that Americans liked to exert their control through speech. They made big declarations. They had a sense of bravado to them. He knew this came from the movies. Heroes in American cinema believed they could single-handedly take down a gang of twenty men. In reality, it took the brutal murder of one person in the gang to teach the others that they shouldn't mess with him.

He took a sip of his drink. The vodka tasted stale in his mouth. He preferred the Russian brand—it was much stronger and more potent—but the bartender didn't have it. This would have to do for now.

Every action he'd taken had a reason. When Wayne Lemont had contacted him about a woman who was acting suspicious, Kristoff wanted more information. Lemont told him the woman's name was Danielle Perkins. Kristoff didn't know anyone by that name. When Lemont gave him the address on the woman's driver's license, Kristoff decided to go check it out. He found himself in front of an office building in an industrial part of town. He realized it was a fake, and that's when he knew he had to go to the motel and check it out for himself.

He and Andrei waited in the parking lot until they saw her come back to her room. When he went in, she was gone. And then everything fell apart.

Kristoff cursed himself for wasting time checking out the address on the woman's driver's license. When Lemont had called, he and Andrei should have driven straight to the motel that very night. In the comfort of darkness, Kristoff was certain they would have completed the task that had been hanging over them for almost three years.

But what was done was done, he knew. He was not one to ruminate on a situation for long. He was a man of action, and he would find a way to rectify the problem.

His cell phone buzzed on the table. The name Crenshaw appeared on the screen. Andrei saw it and grunted dismissively.

Kristoff answered anyway, and after listening, he said, "We're on our way."

## SEVENTY-SEVEN

When Callaway received the text, he was at first puzzled by who had sent it. He didn't recognize the telephone number. It was only when the sender mentioned a name that he took it seriously.

He drove around the block for fifteen minutes until he found a spot in the parking lot of a fast-food restaurant. He checked his watch to see if he was early. He wasn't. A woman got out of a BMW. He recognized her immediately. She went into the restaurant. He quickly got out and followed her inside.

The line was short. Within minutes she had her tray of food. She moved to a booth in the corner and sat down. He bought a combo, and with his tray in his hand, he approached her.

"Do you mind if I join you?" he asked.

She shook her head. He sat across from her.

She was dressed in a business suit that probably cost more than any of the restaurant's employees made in a month. Everything about her shouted money. She stuck out in the fast-food joint, but she didn't care. She was here for a reason. And so was he.

*Tara Sandhu.*

That was the name on the text she had sent him.

"Who are you?" he asked.

"Denise Hollins," she replied.

"Why are we here, Ms. Hollins?"

"It's Mrs. Hollins," she said. "And my maiden name is Graft."

Callaway's eyes narrowed. "Is your father Wilbur Graft, the founder of Carta Aluminum?"

"He is," she said. "And I'm Carta's current CEO."

"Why do you say *current*?"

"Because my father is doing everything in his power to remove me."

"Why would he do that?"

"It's a family dispute—a power play on his end. And to teach me a lesson, that he is still in charge."

"Okay, but what does this have to do with Tara Sandhu?" he asked.

"There were rumblings in the family that my father was recently involved with someone. He's never been a saint. People like him who have achieved a lot, they think they own everything and everyone."

"He was involved with Tara Sandhu?"

"My father's had multiple affairs in his lifetime, to the dismay of my mother. She ignored his indiscretion just as long as it didn't interfere with the family dynamic, or as long as he didn't bring his mistresses into our house or to public events and embarrass her. I mean, it was no secret that he was always sleeping around, but this time it was different."

"How so?"

"I don't know. When I became CEO, I began to hear that he was in a relationship with an employee. This was something he had never done before. He knew better than to mix business with pleasure. All the girls he'd found before were waitresses, models, or aspiring actresses."

"What did Tara do at Carta Aluminum?" Callaway asked.

"She started out in our HR department, but somehow she became one of his secretaries."

"He had multiple secretaries?" Callaway asked, surprised.

"Edith was his longest secretary. She worked for Carta for thirty-five years. But the last couple of years before his retirement, she had begun to take on less and less responsibilities. She was in her early seventies. She was the one person my father couldn't get his way with. She had rebuked his attempts at seduction very early on when they were both younger. When Carta was still in its infancy, she had a no-nonsense attitude about her. She also kept him on his toes, which I think he admired. He relied on her more than anyone in the company, including some of the members of his upper-management team. Even when she was contemplating retirement, he kept encouraging her not to. In order to induce her to stay longer, he offloaded some of her duties to other secretaries. And I believe one of them ended up being Tara Sandhu."

"Tara Sandhu's been missing for three years now," he said. "Did you know that?"

"I've never bothered getting into my father's personal affairs. I have a company to run, and I have a family of my own. But someone recently told me about her disappearance."

"Who? Who told you?" Callaway asked.

"I don't know. They never gave me their name."

"How did they contact you?"

"I received an anonymous call. The caller said they had some information for me. It had to do with my father—and Tara Sandhu. At first, I ignored them. I know my father is a philanderer, but again, this had nothing to do with me. But then something happened that changed my mind."

"What?"

Denise fell silent. She looked down at her tray. She had not touched her meal. Neither had he. He wasn't very hungry, to begin with. She then plucked a French fry and put it in her mouth.

"I don't want to go into the details," she said, "but I believe someone is blackmailing me."

"Who?"

"I don't know. But I also believe my father is behind it."

"He's doing it to remove you from your position at Carta Aluminum?"

Denise nodded. "I then sent a message to the number where I had received the anonymous call. I got a quick reply. They wanted to meet."

"Where?"

"At a food court in a shopping mall."

"And what did this person say when you met them?" Callaway asked.

"I never got the chance. Someone was following us... or perhaps, following *me*, and it spooked this person. I haven't heard back from them since."

Callaway fell silent. He mulled this over. "You were hoping whatever this person had on your father, you could use it against him?"

"That was the plan," Denise replied. "But the more I looked into this, the more concerned I am now."

"About what?"

"What really happened to Tara Sandhu. Six months before she disappeared, she had stopped coming into work. But according to our HR department, she was still on the payroll. I mean, we kept paying her even though she wasn't working. Why would we do that? And what's even more strange is that *one* day before she was reported missing, we abruptly ended her employment at Carta Aluminum. And there was no reason given as to why that was done."

"Who would do that?"

"As the CEO, people can't easily say no to me. I write their checks. And when I pushed for more information, I found out it was my father."

"Are you saying that Wilbur Graft fired Tara Sandhu from Carta Aluminum?"

"I am."

Callaway stared at her for a moment. "Do you believe your father is somehow responsible for Tara Sandhu's disappearance?" he asked.

"That's a question I've been grappling with ever since I started looking into it," Denise replied. "I would love to say I know my father well, but I don't. He has always operated in his own universe, where he makes his own rules. However, it wouldn't be beneath him to do something if he somehow felt threatened."

"Threatened how?"

"I don't know, but I'm his daughter, and he's willing to blackmail me so I wouldn't affect his way of doing things. I can't imagine what he would do to someone like Tara Sandhu."

Callaway felt a shiver go up his spine.

## SEVENTY--EIGHT

The DNA test results came back. The saliva on the envelope sent to J.J. Turner belonged to Laura Sinclair.

Fisher was familiar with the story. Everyone in Milton had heard about it. A successful engineer had murdered his wife, who also happened to be an accomplished doctor. He then burned the couple's house down in order to hide his crimes. He later confessed to the crime and was sentenced to life in prison with no chance of parole.

"That can't be right," Holt said in disbelief.

"That's what the DNA results say," Fisher replied.

They knew DNA testing was reliable and accurate 99.9 percent of the time, which made this discovery even more shocking.

"She's dead," Holt said, looking up from the results.

"I know," Fisher said.

There was a moment of silence as they pondered this new revelation.

"Let's go over this for a moment," Fisher said. "The victim's husband was seen outside the house while it went up in flames."

"Yes."

"The victim's husband later gave a statement to the police that he was responsible for her death."

"Okay."

"But as far as I can tell, no dead body was ever found."

Holt frowned. "I did read about that when it happened, and I was somewhat troubled by it."

"We can't blame the detective on the case," Fisher said. "The victim was missing, and her husband had taken responsibility for that. Most domestic murders are perpetrated by a spouse or partner. It's rarely a stranger committing the crime."

"So, for the detective, it was an open-and-shut case," Holt said.

"It was," Fisher said. "And if we were in this detective's shoes, we would have done exactly as he did."

"I don't know about that," Holt said. "I would have looked into it further."

"For what?" Fisher said. "What purpose would it have served?"

"I mean, to get to the bottom of the truth. The real killer could be free."

"The real killer's not free. Laura Sinclair is still alive, remember? That means this was all staged. Her disappearance was made to look like a crime, and her husband took the fall for it."

"Why would he do that?" Holt said, surprised. "People like to stay *out* of prison, not the other way around."

"Maybe there was a bigger threat outside."

"What do you mean?"

"I don't know," she said, rubbing her chin. "But think about it. She's dead, and everything is quiet. But then she reappears at the motel after all these years, and a man shows up to her room with a gun. This tells me her life was always in danger. Maybe her entire family, too. It was probably out of necessity that she and her husband came up with this plan."

"It's a foolish plan if you ask me," Holt said. "Why didn't she just come to us? The police could have protected her."

"Could they, really?"

"Yes," Holt said with conviction.

"We couldn't protect Wayne Lemont or Trevor McGinty."

"We didn't know their lives were in danger."

"The man who killed Wayne Lemont and Trevor McGinty is a professional. We've believed that ever since we took on this case. There is no telling what lengths he would have gone to harm Laura Sinclair. And if I remember correctly, she has a daughter. Any parent would be willing to risk everything for the safety of their child."

Holt fell silent.

Fisher said, "Laura Sinclair's return to Milton—from wherever she was hiding—had a domino effect. This resulted in the deaths of Wayne and Trevor. We have to find her before there are any more dead bodies."

## SEVENTY-NINE

Callaway drove back to his office. His talk with Denise Hollins had answered some questions, but had raised many more. He knew a little bit more about Tara Sandhu, but he still didn't know what happened to her.

Graft's daughter believed her father may have had something to do with Tara's disappearance. She had no proof of this, though. Her reasoning could be out of spite. Her father was doing everything in his power to remove her from her position. He was willing to blackmail her to get what he wanted.

Callaway had seen his share of family disputes. As a private investigator, he was usually hired to go after cheating spouses. Sometimes he would have to find out if a strange woman or man was trying to seduce a client's elderly father or mother in order to get into their will. Those cases were hard to prove. They had to show that the seducer was clearly manipulative in the relationship. They had to also prove that the elderly parent was not of sound mind, that they were not aware they were being taken advantage of. Psychiatrists would have to be brought in to determine the mental capacity of the elderly parent.

Luckily, Callaway didn't have to get too involved in those cases. He didn't focus his attention on the elderly parent. He would learn nothing about the interaction between the seducer and the elderly parent. Even if they went out together, anyone seeing them would think they were in a mutual relationship. Callaway focused his attention on the seducer. He would follow him or her, see where they went, who they interacted with. He would try to gather as much information as possible in order for his client to present to the judge that the seducer had ulterior motives. Perhaps the seducer had a family in another country he or she needed to support. History of bad credit or debts that needed erasing. Anything to show that the seducer saw monetary benefits in the relationship.

There was no telling if Tara Sandhu and Wilbur Graft's relationship was genuine, even with the age difference. Graft was in his seventies, and Tara Sandhu was in her twenties. He was old enough to be her grandfather. But love is complicated. Love is blind. Maybe he was her sugar daddy.

But Callaway could not see why Graft would want Tara Sandhu gone. His affairs were no secret. Graft was proud that he had bedded many women, and he didn't even bother hiding it from his wife. Callaway understood the rift between father and daughter. No child wanted to see one of their parents get hurt, especially their mother.

There was more to this, Callaway believed. He just couldn't put his finger on it.

He parked his Charger on the street and walked to his office. As he passed the noodle shop, he saw that the interior lights were on.

He peeked through the windows and spotted a silhouette inside.

He knocked on the glass door. The silhouette waved and pointed to the CLOSED sign.

He shook his head and waved back.

The silhouette came closer and quickly opened the door.

Ms. Chen said, "I thought you were a customer."

"Are you planning to open the shop?" he asked.

"No. I just came in to pay some bills."

"How is Bruce doing?"

"The doctors said he is in critical, but stable condition. I don't know what that means." Ms. Chen looked at Callaway. "Does that mean he'll get better?"

"It means he won't get worse in the short term, so that's good news."

She gave him a weak smile. "Did you find who took our money?" she asked.

"It's not that easy. The money could be halfway across the world."

She looked down at the floor. She nodded. "Thank you for trying," she said. "I know we put you in a difficult spot."

"I'm still looking," he said, trying to sound reassuring. But she could tell he wasn't successful.

"I always knew one day I would have to close the shop," she said. "I never wanted Bruce to take over. He had bigger things to do in his life than run a small noodle shop. Maybe now is a good time to sell the business."

"Are you at least going to keep the building?" Callaway thought of his cheap rent. He didn't know where he'd go if she sold the entire property.

"The shop has been losing money for years, but because of our savings, we got by. I don't know if that will be possible anymore."

Callaway felt his heart sink.

# EIGHTY

Callaway kicked himself for getting distracted with Millie's case. In the process, he had neglected Bruce's case. But what could he have done? Dr. Reza had called him out of the blue, and Callaway had to drop everything to meet him.

Not anymore. He was determined to find who was behind the Grannex scam.

He had a lead. If that didn't pan out, he would have to abandon it. There was only so much he could do. He wasn't the police or the FBI. He didn't have the jurisdiction or the means to conduct a statewide investigation. He was a lowly private eye. He worked on one case at a time, sometimes two, when the heavens shined on him. Most of the time, though, he sat on his hands, waiting for the phone to ring.

Callaway drove to Bellview County. It was a small town with working-class people. All the houses were either bungalows or townhouses. He saw pickup trucks and minivans in the driveways. He entered one part of town where the houses were suddenly bigger. He saw metal front gates. Six-foot walls, manicured lawns, and double or triple garages. All towns had neighborhoods where the more affluent congregated together. The rich liked to live among the rich, and this place was no exception.

He pulled in front of a large house. Through the front gate, he could see several high-end cars in the driveway.

The house belonged to Rick Wallen, and if Callaway was right, Wallen was a recruiter for Grannex Investments. How else could he afford all the finer things in life?

Callaway had no proof that Wallen was making money off Grannex's victims. He could be legally making money by helping others as a lifestyle guru. A lot of them had online videos and courses. They also held seminars or wrote self-help books.

Rick Wallen only had a high school diploma, but on his website, he stated he went to Stanford University. He may have gotten into Stanford, but that didn't mean he graduated from there.

Everything on Grannex Investments' website was fabrication and lies. None of their board members or employees even existed. It was a scam, through and through. And Wallen was complicit in promoting that scam.

As he sat in his Charger, Callaway considered what to do next. *Should I go up and ring the bell? But what will I say?* he thought. *I know you are a scammer, and I want you to return my client's money? He'd laugh in my face, or maybe call the cops on me.*

He had only one option: he would try to dig up as much dirt on Wallen as possible. There had to be a weakness Callaway could exploit. He hated doing it. It was underhanded, and, in some ways, outright blackmail. But if Wallen was who he thought he was, Callaway had no qualms about doing it.

People like Wallen were predators. They took advantage of the vulnerable. Most regular folks wanted a leg up. They weren't savvy enough to know that all get-rich-quick schemes were scams.

A majority of the laws were lenient toward white-collar crimes. A scammer could get five years for the crime, but he would only serve a third of that before he was let out. These people knew how to hide the money they had stolen, and once free, they continued to enjoy the fruits of their crime. The victims, on the other hand, would have to start their lives from the bottom again. Some would be so devastated by the loss that they would turn to alcohol or drugs to numb the pain, and others would see no other way out but to end their lives.

Callaway despised people like Wallen. He would not leave here until he had spoken to him. He didn't have to wait long.

The gates began to open, and a moment later, a red Ferrari pulled out.

Callaway decided to follow.

## EIGHTY-ONE

Crenshaw was used to dealing with stress. It came with the profession he had chosen. Blackmail at the highest level was not for the faint of heart. One had to roll with the punches and deal with whatever came their way. For that reason, he rarely became rattled. He knew fretting about problems he couldn't control would do him no good. There was always a solution to every situation. He was confident he would find a way out.

This was different. This was uncharted territory.

He was accustomed to being in control. Dark Box worked on the fringes of society. They were a ghost, an enigma to those who had the misfortune of dealing with them. They didn't just skirt the law. They broke it. This made them dangerous and highly unpredictable. Their victims didn't know how far they would go. Dark Box went as far as necessary to get the job done.

If they had to destroy someone's reputation, they did just that.

If they had to coerce someone into doing something they weren't willing to do, they did that too.

If they had to commit murder to rectify a problem, they did that as well.

Nothing was off-limits. Everything was fair game. Women. Children. The elderly. It didn't matter.

What mattered was that their clients were satisfied, and Dark Box was compensated for their services.

But things were suddenly different. The game had changed, and not in their favor.

They now had to deal with two problems instead of one.

Laura Sinclair was back in town.

Crenshaw never believed Dr. Sinclair was dead and that her husband was responsible for her death.

The news of her so-called demise had come unexpectedly. It had taken him by surprise. He could see why she and her husband had gone to such lengths.

They were right to fear Dark Box, he believed. He would have done everything to shut her up. Even if it meant going after her daughter.

A parent's love for their child knows no bounds. They would do anything to protect them. Crenshaw never had any children of his own. He knew it would have been a liability in his line of work. His enemies would have used them against him.

When Roger Sinclair had gone to prison for the crime, Crenshaw had to back off. He had to leave the little girl alone. Plus, if by some miracle, Dr. Sinclair was still alive and well, they could use the girl as leverage.

Crenshaw always kept an eye out. He had tapped the grandmother's phone for any suspicious calls. He had paid guards at the prison in case Dr. Sinclair decided to contact her husband. He had informants everywhere feeding him information.

One of those informants had seen a mysterious woman appear at a motel. Had Kristoff not messed up and let this woman slip away, this problem surely would have been resolved.

But now Crenshaw had another problem to deal with.

The private investigator was seen at Carta Aluminum's headquarters. He had gone there asking about Tara Sandhu. How much did this private investigator know? Was he aware that Dark Box was blackmailing Denise Hollins at the behest of her father?

Wilbur Graft would not be forgiving if he found out a private eye was snooping around his business. If Graft went down, he would use his considerable power to take Crenshaw and Dark Box down with him.

Crenshaw would not let that happen. It was time to clean this mess up.

He had already called Kristoff with specific instructions.

Kill the private investigator before he exposed the truth—the very truth that could be the undoing of him and Dark Box.

## EIGHTY-TWO

Callaway spent several hours following Rick Wallen's red Ferrari around Bellview County.

He took photographs of each place Wallen visited. He even took a moment to find out more about Wallen, things only a private investigator would be able to dig up.

When Wallen returned to his estate, Callaway decided to go speak to him.

He rang the buzzer at the gate.

"Who's this?" asked Wallen over the intercom.

Callaway saw a camera above the gate. He smiled and waved at it.

"What do you want?" Wallen asked.

"We have to talk, Mr. Wallen," Callaway replied.

"I don't know you, so we have nothing to say to each other."

Callaway held up his digital camera. "I know you just came back from a place called the Dragon Massage Parlor. I have photos if you don't believe me."

There was silence on the line. "I… I went there for a massage. I have a sore back."

"I'm sure you do. But from what I know, the parlor is known for other services as well."

"I wasn't aware of that. I didn't get any other service except for a back rub."

"That's fine. I'll just pass these photos on to your parole officer. He can go and speak to the girls to see which service was performed. I'm sure one of them will tell the truth. Most of those girls are undocumented, and they wouldn't want any trouble with the law."

There was heavy breathing on the line.

The gate buzzed open.

Callaway walked up to the house. Rick Wallen came out. He was wearing a light-colored golf shirt, white shorts, and white runners. His tattooed, toned arms were exposed. He also wore a diamond-encrusted watch.

"Who are you?" he demanded.

"Lee Callaway. Private Investigator."

"Who hired you to follow me?"

"That's not important. What's important is that as part of your parole, you weren't supposed to frequent strip clubs, exotic massage parlors, or even nightclubs. You must have really roughed up those escorts for the judge to place all these restrictions on you."

Wallen shook his head. "I got carried away, okay? I thought those girls would be okay with that kind of stuff."

"They weren't. And that judge wasn't okay with it, either."

Wallen stared at him. "Do you want money? How much?"

"Fifty-eight thousand dollars."

Wallen almost fell back. "Fifty-eight grand? Are you crazy? I don't have that kind of money."

Callaway pointed to the Ferrari and the yellow Lamborghini in the driveway. He then pointed to the house. "Seems like you can afford it."

Wallen looked away and fell silent.

"Listen," Callaway said. "What do you do for Grannex Investments anyway?"

Wallen's eyes widened. "Is that why you're here?"

"I am. Grannex stole money from one of my clients."

"Grannex didn't steal anything. Those people aren't victims. They're investors."

Callaway's blood was about to boil. "Don't give me that crap. You, or whoever is in charge of Grannex, is running a Ponzi scheme. There are no investments. People aren't earning a return. In the beginning, you were paying people from their own investments. And when the money started running out, you brought in more so-called investors to keep the entire thing from falling apart. Isn't that right?"

"You got no proof of that," Wallen said, crossing his arms over his chest.

"I don't have to prove anything. I just have to send these photos to your parole officer."

"Okay, okay." Wallen put his hands up. "Please don't do that. I can't go back to jail."

Callaway stared at him. Wallen looked like he took very good care of himself. His hair was dyed, his eyebrows were plucked, and his skin was without a blemish. He wouldn't last a day behind bars. The inmates would eat him up.

"First, tell me what you do for Grannex," Callaway said.

"I get investors."

*I was right*, Callaway thought. "So, you're a recruiter?"

Wallen nodded.

"And they pay you a referral fee for each new investor?"

"Not exactly."

"Then what?"

Wallen hesitated.

## EIGHTY-THREE

"Don't make me walk out of here upset," Callaway said to Wallen.

Wallen sighed. "I also get a percentage of the amount people invest."

Callaway's eyes narrowed. "That's why you push people to invest more and more money into Grannex. So you can get your cut."

"Yes. I encourage them to get a line of credit. A second mortgage. Borrow money from family and friends. Anything to get them to keep the cash flowing in."

"Is that what you did with Bruce Chen?" Callaway asked.

Wallen blinked. "Who?"

"Don't play with me. Bruce Chen. You took fifty-eight thousand from him and his mother."

"I don't know that name, I swear. If I did, I would tell you."

Wallen had no reason to lie, Callaway knew. He had incriminating evidence against him.

"Who's behind Grannex Investments?" Callaway asked.

"I don't really know. No one's ever told us who's running it. I think it's someone from Europe. Could be Portugal or Spain."

"How did you get involved with Grannex?"

"I was hired by someone online. I never met him in person. We messaged each other, and then he told me to take a plane to Vegas for a conference. He knew I had done online marketing, so he said I was the perfect candidate they were looking for. When I got there, I found there were other people like me— young, motivated, eager to change our lives."

"How many were at this conference?"

"I didn't count, but a couple of dozen for sure."

"Who was the guy running it?"

"He just told us his name was Marcos. He said if we listened, he could teach us how to make a lot of money. So, over the course of four days, he taught us how to find and convince people to invest in Grannex."

Callaway scoffed. "And you willingly went along with the scam?"

"I didn't know it was a scam until I started getting big checks from them. Next thing I knew, I was hooked. I just kept hustling. Bringing in new investors each and every day."

"And that's how you're able to maintain this lifestyle," Callaway said.

"This is really all for show, man," Wallen said. "I don't own anything."

"What about that watch?"

"It's on loan from a jeweler."'

"Those cars?"

"On lease."

"The house?"

"Rented."

Callaway was confused. "Why?"

"It's to convince people I'm successful, or else they won't invest their money through me."

"What about all the money you made from fees?"

Wallen looked away. "I spent most of it on nice trips. Flying on private jets. On girls. It's so I can promote my brand online."

"Your brand?" Callaway asked.

"Yeah, you know… get more subscribers to my channel. More likes on my page. I look at it as an investment."

*That's pretty big talk coming from a hustler,* Callaway thought. He shook his head. "Listen, I don't care what you did with the money. You are part of the problem. You benefited from Grannex's scam. You owe my client fifty-eight thousand dollars."

"I told you, I don't have that kind of money, man."

"Go to the bank and get a line of credit."

"You don't think I've tried?" Wallen said. "When they see I don't have much collateral, they decline my request."

Callaway's ears began to ring. He felt like his head was about to explode. He took a deep breath and said, "The money Grannex took affected two people I know. One's in the hospital fighting for his life, and the other may lose her business and property."

"Sorry to hear that, but there's nothing I can do."

Callaway knew he couldn't leave here empty-handed. Wallen was a scammer, a low-life thief. He would find a way to leave the country and disappear for good. His parole violation wouldn't extend beyond international borders. He wasn't a convicted murderer or a high-profile criminal. The local police wouldn't bother going after him until he returned to the United States, which could be years from now, or never.

Callaway was not about to take any chances.

"Get in your car," Callaway said. "We're going for a ride."

"Where're we going?" Wallen asked. There was a glint of fear in his eyes.

"Some place where you can get me the money I want," Callaway replied.

## EIGHTY-FOUR

Fire Chief Brian Dawkins had a gravely voice. His hair had begun to show patches of silver. He had a slight paunch, which hung over his belt. His wedding ring was wrapped tightly around one of his pudgy fingers.

Behind him on the wall of his office were photos of Dawkins with the mayor, the governor, and one with a former president. There were also medals and plaques in recognition of the outstanding work he had done.

After thirty years of serving the community as a firefighter, Dawkins had earned the respect of his peers.

Holt and Fisher sat across from him in his office.

Dawkins frowned. "I remember the case," he said. "But it was a couple of years ago, wasn't it?"

"Three years, to be precise," Holt said.

Dawkins nodded.

"What can you tell us about the case, sir?" Fisher asked.

"What do you want to know?"

"Everything."

Dawkins took a deep breath. They could tell he wasn't pleased with someone from the police questioning him about an older case. The police department and the fire department had never gotten along. Holt and Fisher didn't understand why. The fire department wanted to know if the fire was deliberate or an accident, and the police wanted to know who was behind it. They both served a common purpose, to get to the bottom of the truth. It was egos at the higher levels that prevented them from doing so.

"It was arson, no doubt about it," Dawkins said. "The fire was started with lighter fluid—the kind you use for most charcoal barbecues. But it was something else that spread the fire quickly and violently."

"What was the accelerant?" Fisher asked.

"Gasoline. The arsonist had doused every corner of the house with gasoline. He wanted that house to go up in flames, and fast."

"Then how did you know it was lighter fluid that started the fire?" Holt asked.

"The arsonist was standing in the driveway holding the bottle of fluid in his hand, so it wasn't that hard to put two and two together." Dawkins paused. "It took my boys several hours to control that fire. We were lucky it didn't spread to adjacent houses."

"Did you find something once you dug through the rubble?" Holt asked.

"Find what?" Dawkins asked.

"A body, perhaps."

Dawkins almost laughed. "The fire was so intense, there was nothing left but ash. The arsonist wanted this outcome so that we couldn't find anything." Dawkins stared at them. "Why are you looking into it now?"

"We have reason to believe the victim is still alive," Fisher said.

Dawkins blinked. His eyes narrowed. "Didn't the arsonist confess to killing his wife and burning her body in the process?"

"He confessed to burning the house, but he never confessed to murdering his wife," Fisher replied. "We always assumed she was inside when he torched the house."

"So, why are you questioning me about it now?"

"We wanted to know if you'd found his wife's body."

Dawkins's face hardened. "You want to know whether we messed up."

"That's not what we're saying, sir," Holt quickly replied.

Dawkins leaned forward in his chair. "We didn't go looking for any evidence of murder. That's not our job. When we got word from the state attorney that the perpetrator had confessed to the crime, we went from searching for survivors to cleaning up the scene. Our priorities suddenly changed. We had to make sure there was nothing left on the property that could reignite the fire, so we had to clear it out as quickly and safely as possible."

"We understand, but…" Fisher began.

He glared at her. "No, you don't understand, detectives. You have no idea how we operate. Most of the guys in my station are volunteers. They have other jobs to pay the bills. To make matters worse, our budget keeps getting slashed each year. Our vehicles and equipment are at least twenty years old. Unless the state or any other department was willing to pay for us to go in and dig for clues, we just clean it up."

Holt and Fisher were silent. They knew he was right. The government was constantly reducing funding to cities and municipalities.

"Listen, guys," Dawkins said, his voice calmer. "The arsonist's lawyer didn't ask to see a body, either, so there was no pressure on us to do anything. We determined the cause of the fire and provided our findings to whoever was interested in looking at it. This included the prosecution and defense. When no one contacted us, we closed the case. If the victim is alive as you say she is, then you have an innocent man in prison. He's guilty of property damage, but maybe he's not guilty of murder. That's for you guys to determine, not us."

## EIGHTY-FIVE

Callaway was back at the hospital. He peeked through the window and saw Ms. Chen at Bruce's bedside. She was holding his hand to comfort him. Bruce was still hooked up to tubes and monitors, but he no longer required an oxygen mask.

Callaway didn't feel like disturbing them. He could always speak to Ms. Chen when she returned to the shop.

He had turned to leave when the door opened.

"Mr. Callaway," Ms. Chen said. "What are you doing here?"

"I wanted to see you… and see Bruce."

"Come in."

He went inside. The beeping from the heart monitor was much louder now.

"The doctors came by earlier," Ms. Chen said. "The paramedics did a great job of pumping the painkillers out of his body. If it wasn't for their quick action, Bruce might have gone into a severe coma. But now the doctors believe Bruce will make a full recovery."

"That's good to hear," Callaway said, relieved.

She smiled. "I keep telling him that I forgive him," she said. "I don't care what happened to the money. I just want him to open his eyes. He's more important than the shop. He's more important than anything I own. I will start saving again for retirement. I did it before. I can do it again. It might take a little longer, but it doesn't matter. Just as long as my son is okay."

"I hope you won't have to save for retirement for too long."

Callaway reached into his jacket pocket and pulled out a thick and heavy envelope. He held it out for her.

"What is this?" Ms. Chen asked, confused.

"Fifty-eight thousand dollars. That's the amount of money Bruce invested in the scam."

"How… how did you get it?" she stammered.

"I have my ways."

Callaway had driven Rick Wallen to Mason and Baxter. Mason was a ruthless loan shark, and the only thing he cared about was making money. And Baxter, Mason's muscle, made sure people paid back the money they had borrowed from Mason—plus interest, of course. Baxter was a brute. If Wallen tried to renege on repaying his debt, Baxter would be on him like a hound. He would go to great lengths to punish Wallen.

Mason was grateful for the business, and he offered Callaway a discount on the interest the next time he came in for a loan, which Callaway hoped would be never.

Callaway hated having to throw Wallen to the wolves, but Wallen was no sheep. He was a wolf in sheep's clothing. He knew that what he was doing was wrong, but he still kept roping people into the scam.

*Maybe this will teach him a lesson*, Callaway thought. *Maybe he can stop cheating people out of their hard-earned money.*

There was also a possibility that Wallen could ramp up the promotion of the scam. After all, he now owed sixty-grand to Mason and Baxter. But Callaway had warned him that he would be keeping an eye on him, and if it looked like Wallen was back to his old habits, a copy of the photos would be couriered to his parole officer.

Callaway didn't take his word that he would find other ways to pay the money back. Once a liar, always a liar, Callaway believed. Mason would keep Wallen honest. At Callaway's behest, Mason let Wallen go on a monthly repayment plan. Callaway believed him when he said that everything was either a lease or a rental. Wallen would have to find a legitimate way to earn a living, just like everyone else.

Ms. Chen stared at the envelope but didn't touch it.

"Don't worry," he said. "It's all in there."

She slowly reached over and took the envelope. She then fell into the chair and clutched the envelope to her chest. Tears streamed down her face.

"Thank you," she said, looking up at him. "Thank you so much."

Callaway's eyes turned moist, too.

"You're welcome," he quietly replied.

## EIGHTY-SIX

Holt and Fisher decided to go speak to Diane Aldershot, mother of Laura Sinclair. Maybe she could shed some light on what might have happened to her daughter.

*How is it possible that a person who was murdered is still alive?* Fisher thought. She knew the answer was simple.

*Laura Sinclair never died.*

They didn't blame Chief Dawkins, nor did they blame the detective at the scene. That detective was retired and was living on a beach in Puerto Rico. Holt and Fisher decided against contacting him. They knew he would say the same thing Chief Dawkins had said: There was no need to dig up a body. Roger Sinclair had confessed to the crime. Also, Laura Sinclair had disappeared at the exact moment her husband had torched the house. This fit the time of her death perfectly. She was, perhaps, strangled or stabbed (the method of death was never determined), and then her body was burned to cover the crime. Had someone seen her after her supposed death, it would have raised more scrutiny.

Holt and Fisher planned to speak to Roger Sinclair at the state penitentiary. They doubted he would give them anything useful. After all, he had kept his mouth shut for the past three years. But they wanted to see his reaction when they told him what they'd found on the envelope.

This raised another set of questions for them. What if someone had *planted* the DNA on the envelope? They weren't sure how it could be done, but it wasn't out of the realm of possibility. Stranger things had happened before. People who were pronounced dead were suddenly alive. People who were deemed guilty with certainty were suddenly innocent. Nothing could be ignored.

They rang the bell.

A woman answered the door.

"Diane Aldershot?" Fisher asked.

"Yes," the woman replied.

"I'm Detective Dana Fisher, and this is my partner, Detective Gregory Holt."

"What's this about, detectives?" she asked.

"It's about your daughter, Laura."

Diane Aldershot crossed her arms over her chest. "What about her? She died three years ago."

"We have found something that may contradict that."

"Are you saying my daughter is not dead?"

"That's exactly what I'm saying."

If they expected Diane Aldershot to fall to her knees at the thought of her daughter being alive, they didn't get that. Instead, she glared at them. "Do you have proof of this?"

"We have found her DNA on an envelope she mailed to someone."

"But have you found *her*?"

"No... no, we haven't," Fisher stammered in reply.

"Then you've found nothing," Diane said. "I held a funeral for my daughter three years ago. I don't need you to tell me—"

She was interrupted when a little girl appeared next to her.

"Are you the police?" the girl asked.

"Millie," Diane said, "please go inside."

The girl didn't move.

Fisher leaned down, smiled, and said, "We're police officers."

"And are you looking for my mom?" Millie asked.

"We... we would like to find her, yes."

Millie broke into a wide smile. "There's someone else looking for my mom, too."

"Who?" Fisher asked.

"Millie," her grandmother scolded her.

"He's a private investigator," Millie continued. "I hired him to find my mom."

"Can you tell me his name?" Fisher asked.

## EIGHTY-SEVEN

Callaway was back at his office. He felt good about what he'd done for the Chens. His landlady was overwhelmed. She couldn't stop crying and thanking him. He was overcome with emotion, too.

Ms. Chen tried to pay him something from the envelope. Callaway didn't feel comfortable taking any money. Her son was still not out of the danger zone. The doctors believed he would be back to his normal self, and Callaway had no reason to doubt that. But more than that, he had a soft spot for the Chen family.

Ms. Chen could have kicked him out a long time ago for not paying his rent. He could've returned to his office one day to find the lock had been changed and all his belongings at the curb. The fact that she had never raised the rent by a single penny, even though the rent was the cheapest in the city, spoke volumes to him.

He had made two requests to Ms. Chen, though. One was that she let him stay in his office rent-free for the next couple of months, which she agreed to without hesitation. And the second was that she promise not to sell the shop or the building. She smiled, and while clutching the envelope tightly, she assured him there was no need for her to do that. She wouldn't be going anywhere anytime soon.

That was all Callaway needed to hear.

He smiled as he sat behind his laptop. He didn't bother turning the machine on. He just wanted to savor this moment. In his line of work, there weren't that many happy endings. Most of his investigations were chasing cheaters, which led to the end of marriages, where families were shattered, and people were no longer sure who they could trust.

This small victory with the Chens, he would hold on to for as long as he could.

His smile instantly faded when he heard a sound.

Someone was rushing up the metal stairs.

Before he could pull out his cell phone and enable the camera app to see who was outside, there was a knock at his door.

He opened the drawer on his desk and pulled out his weapon. He checked to see if the safety was off.

He moved to the door. "Who is it?" he asked.

"Mr. Callaway?" a female voice replied.

"Yes," he said slowly.

"Please open the door. I need to talk to you."'

"Talk about what?"

"Millie," she said.

He blinked. He then unlocked the bolt and opened the door slightly. He held his weapon by his side. "Who are you?"

"I'm the woman you've been searching for," she replied. "I'm Laura Sinclair."

## EIGHTY-EIGHT

Dr. Laura Sinclair sat on the sofa with her arms wrapped around her body. She had on a sweatshirt, blue jeans, and running shoes. She had a baseball cap on her head. Strands of blonde hair hung out from the sides. She was small, around five-foot-two, but she was skinny to the bone, which made her look even smaller.

She looked like a scared girl rather than a medical doctor.

"How did you find me?" Callaway asked.

"I've been keeping in touch with my mother," she replied. "It's not easy communicating with her. I know they're listening in on our conversations."

"Who is?"

"I don't know, but they are. The last time I spoke to my mother, I acted like I was an old friend from out of state. My mother jokingly mentioned that Millie had hired a private investigator. She told me your name. If someone was listening in, they would think these two women were amused by what a nine-year-old was up to, that it was harmless fun, but I knew it was serious."

Callaway smiled. "So, *you* were sending Millie those birthday cards."

Laura nodded.

"Is that why you came back?" Callaway then asked. "Because I was looking for you?"

She shook her head. "That was a coincidence. I came back to meet someone."

Callaway's eyes widened. "You were supposed to meet Denise Hollins at a mall's food court, isn't that right?"

Laura nodded again. "I always kept an eye on what was going on at Carta Aluminum. I heard rumblings that their CEO was under siege, that someone wanted her gone. It wasn't a secret what was going on with her family, considering Wilbur Graft is her father and the founder of Carta Aluminum."

*Now the puzzle is starting to come together*, Callaway thought.

"You knew Tara Sandhu. She was one of your patients."

"I knew her well enough."

"You also knew she was in a relationship with Wilbur Graft, didn't you?"

"I did."

"You came back to tell Denise Hollins all about the affair."

"But I never got that chance. There were people following her, and I feared once they saw me, I would be exposed, and everything we had worked so hard to create would be for nothing."

"When you say *we*, who do you mean?" Callaway asked.

"Isn't it obvious by now?"

*It is*, he thought. "Your husband, Roger," he said.

She nodded.

"But why?" he asked. "Why fake your death and have your husband take the fall for it?"

"I know it doesn't make sense. My husband made the ultimate sacrifice. Knowing that he was locked up in a cell tore away at me, but I didn't fare any better. I had to run away, leave our daughter behind." Her eyes welled up. "I had to constantly look over my shoulder. I didn't know when they would show up and finish what they had started."

"Where did you go?" Callaway asked.

"I knew I couldn't stay in Milton, or in the country for that matter. Sooner or later, someone I knew would see me. It would not only be dangerous for me, but also for Roger and Millie. I found a truck driver, and he smuggled me across the border to Mexico. The border agents aren't too picky about people going from America to Mexico, but they are the other way around."

"So, how did you get back into the country?" Callaway asked.

"It was actually quite easy. I still had my US passport and IDs. I'm supposed to be dead, but that doesn't show up anywhere unless someone goes digging further. I'm also not flagged for any violations in any government databases. Nothing would come up from the local police or from the FBI. The only concern was if the border agent recognized me from the news. When the border agent ran my name through the system and it came back clear, he let me drive straight through and moved on to the next person. It helped that I picked the busiest time of day to pass through."

Callaway said, "You still didn't answer my question. Why go through this charade anyway?"

"It was to protect our daughter."

"Millie was in danger?" Callaway asked.

"We started getting anonymous packages with photos of Millie playing in the school yard, of her getting in and out of the car, of her buying groceries with us. It was a message to us. They were watching our every move, and they were particularly keeping an eye on Millie. We thought about taking her out of class, keeping her at home, but even that didn't feel safe enough."

"Why didn't you go to the police?"

"That's the first thing we thought of. But we had no proof that our lives were in danger. All we had were these photos. They could have been taken by anyone, for any reason. The police may not have taken us seriously unless there was a clear threat made against us. Even if they had, they would only send a patrol car to our house a few times a day, but who's to say how long they would've done that? Eventually, we would have been on our own. We would have had to fend for ourselves." Laura paused and stared at her hands. "The danger was real and imminent."

"How can you be so sure?" Callaway asked. "These people could've been bluffing."

She looked him in the eye. "I know because of what happened to Tara."

Callaway sat up straight in his chair. "What *did* happen to her?"

"As you know, Tara was one of my patients. I would see her regularly."

"For what?"

"I can't say."

"Why not?"

"I'll cite doctor/patient relationship."

"You're the second person who's cited that."

"Dr. Reza?" Laura asked.

He nodded.

"He's a good man and a good doctor."

"Did he know you weren't really dead?" Callaway asked.

"He knew enough to keep the lie going."

"Okay, let's go back to Tara. What happened to her?"

"I don't know exactly," Laura replied, "but I believe these people killed her."

"How can you be so sure?"

"A few days before her disappearance, she told me her life was in danger. That someone wanted to kill her."

"Who?"

"I would rather not say right now."

Callaway rubbed his chin. He shook his head. "That still doesn't mean she's dead. Her body hasn't been found. She could have run away like you did."

"I know she's gone because…"

Dr. Sinclair went silent.

"Because of what?"

"I'm sorry, but I'll cite doctor/patient relationship again."

Callaway stood up and paced about the office. "You know, because of you, your husband is still in prison."

"It was only supposed to be for a short time, until I could find a way back home and expose what had happened. I thought that opportunity would be with Denise Hollins. She's still the CEO of Carta Aluminum. She has the resources and the power to fight back."

"But you didn't suspect that she was also being blackmailed?" Callaway said.

"I wasn't aware of the full scope of the problem. I knew her relationship with her father was strained, which I knew would work in my favor. I just didn't know she was in the same predicament as me—having to decide between protecting her family or doing the right thing."

"Do you think she would still help you if you told her the truth?"

"I do. She's a mother. She would understand."

Callaway was about to ask her what she meant when there was a knock at the door.

## EIGHTY-NINE

Kristoff and Andrei were stationed outside the private investigator's office. The moment he received the phone call from his boss, they drove straight over. Crenshaw was losing his nerve. He wanted immediate results. He had given Kristoff the go-ahead to eliminate the private investigator. It was something Crenshaw had never done before. He preferred not to think about things like this. He didn't want the weight of someone's death on his mind and soul. That didn't mean Crenshaw was against such methods. On the contrary, he believed in the use of force. He just didn't like giving kill orders.

If you asked Kristoff, Crenshaw was just as guilty as them. Nazi commanders who ordered their men to execute innocent civilians were also punished for those crimes along with the soldiers. No one was innocent. They all had blood on their hands. Crenshaw's hands were soaked deep in red. He was the mastermind behind Dark Box. He was one who met the clients and decided which jobs to take.

In the time Kristoff had worked for Crenshaw, his boss rarely turned a job down. The more complex the job, the more money Crenshaw demanded. And Crenshaw worshipped money above everything else.

Crenshaw didn't care who got hurt and who didn't. This was business for him. Nothing more and nothing less.

Kristoff held no opinion either way. He liked what he did. So did Andrei. They were survivors. They did whatever was necessary to take care of themselves. That didn't mean they wouldn't turn on Crenshaw. The moment Crenshaw tried to stiff them on their agreed-upon fee, he could expect a bullet in his head. They operated on the premise of *eat or be eaten*. Crenshaw knew that. He wasn't stupid enough to try anything funny with them. He would keep the money flowing, but that would only be possible if they kept completing their tasks.

Kristoff was aware that the client was not pleased with their results. And Kristoff took full responsibility for this. He couldn't blame Andrei for the failure. Andrei followed his lead. He did whatever Kristoff asked of him. Unlike Crenshaw, who would turn on even his mother to save himself, Kristoff was loyal to Andrei. He would not let Andrei suffer for his mistakes. Kristoff would make sure the job was done.

And this was the perfect opportunity to do it right.

A moment ago, he had seen the private investigator go to his office. And as luck would have it, he saw the woman follow right after him.

Kristoff was brimming with glee. He couldn't believe he could kill them both at the same time. It was the perfect opportunity, one that he was not about to lose.

*It's time to end this,* he thought.

# NINETY

"They found me," Laura Sinclair said.

"Who found you?" Callaway asked.

"The people I'm running from."

"Right," he said, feeling stupid for asking. He reached over and pulled his weapon from the desk drawer again. He had thumbed the safety and put the gun back when he realized Laura Sinclair was not a threat.

"Don't open the door," she said, standing up.

He put his finger to his lips. "Stay back," he whispered to her.

He walked over to the door. It was metal, but he wasn't sure how thick it was. *Could it withstand a barrage of bullets?* he thought. *Maybe it depends on the type of weapon.*

If the people behind the door had a shotgun or even an assault rifle, the chance of Callaway avoiding serious injury was slim to none.

He took a deep breath and said in a loud voice, "Who is it?"

"It's me, Dana."

"Fisher?" he said to confirm.

"Yes. Open the door."

*Fine time to forget to check the security camera app*, Callaway thought.

He flicked the safety back on and tucked the weapon in the back of his belt.

"You can't tell them I'm here," Laura Sinclair said.

"I know her," Callaway said, trying to calm her.

"You can't trust anyone."

"I can trust her. She's a friend."

Laura Sinclair stared at him. She then nodded.

"Okay," he said to her. He turned and then opened the door an inch. He saw Fisher and Holt standing on the landing. "What's up, Dana?" he said with a smile.

"We need to talk," she said.

"About what?"

"About Laura Sinclair."

"Who?" Callaway said.

Holt jumped in. "Don't play dumb. We know you were hired to find Dr. Sinclair."

*Still warm and fuzzy, aren't you, Holt?* Callaway thought.

Callaway and Holt had a testy relationship. Holt had no respect for private investigators. He thought they were unnecessary, when there were real police officers to solve crimes. Callaway thought Holt was a hard ass. Once he got someone in his sights, he rarely changed his mind. Over time, though, the relationship had thawed. But that still didn't mean they liked each other.

Callaway turned to Holt. "And who hired me exactly?"

"Laura Sinclair's daughter."

"How old is she?"

"Nine."

"Do you think I would take a case from a nine-year-old?"

"You would take a case from a leper just as long as he paid," Holt growled.

"Ouch," Callaway said. "That actually hurt."

"Stop it," Fisher said. "We're not here to see you go at each other."

"Well, he started it," Callaway said.

"I did not," Holt said.

"You did when you called me dumb."

"I said you were *playing* dumb."

"Same thing."

Fisher yelled, "Enough! Both of you!"

Holt crossed his arms over his chest. Callaway looked away.

Fisher took a deep breath to calm herself. She then said to Callaway, "We have reason to believe that Laura Sinclair might not be dead. And we also have reason to believe that her life might be in danger."

"How can you be sure of either of those things?" Callaway inquired.

She looked over at Holt, who was not pleased with what she was about to tell him. Holt didn't like sharing information on active cases, especially not with a civilian. But Fisher didn't care.

She looked at Callaway. "We have DNA evidence that shows she could still be alive. And we have footage of a man with a gun looking for her at a motel."

"Okay," Callaway said.

"We want to know if you've discovered anything that might help us."

"I can say you are correct on both accounts."

"What?" Fisher said, looking unsure.

"Laura Sinclair is alive, and someone does want her dead."

"How can you be so sure?" Holt interjected.

Callaway looked at him. "Because she's inside my office right now."

## NINETY-ONE

Kristoff and Andrei were about to get out of the car when they saw a truck pull up in front of the noodle shop. Construction workers quickly got out and began patching up a pot-hole next to the sidewalk.

Kristoff let out an audible curse.

This was their chance to get the woman and the private investigator. Their targets would be helpless once Kristoff and Andrei made their way up to the office.

But their entry to the office was blocked by the construction workers. Even if Kristoff and Andrei got past them, their exit would be complicated. If either the woman or the private investigator made a noise, the construction workers would hear it.

Kristoff was not prepared to shoot the workers just to make his escape. There were three of them. One in the truck and two working on the pot-hole. There would be five dead bodies if Kristoff and Andrei made their move.

Crenshaw would lose his mind if that were to happen. The carnage would alert not only the local authorities, but the federal as well. The heat would be too much. Kristoff and Andrei would have to go into hiding.

They might even have to leave the country, something neither of them wanted to do. They had come from an authoritarian regime. Kristoff and Andrei had come to enjoy the freedom America bestowed on its people, even if they blatantly broke its rule of law.

Andrei stirred next to him. He was itching for a fight. Ever since the problem at the motel, Kristoff had to keep him muzzled. Andrei was not known for his patience, and he was a firm believer in the saying, *Shoot first, ask questions later.*

Sooner or later, Kristoff would have to unleash Andrei and let him do what he was good at. But this was not the time. Any decision he made could have consequences down the road.

Fortunately, the construction workers were done patching up the hole. They got in the truck and moved on.

Now was their time.

Andrei opened the passenger door.

Kristoff put his hand out to stop him.

He nodded in the direction of the noodle shop.

Two people were making their way to the side of the building. They were on their way to the office above the noodle shop.

Kristoff recognized them. They were the detectives he'd seen at the motel.

He turned to Andrei and shook his head. His partner didn't need much convincing. Even he knew the risks were suddenly too much to take.

Kristoff couldn't believe they had lost a golden opportunity. He had them in a perfect spot. All he and Andrei had to do was go up, put a bullet in each of their heads, and get out.

Anger rose inside him, but he had to control himself. This was no time to let his emotions get the best of him.

They would have their chance.

## NINETY-TWO

Laura Sinclair told them everything. How she and her husband planned her supposed death, how she left the country for Mexico, and why she came back.

Holt and Fisher listened attentively. They had no reason not to believe her.

When she was done, Fisher asked, "Were you the one who called 9-1-1 about Trevor McGinty's murder?"

"I didn't know his name at the time," Laura Sinclair replied. "I mean, I had just moved into the room across from him the night before. But yes, I called 9-1-1."

"How did you know he was dead?" Fisher asked.

"After I had made my escape through the bathroom window, I returned to the motel to retrieve some of my stuff. I noticed the blinds were down in the unit across the hall. They were up the night before and even in the morning." Laura let out a tiny laugh. "It's absurd how much you end up noticing when you're on the run. Every little thing can mean life or death. That's how I was able to get out of the motel room so quickly. I had stuck a piece of paper between the door and the lock. When it fell to the ground, I knew someone was trying to get in. I didn't hesitate to get out. Anyway, the night I moved into my room, I did a reconnaissance of the motel. I made a note of each unit and who might be staying inside. The tenant across the hall from mine had a security camera installed. I could see the red light blinking whenever anyone passed his room. I debated moving to another room, but I didn't want to arouse any suspicions. The motel owner was already asking me too many questions."

"Like what?" Holt asked.

"Where did I come from? How long was I planning to stay at the motel? What did I do for a living? Things like that may seem innocuous, but like I said, your senses become heightened when you're always looking over your shoulder. Plus, I didn't switch rooms because I didn't plan on staying long anyway. After my meeting with Denise Hollins, I would go into hiding again. Not out of the country, but still somewhere far from Milton. I would let Denise use the information I gave her to get things in motion."

"I apologize for focusing on Trevor McGinty," Fisher said, "but it's still an ongoing investigation for us."

"Oh, right. When I didn't see the red light blinking through the window, I went inside to take a look. I also wanted to see if he could delete any recordings of me. I was even prepared to pay him to do it. I had come up with a story to go along with it. That I was running away from an abusive partner and that he was a former police officer—anything to show that my life was under serious threat and that I needed his help. But it didn't come to that. I found him in the bathroom, and that's when I called 9-1-1 from a payphone down the street."

Fisher asked, "You don't know who's after you?"

"No."

"Have you heard of an organization called Dark Box?"

"Dark Box?" Laura Sinclair repeated.

"Yes."

"I'm sorry I haven't. Who are they?"

"We did a search on them, and we came up with nothing," Fisher replied.

The room was silent. Callaway stood in the corner. He wanted to give the detectives enough space to speak to Laura Sinclair.

Fisher said, "The person who shot Trevor McGinty and Wayne Lemont is still out there looking for you, which means your life is still in danger."

"Now that I'm exposed," Laura Sinclair said, "my daughter and my mother are in danger as well.'"

"Where is your daughter now?"

Laura Sinclair looked at her watch. "She must be in school right now."

"Which school does she go to?"

Callaway chimed in. "It's the same school as Nina's. Millie is Nina's classmate."

Fisher mulled this over. "We should get your daughter someplace safe. I'll send a police cruiser to pick her up from school."

"Can you trust the officer?" Laura Sinclair asked. "These people have informants everywhere, even the police."

Fisher smiled. "You can trust Officer Lance McConnell. He'll risk his life to protect your daughter."

Holt said, "We should also take you someplace safe."

"Where?"

"We'll figure it out, but you have to come with us."

Laura Sinclair looked at Callaway.

"You should go with them," he said. "You can't keep running forever. This has to end now."

Laura Sinclair nodded.

## NINETY-THREE

As the clocked ticked, Kristoff was more agitated than ever. There was no telling what the woman had told the detectives.

He was certain she did not know about them or Crenshaw or even Dark Box. Crenshaw was careful not to reveal who was behind the blackmail or the murders. Kristoff and Andrei also never carried anything on their persons that could link them to Dark Box. But that didn't mean they wouldn't reveal their secrets to save themselves. If that happened, it would be every man for himself.

Kristoff was confident it would never come to that. Sure, there had been mistakes—the woman escaping from a second-floor room, Trevor McGinty recording him on his security camera, Wayne Lemont trying to squeeze him for more money—but two out of three had been taken care of. McGinty and Lemont would never utter another word from their graves. The woman would see her grave soon enough.

The detectives came out from the back of the noodle shop. They were followed by the woman.

Andrei shifted in his seat.

"No, Andrei," Kristoff said. "Not right now."

Andrei wouldn't hesitate to shoot and kill a police officer. Andrei had no respect for the badge. Anyone who got in their way was fair game.

Kristoff couldn't take that chance. He knew the detectives were armed. Any one of them could shoot Kristoff and Andrei. On top of that, a dead police officer would place a giant spotlight on them. Kristoff wasn't looking forward to being in the middle of a statewide manhunt.

The detectives and the woman got into an SUV.

"Let's see where they take her," Kristoff said.

"What about the private investigator?" Andrei asked. "He's still in his office."

"We know where to find him. We can always come back later to finish him off. Right now, we need to know what the police are up to. Our objective is to silence that woman, once and for all."

Andrei liked the sound of that.

## NINETY-FOUR

Alone in his office, Callaway suddenly felt relieved, but exhausted at the same time. He had just gotten a text from Ms. Chen that Bruce had opened his eyes. He was still under heavy medication, but that was one small step toward a long, but hopefully, complete recovery.

Ms. Chen would be by her son's side as he transitioned from the hospital back to his normal life. She could focus on his health and not have to worry too much about money anymore. The fifty-eight thousand dollars would be a nice buffer until she opened the noodle shop again.

Laura Sinclair was alive. Millie would have her mother again. Although Callaway didn't locate her—she came to him—he still had a hand in making certain she was safe. Holt and Fisher would make sure of that. They would also make sure that whoever was after Laura Sinclair—who made her abandon her career, her life, and her husband and daughter—would be found and punished.

Callaway would leave the latter for the police to deal with. He had done his job. He had fulfilled his duty to his clients.

He suddenly felt parched. He needed a drink.

He shoved his hand in his pocket and pulled out a few bills. He hadn't made a penny on either case. He stuffed the bills back in his pocket.

*This is no time for a drink*, he thought.

One misstep, and he could fall back into a life of self-destruction.

Nina and Patti gave meaning to his otherwise chaotic life. He wasn't living aimlessly anymore. His purpose was to make them happy and to make them proud of him.

He'd been a failure for too long. He didn't have a stable job or any savings he could tap into on a rainy day, and he owned nothing of particular value— if you didn't count the Dodge Charger, of course.

This wasn't a bad thing. People sometimes became too focused on material possessions. Callaway didn't have that problem. He never had enough money to spend on frivolous things.

But now, he had something to keep him grounded: his daughter and his ex-wife.

His main focus was to get his family back.

Instead of heading to the nearest bar, he decided to head home.

## NINETY-FIVE

Laura Sinclair was in a secure room inside the Milton Police Department. There was a keypad outside the door with a password only Holt and Fisher knew. They hoped this alleviated any concerns Laura Sinclair had about officers working for the people who were after her.

Fisher never believed for a moment that a member of the Milton PD would jeopardize the life of another person. But anything was possible. Only an hour ago, Laura Sinclair was presumed dead, and now she was alive and waiting inside a room.

Prior to coming to the Milton PD, Laura had made one request. Fisher had no reason not to oblige. In fact, she understood the urgency of it.

Fisher was standing in the lobby of the station. She watched as three people came in through the door. Officer Lance McConnell was followed by Diane Aldershot, who was holding the hand of Millie Sinclair.

"You must be Millie," Fisher said with a smile.

Millie looked hesitant. "Why are we here?" she asked.

"There is someone very special who wants to meet you."

"Who?" Millie asked, confused.

Fisher looked over at Diane Aldershot. Millie's grandmother smiled. She already knew, but hadn't told her granddaughter. She wanted it to be a surprise.

Fisher extended her hand to Millie. "Why don't you follow me, and I'll show you."

They walked down a narrow hall, through three sets of secure doors, and then made their way down a second hall.

Holt was standing before another door.

"This is Detective Holt," Fisher said.

He smiled. "Hi there."

Millie managed a smile, but she was still not sure why they had brought her here.

Fisher punched in the access code and then held the door open. "Come on," she said. "It's okay."

Millie went inside.

A woman was standing in the middle of the room.

Millie froze.

"Hi, Millie," the woman said.

Millie looked up at Fisher. Her grip tightened around her hand.

"It's okay, darling," the woman said. "It's Mommy."

Millie still did not let go of Fisher.

The woman then got down on her knees. She began to softly sing a song. "*Mommy loves you. Daddy loves you. Forever and ever. Because you will always be our cupcake.*"

"Mommy?" Millie said.

Laura Sinclair held out her arms. "Yes, baby. It's me."

Millie ran over, and Laura quickly wrapped her arms around her.

Tears flowed down her cheeks. "I'm so sorry, baby," she said. "I'm so sorry."

"Where have you been, Mommy?" Millie asked. "I missed you so much."

"I missed you too. I just had to go away for a little while, but I'm back now, and I'll never leave you again."

"You promise?"

"I promise. I love you so much, Millie."

Laura Sinclair held her little girl and cried uncontrollably.

Fisher's eyes turned moist. She worried she would break down, too.

She left the room. She wanted to give Laura and Millie this moment they'd been waiting for, for three years.

## NINETY-SIX

Callaway lived in a two-bedroom apartment on the fourteenth floor of an apartment complex. It was far bigger than any place he'd ever lived in, but the extra space was worth it. The first bedroom was for him. The second bedroom was for Nina when she came over to stay. He had even let her decorate it. He thought she would paint the walls pink. Instead, she painted it a darker shade of purple. She found the color calming. He thought it was an eyesore, but he said nothing.

*I guess I still have so much to learn about my little girl*, he had thought at the time.

He entered his unit and headed straight for the kitchen. He opened the fridge and pulled out a bottle of lemonade. He drank it down in one gulp. It was cold and refreshing.

He still kept a case of beer in the fridge. When he felt like it, he would open a bottle and drink it while sitting on his balcony.

Today he didn't reach for it. His mind was still unsettled. He was still thinking about Laura Sinclair and the people who were after her. Until they were caught, Laura and her family's lives would never be normal.

His apartment was sparingly furnished. In the living room, he had a futon, a coffee table, and an older model television. He had finally bought a dining table, but only because it was getting crowded having meals on the coffee table whenever Patti and Nina came over.

Callaway was now seeing his daughter and ex-wife several times a week. One night they would come over to his place, and the other nights he would go over to theirs.

He still held out hope for the day when they were all under one roof. He didn't care how long it took for that to happen. He just wanted it to happen. Period.

He checked his watch. It was still early. Nina was likely still in class, and Patti was probably finishing her shift at the hospital.

Callaway suddenly missed them. He couldn't wait to see them later that night.

## NINETY-SEVEN

Millie was doing her homework in the station's cafeteria. Her grandmother was helping her.

Fisher wanted to speak to Laura Sinclair in private, so she pulled her aside.

"We'll take you someplace safe," Fisher said. "It's not going to be your mother's home, I'm afraid. There's no telling who's watching it right now. So, I just need some time to arrange where to take you guys."

"No," Laura said.

Fisher blinked. "Sorry?"

"I want to help you find the people who threatened me, and whom I believe killed Tara Sandhu."

"How are you going to do that?"

"I want you to use me as bait."

"What?"

"Yes."

"But why?"

"I can't keep running like this. I can't leave my daughter again."

"You don't have to run anymore," Fisher said. "We will protect you."

"For how long?" Laura said. "These people will not stop until I'm dead."

"Why won't they stop?"

"I have a secret they want buried forever. It's a secret that made them go to great lengths to threaten me, my family, and my daughter. They will do everything they can to prevent it from coming out."

"What is this secret?"

"I can't tell you."

"That doesn't help me."

"You need to trust me," Laura pleaded. "I wouldn't put myself on the line if it wasn't important."

Fisher stared at her. "Okay, what do you want to do?"

## NINETY-EIGHT

Wilbur Graft entered the establishment. A man took his coat and then led him to an elegant room. The space was open with twelve-foot ceilings, a glass chandelier, and it was decorated with the finest furniture money could buy. The Persian rug alone cost ten thousand dollars.

Graft walked over to his usual chair. The leather came from Italy and was soft to the touch. The man quickly brought him a box of cigars and a bottle of cognac—Graft's favorite. He assisted Graft in lighting the cigar and then poured a glass of the cognac. He asked Graft if he needed anything else—a newspaper, a magazine, or even a light snack, which consisted of caviar and an assortment of other delectable foods. Graft waved him away.

Graft was at a gentlemen's lounge.

It was one of the oldest in the city. Only men were allowed to become members, and they had to have a high net worth. A group of older stalwarts decided who got in and who didn't. Graft was one of the decision-makers.

Whenever he was stressed, he came down to the lounge to relax.

He liked the atmosphere—quiet and peaceful. The members rarely spoke to each other. If they had anything to say, they would leave the room and go out into the hall.

Right now, the room was empty. All the members were worth millions, if not hundreds of millions of dollars. You didn't see them at the club at this time of the day. They were busy making more money. It was only later in the evening that the place became busy.

Graft wished he hadn't retired early. He wished he could still be running Carta Aluminum, but he figured the company would be in safer hands. By handing the reins to his daughter, Graft always assumed he would still be in control. And why not? He had built the business from the ground up. He had poured his blood and sweat into it. It was *his*.

He never imagined his own child would betray him and seize control of something *he* had bestowed upon her.

His jaw tightened, and he angrily bit into the cigar.

She would be punished for her ungratefulness, and Graft would be the one to do it.

He was not some old-timer who cashed his pension checks while sitting at home watching game shows. He was Wilbur Graft. A man not to be reckoned with.

He would take his company back, and he would destroy everyone who got in his way—even his daughter.

In fact, he would relish seeing the look on her face when he did just that.

Right now, though, he had another matter to deal with.

*Tara Sandhu.*

He shut his eyes as pain shot up through his head.

It was a mistake getting involved with her, but he always had a soft spot for women. He prided himself on the fact that he could get anyone he desired. He never forced himself on them. He didn't have to; they came to him. They knew who he was and what he could do for them.

Tara was just like the others. She was a lot of fun until he got bored with her. He would usually write them a nice check, buy them a house, or even pay for their entire education. But with Tara, it was different. It was complicated.

He knew it was time to make her go away, and he regretted waiting too long. Because of his hesitation, he now had a bigger problem on his plate.

The same man who had brought the cigar and cognac came over to him. "Sorry to bother you, sir," he said.

Cellphones were prohibited in the room. If someone needed to make or receive a call, they would have to go to another room.

"Who's on the line?" Graft grumbled. He didn't want to be disturbed. He had too much on his mind already.

"There's actually someone here who'd like to speak to you."

Graft looked at him. "Who?"

"It's a woman, sir."

"And does she have a name?"

"She said it's Dr. Laura Sinclair."

Graft stared at him for a moment, his fingers tight around the cigar. He then said, "Well, send her in."

"But sir, there's no speaking inside—"

"I know the damn rules!" Graft roared. "I made them. Just send her in."

"As you wish, sir."

## NINETY-NINE

Laura walked over and sat across from the man who had ruined her life. A part of her wanted to reach over and slap him across the face. The pain would be nothing compared to the loss she had endured, and it would be insignificant compared to what Tara Sandhu had lost.

Wilbur Graft glared at her. "We finally meet, Dr. Sinclair."

"I can't say it's a pleasure meeting you," she replied curtly.

"What do you want?"

"I want to talk about Tara."

"What is there to talk about?" he said, taking a puff of his cigar.

"How you seduced her."

"She knew what she was getting into. All my mistresses know that."

"She was only twenty-three. You were old enough to be her grandfather."

He chuckled. "If you are trying to insult me because of my age, I would advise you to stop. I was poorer than dirt when I was young. It was only when I got older that I was able to enjoy life to the fullest, so being old doesn't bother me. And I can assure you, it didn't bother any of the girls I was involved with, either."

"But she was just a child. She didn't know any better."

"She was fully aware of what she was doing. She got what she wanted out of the relationship. I bought her nice things. I even helped pay off her student loans."

"And what did *you* get out of the relationship?" Laura asked.

Graft let out a long plume of smoke. "I got the company of a beautiful woman. There is no law against that, is there?"

Laura was silent.

"She was of legal age," he said. "The relationship was consensual."

"Then why did you get rid of her?" Laura asked bluntly.

He paused. "I'm not sure what you mean."

"Don't play dumb, Mr. Graft," she said. "Tara has not been seen in three years. What happened to her?"

"How would I know?" Graft said with a smile. It was pure evil, and it sent chills up Laura's spine. "Maybe she decided she needed to get away, start a new life somewhere else."

"I highly doubt that."

The tension between them was so thick you could slice it with a knife.

Laura asked, "Did you know that Tara was pregnant?"

He shrugged. "I'm not sure how it's relevant to me."

"At the beginning of her pregnancy, Tara hid it from everyone. But as she began to show, she wore large clothes to conceal her belly. Eventually, when she couldn't hide it anymore, she stopped going to work and seeing her friends."

"Forgive my age, which you have aptly reminded me of, but I don't follow how this—"

"At the time of her disappearance, Tara was *not* pregnant."

He stared at her. "What do you mean?"

"I mean, she had already delivered her baby."

"How can you be so sure of this?" he asked.

"I can, because I delivered her baby," she replied.

Graft's face was hard.

"But you already knew that, didn't you? It was why you came after me once Tara was out of the picture. You wanted to know what I knew. You threatened my family—my *daughter*." Laura gritted her teeth. "You wanted to get rid of me just like you got rid of Tara."

"I don't know what you are talking about," Graft said.

"I was Tara's family physician," Laura said. "When she got pregnant, I advised her to go to a gynecologist, but she wanted to keep seeing me. She was afraid. She didn't trust anyone else. I didn't know why at first, but she later told me that the baby's father wanted her to get an abortion, that he was a very powerful man and that he wouldn't let another child come into this world because it could ruin him. But Tara was adamant about keeping the baby, a little girl. She had the same dark hair as her mother."

"How do I know you're telling the truth?" Graft asked.

Laura pulled out an envelope and dropped it on the table next to him. "Inside, there is a photo of Tara holding her daughter minutes after she was born."

Graft was silent.

"Aren't you going to look at it?" Laura asked.

His eyes were cold as steel, and his nostrils flared. "I'm going to ask you again… what do you want?" he growled.

"I want you to know that I'm not scared anymore. I can't prove that you were behind Tara's disappearance, but I can make sure the truth finally comes out."

"And what truth is that?"

"When a paternity test is conducted, it will reveal that you are the father of Tara's baby. That Wilbur Graft had produced a child out of wedlock. I'm sure it'll make great fodder for the press."

Graft's face was beet red. "Where is the child now?"

"You'll find out in court soon enough."

Laura stood up and left the room.

## ONE HUNDRED

With nothing else to do, Callaway decided to watch some TV. He still had time before he went to see Patti and Nina. He flipped through several stations. Nothing particularly interested him. Most of the talk shows were geared toward women. They talked about diet, exercise, and healthy cooking. Callaway was good at none of those things.

He took an escalator instead of the stairs, he ate fast food whenever he could, and he ate fast food *because* he couldn't cook.

He despised watching soap operas. It was nothing more than attractive people doing bad things. Sleeping with a friend's spouse, lying to one another, fighting over money and possessions. It reminded him a lot of his life, minus the money and possessions, of course.

He stopped on a game show. He always found them entertaining. People's excitement at being selected to play was overwhelming. In fact, he would begin to root for contestants to win. When they won, he felt like he had won.

His cell phone buzzed. He answered it.

"Hi, Daddy," Nina said.

Callaway had bought Nina her own cell phone. Patti was against it. She feared boys would coerce her into taking and sending provocative photos of herself. As a compromise, he had gotten Nina a basic phone. It had no camera and only a touchtone keypad for texting, but it had a great battery that could last for days on a single charge.

"Hey, baby," he said, excited to hear her voice. "What's up?"

"Mommy isn't here."

"Where?"

"To pick me up from school."

Callaway sat up straight. "Did you call her?"

"I did. I called her like five times, but it goes straight to her voicemail."

"Maybe Mommy's running a little late."

"She's never late."

"Never?" he asked, surprised.

"No. She always makes sure to be here."

"Okay," he said, suddenly thinking. "Are you still at school?"

"I'm in the principal's office."

"Don't worry, baby. I'll be there to pick you up."

He grabbed his jacket and rushed out of the apartment.

## ONE-HUNDRED ONE

Holt and Fisher sat in Holt's Volvo, which was parked across from the gentlemen's lounge.

Several minutes had gone by since Laura Sinclair had returned. She was in the back seat. The envelope she had left behind for Wilbur Graft contained a small listening device. It was tiny and as thin as a watch battery. The device was glued to the bottom of the large envelope. It had enough power for three hours. It didn't have the capacity to record or store anything. It only transmitted audio in one direction.

Holt and Fisher wore earpieces. They heard every word between Laura and Graft. They knew Laura had done an exceptional job of spooking Graft, and if their plan worked, they were waiting for Graft to do something.

They didn't have to wait long.

They listened as Graft made a frantic call. A moment later, Graft came out of the lounge, bound for a waiting car. His driver held the door for him as he got into the back seat.

Holt started the engine.

Fisher's cell phone buzzed.

She answered, listened, and then turned to Holt. "We have a problem," she said.

## ONE-HUNDRED TWO

As per Crenshaw's instructions, Kristoff and Andrei had the private investigator's ex-wife in their possession.

She was tied up in the trunk.

They were told to get his daughter as well, but she was in school, and there was no time to wait for her to return home. The ex-wife told them she was supposed to pick her up. They had no doubt she would raise the alarm once they got to the school.

*She would have to do, for now*, Kristoff thought.

The plan was to make the private investigator exchange Laura Sinclair for his ex-wife.

They knew the police were now involved, which complicated things, but they had no choice. These were desperate times.

Kristoff had a much simpler plan in mind.

Andrei would park the car under a bridge and wait for further instructions. Kristoff would go to meet Laura Sinclair at a busy park. When she showed up, he would shoot her from afar. Once she was dead, he would inform Andrei, who would then put a bullet in the woman in the trunk. She had seen their faces. She had to die.

The police were not expecting two killers— only one. And Kristoff and Andrei would use it to their advantage. They could be in two places at once.

If their plan went awry and Kristoff was somehow caught, Andrei would still kill the private investigator's ex-wife and disappear.

Regardless of what happened, someone would die today.

# ONE-HUNDRED THREE

Callaway and Nina were standing outside Patti's house when Fisher pulled up in her SUV. She was accompanied by Laura Sinclair.

"What exactly happened?" Fisher asked.

"Patti was supposed to pick Nina up from school, but she didn't," Callaway replied. "I just spoke to a neighbor. He said he saw Patti get into a car with another man. Patti didn't look happy about it."

"Did the neighbor get the license plate?" Fisher asked.

"Fortunately, he did."

"We can use it to track it."

"But that's not all," Callaway said. "Right before you arrived, I got a call from a blocked number. The caller said he had Patti and was willing to exchange her for Dr. Sinclair."

They were silent for a moment.

To break the tension, Laura asked Callaway, "Is that your daughter?"

"It is. Her name is Nina."

Laura walked over to Nina. "Hi there, I'm Millie's mom," she said with a smile. "Millie's told me so much about you."

"Is my mom going to be okay?" Nina asked her.

Fisher interjected, "Nothing is going to happen to your mom. I promise."

Laura turned to Fisher. "If it helps bring her back, you can give me up. I'm not going to put someone else's life in danger because of me."

"We're not giving you up," Fisher said.

"I agree with Detective Fisher," Callaway said. "I love Patti with all my heart, but you also have a little girl." He tightened his grip around Nina's hand and gave Laura a reassuring smile. "We can't put your life at risk. There will be no exchange."

"But what choice do we have?" Laura asked.

"I have an idea," Fisher replied. She turned to Callaway. "But we need to find a place where we can keep Nina and Dr. Sinclair safe."

Callaway thought for a moment. "I know just the place," he said.

## ONE-HUNDRED FOUR

Holt followed Graft to a gray concrete building. The Bentley parked in front of the structure. A moment later, a man came out through the front doors and entered the Bentley.

The range of the microphone was several miles, so Holt was comfortable parking a good distance away.

He adjusted the earpiece.

"Thank you for coming, Mr. Graft," the man said.

"Howard, why couldn't we have done this over the phone?" Graft growled.

"As I explained to you, sir, cell phones aren't secure—"

Graft cut him off. "She came to me."

"Who?"

"Dr. Laura Sinclair."

There was silence. "That was unexpected," Crenshaw slowly said. "What did she want?"

"She had proof that I was the father of Tara's child."

"What kind of proof?"

There was a shuffling noise in Holt's earpiece. Holt could tell Graft was removing the envelope from his pocket. If he somehow threw it out the window, then all would be for nothing.

Instead, he heard Graft say, "There's a photo of Tara after she had given birth. She's cradling the baby in her arms."

"Is that right?" Crenshaw said, sounding surprised.

"Yes. Do you want to see it for yourself?"

"I believe you."

"I'm not happy about this." Graft sounded angry. "I thought you had taken care of this problem."

"We did take care of it. Tara Sandhu is buried in a deep hole in Morningside Bluffs."

Holt knew where that was. He also knew he had a confession of murder.

Graft said, "And the child should have been buried with her mother."

"It was a mistake…"

"It was your mistake," Graft growled.

"Yes, it was. And we take full responsibility for it. But in our defense, we should have acted sooner—something we advised you of.'"

Graft grunted.

Crenshaw continued, "My men didn't have much time. We didn't know she had given birth."

"You couldn't tell by her stomach?" Graft asked, cuttingly.

"She was wearing a prosthetic. We only found out after my men were disposing of her body, and we informed you of this right away. Why do you think we went after Dr. Sinclair? We were hoping she'd lead us to the child, but then she disappeared herself."

"This was a monumental disaster," Graft said.

"Where is the child?" Crenshaw asked.

"She wouldn't tell me, but she's vowed to destroy me." Graft was breathing heavily. "Remember what I told you before, Howard. If I go down, then so do you and Dark Box."

*Dark Box?* Holt thought. *I've heard that name.*

"That won't happen, sir," Crenshaw said. "As we speak right now, I have my men making sure Dr. Laura Sinclair never bothers you again."

## ONE-HUNDRED FIVE

Wynford Park was a scenic area in the heart of Milton. It had a concrete section—specifically for skateboarding and rollerblading—on one side of the park. There were dozens of park benches for people to sit and enjoy the view. It had rolling hills of green pastures. There were even vendors selling hotdogs and fries.

Kristoff was standing next to an oversized tree. His weapon was in his coat pocket. The silencer was already on the muzzle. No one would hear the sound of the gun going off.

Kristoff had chosen this location for several reasons. He wanted a spot where Laura Sinclair would feel comfortable. She would be surrounded by other people, which would give her a false sense of security.

He was a good shot. He could shoot a target from half a mile away. The handgun was no comparison to a rifle, but even then, Kristoff was certain if he fired off a couple of rounds, one of them would hit Laura Sinclair.

The second reason for choosing this spot was for *his* security. Laura Sinclair would not be alone. She would bring the police with her. They would scatter throughout the park. But the park had several exit points. There was no way for them to mobilize enough manpower in such a short span to cover all the exits.

After he'd shot her, he would slip out, depending on which exits were unmanned.

In the distance, he saw the park bench. He had given instructions for Laura Sinclair to meet him there. The bench was next to a light pole, one of several in the park, but this one had a sign on it that read, *Please pick up after yourself.*

The city encouraged people not to litter in the park.

The bench was empty at the moment. The worst case would be for someone other than Laura Sinclair to occupy it. If that happened, he would have to improvise. Come up with a new strategy. Something he was not looking forward to doing.

His freedom depended on everything going according to plan. Any deviations could land him in the grasp of the law.

*That's not going to happen,* he thought.

He stood up straight when he saw someone approach the bench. A woman wearing a large sunhat, dark sunglasses, and a long coat walked over and sat down on the bench.

Kristoff couldn't tell if it was Laura Sinclair.

The way the woman kept looking around told him it had to be her. She was searching for someone. She was searching for *him.*

Kristoff scanned the surroundings. He wasn't about to get ambushed. If this was a trap, he wasn't going to walk straight into it. He would wait, however long as necessary. Sooner or later, the undercover police officers would reveal themselves.

Minutes ticked by. Kristoff noticed nothing out of the ordinary. No one in sunglasses talking into their earpieces or acting strange. People were walking around as if everything was normal.

The woman checked her watch. She was becoming agitated. She stood up, looked around, and sat back down.

*She's not going to wait there forever*, he thought. *I have to finish it now.*

He took one look around and then made his move.

He didn't go straight to her. That would be a mistake. She would see him coming and could alert whoever was hiding in the corner.

Instead, he walked over to one of the vendors. He purchased an ice cream cone and then began walking in the woman's direction.

In his left hand, he held the ice cream cone. In his right hand, concealed inside his coat pocket, was his weapon.

When he was ten feet from the woman, he took one last look around and then pulled out his weapon and fired directly at her. Two bullets hit her in the chest, and she fell down in an instant.

He placed the gun back in his pocket and calmly hurried away. He looked behind him and saw people gathering around the woman. They must have seen her go down.

Eventually, they would see what had happened and call 9-1-1. By then, he would be long gone.

He threw the ice cream cone in a garbage bin and then crossed the road. He went down a flight of stairs, turned right, and kept moving. At the end of the street, he spotted his sedan where he'd left it.

Once behind the wheel, he would call Andrei, and Andrei would finish off the private investigator's ex-wife. He would then let Crenshaw know the job was done.

After that, he would get out of Milton for some time, disappear until the police were exhausted from searching for the people behind the slew of murders. He would tell Andrei to do the same. They would have to split up, but it would only be temporary. Once the heat was off, they could resume working for Dark Box.

He pulled his keys out.

"Put your hands up where I can see them," a man's voice said sternly.

He froze. Through the car's tinted windows, he could see a uniformed officer. The officer had his firearm aimed at him.

"Don't think I won't hesitate to put a bullet in your head," Officer Lance McConnell said.

Kristoff hesitated, but he realized the hunter had become the hunted. His gun was in his pocket, and the safety was on. He would be dead if he made one false move.

He raised his hands and began cursing in Russian.

Within seconds, he was in handcuffs.

Just then, the woman in the sunhat, dark glasses, and coat approached them.

Kristoff's eyes widened. "You should be dead," he said, snapping back into English.

Fisher opened her coat to reveal a bulletproof vest. "Not quite."

"You okay?" Lance asked with concern.

"It hurts like hell, but I'll live."

## ONE-HUNDRED SIX

Andrei checked his watch for the umpteenth time. He was getting restless. Kristoff should have called him by now. Regardless, if he didn't hear from him soon, he would finish off the woman and then drive over and dump her body in Morningside Bluffs. There was a spot next to a grave they'd dug three years ago. It would be fitting that both of these women would be buried side by side.

His cell phone buzzed, and he checked it.

There was a text message from Kristoff's number.

He clicked on it.

*She's dead. I got her.*

Andrei smiled. He typed a reply.

*Good job. Now my turn.*

He pulled his gun out and screwed the silencer on the muzzle. He flicked the safety off and got out of the car.

He moved to the back and opened the trunk.

Inside, tied and gagged, was the private investigator's ex-wife. Her eyes were wide with terror.

*You should be scared*, he thought. *You are going to die now.*

He aimed his weapon at her head.

Something cold touched the back of his neck.

"I wouldn't do that if I were you," a male voice said.

He turned his head.

It was the private investigator.

"I've never fired this weapon before," Callaway said. "But I promise you, today I will.

The hardness in the man's voice told him he wasn't joking.

Andrei dropped his weapon. Within seconds, police cruisers descended on the scene.

## ONE-HUNDRED SEVEN

Lance, Fisher, Millie, Laura, Patti, and Callaway had gathered at Joely's restaurant. Callaway knew it was the one place where Nina and Laura would be safe. Joely wouldn't let anything happen to them.

On the drive over, Patti held on to Callaway's arm and didn't let go. He didn't want her to, either. If something happened to her, he wasn't sure how he'd be able to live with himself. She and Nina were the two most important people to him.

It broke his heart to see her tied and gagged in the trunk of the car. She was in tears when she saw him. He had to stop himself from breaking down as well. He kissed her a million times. He told her he was sorry, that it was his fault she was in this position.

But she didn't want to hear it. She knew why he had taken on the case. No apology was necessary, only that he was there for her when she needed him.

Holt came into the restaurant and announced that he had a person in custody by the name of Howard Crenshaw. Crenshaw was in charge of a company called Dark Box, and he had ordered the murder of Tara Sandhu. Wilbur Graft would not go unscathed. He would be charged with conspiracy to murder.

Kristoff Lysenko and Andrei Petrov would spend the remainder of their lives locked up in a six-by-eight prison cell, surrounded by American inmates who wanted nothing more than to get a piece of the Russian hitmen.

# THE UNKNOWN WOMAN

# ONE-HUNDRED EIGHT

Fisher pulled Laura Sinclair aside and said, "Can I ask you something?"

"Of course," Laura said.

"When you spoke to Graft, you mentioned he and Tara Sandhu had a child. Where is this child?"

"Detective Fisher," Laura said, "I spent years away from my family to protect that child. It was a promise I had made to Tara, and I'm not about to break that promise now. But I assure you, the child is safe and well-loved."

Fisher stared at her. "I guess that's the only thing that matters, isn't it?"

Laura smiled. "Thank you for everything you've done for me."

"I'm glad we could help."

Fisher looked over and saw Lance sitting at a table by himself. She walked over and sat down across from him. She winced.

She rubbed the spots where the bullets had hit her.

"You should go see a doctor," Lance said.

"I'm fine," she said. "If it gets worse, I can always get Dr. Sinclair to check it out."

Lance said, "I wanted to say I'm sorry about before."

"What?"

"About the ring and the proposal."

She looked down at the table. "I should be the one apologizing. I shouldn't have walked out like that."

"You did apologize. I listened to the voicemail you left me. In fact, I listened to it several times." Lance was smiling.

She looked at him. "I'm so sorry for the way I acted. You deserved an explanation."

"No. You were right. It wasn't fair to you. We should have discussed this. It's a big step in our lives." He paused and then looked out the window. "After what happened at the farmhouse several months ago—" Fisher knew he was referring to her previous investigation, "I thought I'd lost you for good. That's when I knew I wanted to be with you for the rest of my life."

She put her hand over his hand. "I want to be with you, too," she said.

He said, "We don't need a ring to formalize our commitment to each other. I love you, Dana."

"I love you, Lance."

He leaned over and kissed her. She kissed him back.

Joely walked over. "I'm sorry to interrupt this moment, but can I get you guys anything? The chef can whip up whatever you want in the kitchen."

"I'm actually not that hungry," Fisher said.

"I'm not, either," Lance said.

"No problem," Joely replied.

"You know what?" Fisher said, stopping her. "Can we get a plate of your best combo?"

"Just one plate?"

"I mean, if Lance wants to share it with me," Fisher said, looking at him.

Lance smiled. "I like the sound of that."

## ONE-HUNDRED NINE

The gates of the state penitentiary were imposing and terrifying. The two thousand souls inside the walls were there for murder, rape, assault, and other horrible crimes. They all believed they were innocent, but one man truly was. He had gone there of his own free will. He had done it to protect not only his family but also someone he didn't even know: a child born to a woman who would never get to watch her grow up.

The police had dug up Tara Sandhu's body. She would be given a proper funeral, surrounded by family and friends. Her daughter wouldn't be there. She was far too young to comprehend what all the fuss was about. But one day, she would be told about her mother. A strong and beautiful woman who had risked her life in order to make sure she was born.

Denise Hollins was now fully in-charge of Carta Aluminum. With the people behind Dark Box in prison, she didn't have to worry about being blackmailed any more. She also didn't have to worry about her father, Wilbur Graft, interfering with her plans for the company. He was preoccupied with his trial, which could see him spend the remaining days of his life behind bars.

Callaway had driven Laura and Millie Sinclair to the state prison. They were waiting outside the prison walls.

A moment later, the gates opened, and a man walked out carrying a plastic bag. He looked weaker than when he had first gone inside, but he was stronger for never giving up the truth, no matter how long he was locked up.

Roger Sinclair smiled and held his arms out.

"Daddy!" Millie cried with joy as she ran to him.

Laura had tears in her eyes as she embraced her husband.

When the news broke that Laura Sinclair was alive, it didn't take long to convince a judge to exonerate Roger Sinclair. He was a free man.

Roger turned to Callaway, his eyes moist, "Thank you, Mr. Callaway." He smiled at his wife and daughter. "Thank you for giving us a future together."

At that moment, Callaway knew why he had chosen his profession. All the hardship and disappointments he had endured over the years as a private eye was worth it to see a family reunited again.

He smiled and said, "You're most welcome."

## ONE-HUNDRED TEN

Dr. Sohail Reza drove up to a two-story brick house. He parked his Mercedes Benz and got out.

He went inside and found the house eerily quiet. He placed his briefcase to the side and then walked to the back of the house.

He smiled at the sight before him.

He opened the sliding glass door that led into the backyard.

His wife, Nadia, was playing with a little girl in a makeshift sandpit.

"Look who's here," Nadia said, pointing to him.

The girl looked up, and her face lit up with excitement. She raced over and gave him a hug.

"I love you, Daddy!" she said.

He kissed her and replied, "I love you too, Tara."

Visit the author's website:
**www.finchambooks.com**

Contact:
**finchambooks@gmail.com**

Join my Facebook page:
**https://www.facebook.com/finchambooks/**

## LEE CALLAWAY SERIES

1) The Dead Daughter
2) The Gone Sister
3) The Falling Girl
4) The Invisible Wife
5) The Missing Mistress
6) The Broken Mother
7) The Guilty Spouse
8) The Unknown Woman
9) The Lost Twins

THOMAS FINCHAM holds a graduate degree in Economics. His travels throughout the world have given him an appreciation for other cultures and beliefs. He has lived in Africa, Asia, and North America. An avid reader of mysteries and thrillers, he decided to give writing a try. Several novels later, he can honestly say he has found his calling. He is married and lives in a hundred-year-old house. He is the author of the Lee Callaway Series, the Echo Rose Series, the Martin Rhodes Series, and the Hyder Ali Series.

Made in the USA
Monee, IL
31 December 2021

87615045R00207